Breathe You In

Also by Joya Ryan

Break Me Slowly
Possess Me Slowly
Capture Me Slowly
Sweet Hill Temptation (Novella)

Breathe You In

A SWEET TORMENT NOVEL

joya ryan

Text copyright © 2014 Joya Ryan

Published by Montlake Romance, Seattle

www.apub.com

ISBN-13: 9781477818008
ISBN-10: 1477818006

Cover design by Georgia Morrissey

Library of Congress Control Number: 2013916746

Printed in the United States of America

To Jill.

Thank you for your support over the past couple years. Your belief in me is the reason this book got written. You always go above and beyond. Thank you for everything. You are a wonderful friend.

Chapter One

· · · · · ·

"So you see, sir, the new rehabilitation facility would really benefit the citizens of New York," I said, trying to tamp down my growing anxiety, and mentally chanting that I would not vomit from panic.

House Representative Walter Miller was short, bald, and wore a permanent scowl, which only heightened my already-skyrocketing blood pressure. But he also had influence over this year's proposed state budget.

I shifted my weight. Between the nearby clinking of champagne flutes and the low conversations being held by some of New York's elite, I felt like a sore thumb in the middle of the high-class gala I was attending.

"What was your name again?" he asked, shuffling in his tuxedo and draining his brandy.

"Amy Underwood. I work with New Beginnings, a nonprofit addiction counseling, prevention, and rehabilitation—"

"Yes, I'm aware of your organization. And, young lady, while it's admirable that you're trying to get funding for that little facility, Arbor Hill is not an effective use of state dollars."

"But that's where people need help the most, sir. The substance abuse rate is higher there than in the whole of Albany put together."

His beady eyes looked over the top of his glasses and very much down at me. Suddenly, the cream couture sheath dress I'd borrowed from my roommate, Paige, felt cheap, as Miller's judgmental glare burned a hole right through me.

"And you are so concerned because you grew up there?" He phrased it as a question, but it held a negative, probing undertone.

"No, sir. I live there now, but I'm originally from Indiana. I moved to New York a few months ago."

"I see. Well," he lifted his now-empty glass, "good evening, young lady."

He didn't even bother looking me in the eye. He just waddled off and disappeared into the crowd, leaving me standing with an erratic pulse and LOSER stamped on my forehead.

"Shit," I breathed. Walter Miller had been my one chance, and I'd blown it. Paige had put her job on the line to sneak me into this political function tonight, and I hadn't even hit the two-minute mark before Miller had shut me down.

The whole reason I'd moved to New York and taken the entry-level job at New Beginnings was that people needed the rehab center. There were seven other employees with the same Level One job description as me, and only one Level Two position available. If I got this funding, I'd get that Level Two job and really be able to make a difference—not to mention benefits and a livable wage so that I could afford to stay in New York.

I closed my eyes briefly, hoping the rejection would wash away as quickly as it had come, but it didn't. Instead, I felt like an ignorant, small-town girl in a borrowed dress and stilettos that were both a size too small.

It was a feeling I knew well, and had hoped I'd never experience again.

Everything I had fought for this past year—my fresh start and take-charge attitude, coming to New York to rebuild my life—was crumbling around me. No matter how hard I tried, my sister's death was still a haunting memory I couldn't fix. Smoothing my long blonde hair, thankful I'd worn it down because my dress was more revealing than I was used to, I walked to the bar.

"Ow—" An elbow jabbed into my side and I nearly toppled over, scuffing my—Paige's—pumps along the floor to keep from falling. Regaining my balance, I looked up and saw a tall, well-manicured woman walking away, apparently with no regard for the fact that she'd just run into me. Maybe one of the many shiny diamonds she was wearing had blurred her vision, or maybe she didn't give a damn that she had practically walked right over me. My guess was the latter. Running my palms down my dress, I continued toward the bar.

"What can I serve you, ma'am?" the bartender asked. He was dressed in all white, from his button-down shirt and vest to his pants and shoes.

"May I have a blueberry vodka and tonic, please?"

"Coming right up."

I placed my hands on the counter and reminded myself not to fidget.

Fidgeting shows you're ill-bred and insecure, a voice sizzled through my mind. The same voice I'd been running from for the past two years. For a long time, I had made it a point to stay out of situations that made me feel inferior, that put on display all my shortcomings and flaws. Problem was, the career path I had chosen required me to talk to powerful people.

Powerful people control the money, Paige always said.

Taking another deep breath, I wished for the millionth time that it wasn't true. Not only was my anxiety rising, but I had no interest in politics or money. I just wanted to get this center built.

The bartender placed my drink before me.

"Thank you." I took a long swallow. The cold liquor burned going down my throat, but it was something that I very much needed in that moment.

"You don't belong here," said a rough voice behind me.

I looked over my shoulder and nearly toppled out of my heels. A pair of dark eyes bore down on me. Even more startling, the eyes were attached to a tall, chiseled man with equally dark hair and features.

My lungs stilled and my stupid heart suddenly decided to stop pumping blood. Did he know I hadn't been invited? If he did and tied it back to Paige, her job could definitely be in danger.

Shit, shit, shit!

"I . . . that's just—"

"I meant it as a compliment," he said, forestalling my stuttering.

"Oh." Not the most intelligent thing to say, but getting my synapses to communicate with each other in that moment was a challenge: He was hovering over me and taking up the oxygen I needed.

I couldn't look away from him. He looked familiar, but I couldn't place where I'd seen him. He was younger than most of the men here. Early thirties maybe. Beneath the well-tailored tuxedo, I could tell he was fit. Between the way he held himself and that intense stare, the man radiated power and strength.

"I saw you talking to Walter." My shoulders sank and I took another sip of my drink. "Don't let him bother you. He's an ass, especially after a few brandies."

I smiled at the handsome stranger. He was the first nice person I'd met all night. His strong jaw was cleanly shaven but between the tan skin and thick, chocolate hair, I guessed he could shave every day and still have stubble by five p.m. I wouldn't have been surprised if he had Italian ancestry.

He pulled out a bar stool and offered me a seat. I took it.

"Your feet must be killing you." He looked at the four-inch red heels I was wearing. While they were sexy and gave my usual five-foot three-inch stature a nice boost, they hurt like a mother.

"I'm thinking of writing a letter to my local assemblyman, telling him that torture devices do exist in the US." I wiggled my feet and—holy hell!—Mr. Handsome unleashed a dazzling smile, complete with dimples and so much male swagger it should have been considered a weapon.

He knelt down and cupped my calf in his warm palm. I almost jerked out of my seat at his unexpected touch. Before I could form words, he slipped one stiletto off, then the other, and placed them beneath the stool.

"Can't have you being tortured on my watch."

Trying to relocate my mind and figure out how my panties had gotten a bit damp in a matter of seconds, I folded my lips together to keep from speaking. That onyx glare shot to my mouth. There was an odd contradiction to him. Influence and capability were obvious at the surface, but there was a glimmer of something deeper going on behind the kempt facade. An expression like that came from a man who had seen certain things and lived a life very different from one I could imagine, yet he coaxed me to go barefoot at a thousand-dollars-a-head dinner like I had nothing to be ashamed of.

"What's your name?"

"Amy Underwood." He nodded, continuing his assault on my face with his hypnotic eyes, as though he was trying to see past my scared smile and into my real nervousness. "What's your name?"

"Roman." His voice cut through the air like a fistful of thrown gravel. His glare locked on something behind me. I turned to see what he was looking at, but he gently gripped my knee, which got my attention in several ways. "I was going to get some fresh air on the terrace. Would you care to join me?"

"Um . . ." I looked around, trying to find Paige but had no luck. "Sure."

He held out his hand and helped me up. When I made a play to slip my shoes back on, he bent and picked them up.

"Allow me." He held my pumps in one hand and extended his other arm. There were massive French doors propped open at the opposite end of the ballroom, which I assumed led to the terrace. Problem was, we'd have to walk around or through the entire crowd to get there.

"I'm going to need my shoes."

He frowned down at me. "I thought you said they hurt?"

"Well, yeah. But I can't walk through here barefoot."

"Why not? The floor is clean. I happen to know for a fact they waxed it this morning."

"No, it's not that. It's . . . because it's inappropriate."

"I see." He nodded, glancing first at the floor, then at my feet, as if calculating the best method of travel. "Then how about a piggyback ride?" he winked.

The silly giggle that erupted from my throat couldn't be helped. Roman, with his casual attitude and charm, made me feel like everything was really okay. Like I, in the middle of this shit storm of the elite and entitled, was okay. Scuffed heels or not.

"Lead the way." I smiled.

His palm rested on the small of my back, and I could feel heat radiating from his touch as he steered me around the edge of the room and toward the doors. He didn't seem to want to interact with people any more than I did.

Keeping my eyes generally downcast, I glanced around quickly to try to find Paige. I spotted her in the corner talking to an older woman decked out in what looked like costume jewelry, but I had a suspicion it was all real. Paige's eyes met mine and widened. She mouthed something to me.

I frowned.

She mouthed the same word again, but I had no idea what she was trying to say. Cover? Gopher? Vendor? I shot her a tense smile and slight shrug, hoping it looked more relaxed than it felt.

We finally reached the doors and Roman led me through, out into the crisp fall air. The terrace was massive and wrapped around the entire building. Elegant white lights were strung overhead, and the smell of lavender wafted around. The low hum of the conversations inside grew softer as he led me farther away from the open doors.

The faint sound of traffic from the bustling city streets echoed quietly.

"You're not from New York, are you?" he asked.

"I was born and raised in Indiana. I moved here after college."

He smiled, looking me up and down. "Which was what? Last year?"

Yes. Apparently my age and non-New Yorker attitude weren't hard to spot. "I've been here for six months." *Barely.*

I hadn't realized how far we'd walked until I looked up and saw him standing near the railing, the glow of the open door no longer visible. We were alone. In the dark. With only a few flickering strings of light above. I crossed my arms, holding my elbows.

"Here," he said, putting my shoes down and unbuttoning his jacket. Shrugging out of it, he placed it over my shoulders.

"Thank you." He backed away. Putting his hands in his pants pockets, he leaned back against the railing.

My goodness, the man was beyond sexy. So poised and confident, but in a casual way that made him approachable. Made a girl wonder if the rest of his skin was as tan and edible looking. I looked up at him, my mind doing jumping jacks in an attempt to process the last few moments. Getting lost in the beauty of him was not smart, especially since I still couldn't tell if he knew I had snuck in. Not wanting to push the subject, I went for small talk.

"It's a nice night. I can see why you wanted to come out here."

"I wanted to bring you out here," he corrected, and straightened his stance.

My breath caught as my judgment balanced on a line between danger and excitement.

"Why?" I hated that my voice was little more than a whisper.

"Because you were painfully out of place in there." He stepped toward me and lifted my chin with a single finger, coaxing my gaze to meet his. "Again, I mean that as a compliment."

Once upon a time I'd thought I'd known how to handle powerful, wealthy men. I had been wrong. There had always been a secret expectation I couldn't measure up to, and that knowledge had eaten away at the already-hollow spot in my chest. It had been made clear that I didn't know how to blend into this kind of world, and I had no desire to try. But this man? All I could focus on was him. He wasn't cold and calculated. He was warm and inviting.

"I don't belong here," I admitted and shook my head, hoping that the slight movement would jar my brain enough to keep it from imploding.

"I wish I could say the same," he rasped. There was something so raw and genuine about the way he said it. As if he understood what it was like to have the earth spin around him instead of beneath him.

Once again, I was in over my head, and I had no idea how to dig my way out. Unfortunately, his presence was like gravity. It was hard to break away, and even more difficult to want to.

"I want to know something about you, Amy." He tugged on the lapels of his jacket that covered me, pulling it a bit more securely around my shoulders.

"What would you like to know?"

"Something true." He smiled, and I got a little caught up in it. The more minutes passed, the more comfortable I grew. But I couldn't shake the feeling that something was a touch off. Of all the people—the women—in that room, he had chosen to talk to me. He must have an angle. Maybe he was trying to get me to admit to trespassing?

"You look like I asked you for the codes to a nuke."

"Sorry." I glanced down. "I was just trying to figure out why."

"Why I want to know something about you?"

"Yes."

"Is it wrong to have a conversation with someone who interests you?"

I chewed my bottom lip. He didn't sound like someone who was angry or on the prowl to bust party crashers. Maybe the man just wanted a conversation.

"You want to know something true about me . . . will you return the favor?"

He arched a brow and his grin widened, seemingly pleased with my counteroffer. "Of course."

"Okay, then." I looked over his shoulder at the view of the Albany skyline. "Back home, I used to stand on my parents' porch and just look out at all the acres of green grass. I was a kid and it seemed so big. I remember thinking that it must be the center of the earth, because nothing surrounded our farm for miles. But now, in the middle of all these old buildings and skyscrapers, I don't think I've ever felt so small in my life."

I looked up to find him gazing down at me. A mixture of fascination and raw heat burned through those obsidian eyes. He oozed so much alpha masculinity that it was hard to imagine what he was thinking. Most people wore their generic emotions—happy, sad, angry—rather obviously. Not him.

"Sometimes it's nice to drown in the world instead of always riding at the forefront," he murmured.

He picked up a lock of my hair. The back of his fingers grazed my breast, causing a totally different kind of shiver to race through me. Rubbing the tendril between his finger and thumb, he looked into my eyes.

"Small or not, Miss Underwood," he said, his mouth hovering over mine, "you are certainly striking."

I tried to catch the better judgment that was flying from my mind. I failed. Instead, I tilted my chin up. "Y-your turn to say something true."

His gaze locked on my mouth. "I just did."

He seized my lips with his. His warmth surrounded me, clutching me to him. One strong arm encircled my back while the other cupped my neck. His thumb brushed over my earlobe, and a shot of pleasure raced through my veins.

He delved his tongue inside my mouth, drinking in every small moan I uttered. He tasted good. Like fresh ice and winter mints. Crisp and addicting. My palms slowly roamed over his torso. Hard, cut abdominal muscles jumped beneath my hands, and I grappled with the material of his shirt, suddenly upset that fabric was covering his impressive chest.

"You taste like blueberries," he growled against my mouth. "Sweet and ripe."

He nipped my bottom lip, then sucked it gently to ease the sting. My entire body lit up like crackling embers while my blood turned to lava. He wasn't just kissing me—he was devouring me.

Wanting a deeper draw of him, I rose to my tiptoes, fisting his shirt tighter for balance, and pushed my tongue past his teeth. He growled in response and tilted my head, returning my attentions full force. There was something about this man, something demanding and consuming. I wanted to take everything I could get. Everything he'd give me.

The hand on my back drifted lower. Grabbing my ass, he pulled me into his body. His hardness rubbed against me and my hips shot out of their own accord, seeking more. Fire built and pressure bubbled low in my core. It had been so long since I'd been touched like this . . .

No. I had never been touched like *this*.

From the tips of his fingers to the strength of his biceps, his embrace engulfed me. I had thought I felt small in the world before? Standing within his arms, I felt tiny. Feminine. Protected.

I wanted to tell him. To show him how good he felt . . .

"Governor Reese?" a voice called from behind him.

My eyes snapped open and he released his grip on me, turning to face the person who had interrupted.

"Yes, Andrew?"

"Pardon me, sir, but you're needed inside."

He nodded, then faced me. My entire nervous system shut down, and I felt the blood drain from my face as I stared at him in horror.

"Governor?"

He grinned. "Of New York."

My heart lurched and sped up to an erratic pace, nearly bruising my eardrums with its loud thumping. Now I knew what Paige had been trying to say: *governor.*

"Meet me at Angelo's, Wednesday, at eight." It wasn't a request, it was a command, and I just stood there, dazed and way, *way* beyond confused. Though I was frozen in place, my skin was hot and aching. What should I say? What the hell should I do? I just got caught making out with the governor.

Oh, God . . .

I took off his jacket and handed it to him, then backed up several steps. He put it on, gave it a good tug, and fastened the middle button.

"Pleasure meeting you, Miss Underwood." He turned and left with the man—Andrew—who'd called him. I watched them walk away, staring at his strong back and broad shoulders, realizing that Andrew had an earpiece in. Security. The governor's *personal* security.

Andrew handed him a cloth and judging by his movements, the governor used it to wipe his mouth. The handoff looked practiced, normal.

It hit me hard and painfully: Was this a habit of the governor's?

Chapter Two

. . . • . . .

I have one deadline and miss all the fun," Hazel said, putting her laptop on the coffee table and crisscrossing her legs on the couch. Her black hair was fastened in a messy bun on the top of her head, and her dark-rimmed glasses complemented her cute face and chipper tone.

"How's the writing coming?" I asked, walking through the front door with Paige and kicking my heels off.

"Almost done. Gotta love grad school papers," she groaned.

"Speaking of loving things, sounds like you had an interesting night." Hazel winked.

I turned to scowl at Paige, who was hanging her jacket on the coatrack.

"What?" Paige sounded guilty. "I texted her on the way home."

"Of course," I muttered.

"So you sucked face with a congressman?" Hazel's smile was so big our small apartment could barely contain it.

"Governor," Paige clarified. "And I told you to bat your eyes, not swallow tongue."

"I didn't know who he was," I protested. "He seemed so casual and—"

"Roman Reese seemed casual?" Paige scoffed.

"Well, sort of. I mean, he's got that brooding thing going on, but there was something . . . different."

Which was the only reason I had stuck around as long as I did. I'd been terrified of being found out, but Roman had a commanding stillness that sucked me in and made me want to be near him.

Maybe that's how all women felt around him.

While replaying that kiss, every moment and sensation, it was hard to imagine what he had been thinking. I was definitely not as smooth and practiced as he was. What had probably been just another night in the life of Governor Reese had left me reeling.

"And how could you not know who Governor Reese is?" Paige asked.

"I've heard of Governor Reese, but he introduced himself as Roman. And I blame our lack of cable for not recognizing him."

After Paige and I had maneuvered our way out of the gala and into a cab, she'd spent the ride home telling me the basics about Governor Reese. He was thirty-three, an ambitious young man with a wealthy family and an Ivy League background. Exactly the kind of man I had learned never to tangle with.

Hazel clapped her hands. "Love it! Tell me everything!"

I plopped down on the couch next to her while Paige went into the kitchen and made coffee. Our three-bedroom apartment was cozy and relatively quiet. Paige had been my best friend since childhood. When I'd moved in with her and Hazel, I'd hit it off with Hazel instantly. We'd grown close quickly, and were now a trifecta of awesome friendship.

"Paige, I'm so sorry," I called. Our living room and kitchen were partially divided by a pastel yellow four-foot wall. "I didn't want to put your job in jeopardy."

She was the assistant to the New York communications chief of staff, and not only was she good at her job, she worked hard for it.

Paige started the coffeemaker and looked at me. "Well, that will depend on how good a kisser you are, huh?"

I scoffed.

Hazel's eyes went wide. "Oooh, so it was good?"

"By the time I got to her, the woman was blushing from head to toe," Paige said, smiling.

I rested my forehead in my palm.

"I think this is a good thing," Hazel said, rubbing my back. "You haven't dated since you broke up with Warren. When was that? Like a year ago?"

"Two. And he dumped me," I muttered. "Plus, making out with the governor hardly counts as dating."

After the initial shock had worn off, reality that I wasn't ready for had filtered into my brain. There was a reason I hadn't dated since Warren, several reasons in fact, ranging from heartbreaking to soul crushing. A ping of regret and terror slithered down my spine, and I pushed that familiar ache away.

"Well, you could see Roman again, if you meet him like he asked," Paige said.

"Wait, he asked you out?" Hazel piped up.

"Sort of." I wrapped a strand of hair around my finger. The same one he had been touching when he'd kissed me.

My hair was longer now than it had ever been, falling to just above the small of my back. My mother had told me once that when I kept it long, I looked more like my sister. Aside from the occasional trim, I hadn't cut it since Lauren passed away seven years ago. And in that time, neither my hairstyle nor my accomplishments seemed to matter to my parents. Nothing changed the fact that I wasn't Lauren.

"So . . ." Hazel pushed. "Are you going to go out with him?"

"I don't know. It seems . . . wrong."

"Wrong?" Paige came into the living room, juggling three mugs of steaming liquid. "The whole reason you went to the gala in the first place was to get funding to build this rehab center. To catch the ear of someone who has influence over the budget." She set the mugs on the coffee table and shrugged. "Of course, you caught the *mouth* of someone instead of the ear, but it was close."

"Ha ha," I mumbled.

Paige was right. I had caught something. Maybe bad judgment-itis, or I'm-so-hard-up-I'll-kiss-a-stranger-ism. There was something hypnotic about him, though. I had become used to being ignored and blending in. But from the moment I looked into his eyes, I couldn't look away. Amidst strangers, classy women, and wealthy politicians, he saw me. And it felt good.

"Honey, I love you, and I know this rehab center is your baby. You moved to New York for this opportunity. This isn't like Indiana. If you want to head up a major project, you're going to have to talk to powerful people, plead your case, and get the funding you need. If you can't, you're going to struggle in this profession. You have a golden ticket to sit down with the governor of New York and make your case."

Paige's words were soothing and yes, I knew she loved me. And as usual, she was right. The problem was, this probably wasn't the right profession for me.

Warren Cunningham III had turned me off to the elite and entitled population two years ago. After a few years of dating, and helping him graduate summa cum laude from Notre Dame, I'd found out that he had only been dating me as part of an agreement with his family. If he stayed on the "right path" and "maintained a respectable image," he would get his inheritance. I, apparently, was the brainy, quiet girl who made him study, wrote his term papers, and helped him look like a gentleman while he secretly cheated and lied, and then left me with nothing more than a damaged sense of self-worth and a broken heart.

"Don't," Hazel snapped.

"What?" I looked at her petite finger directed at me.

"I know that look. You're thinking about that douche bag. Don't."

It was hard not to. Everything about tonight had reminded me of what it had been like being around his family and in that world. The Cunninghams had had socialite status, political standing, and oil money, and they hadn't wanted their precious son staining the family name with partying and wild nights. All the while, I was merely his cover, and everyone had known but me. Eight hundred days later, it still stung.

"What he did was disgusting and you're better than that," Hazel said. "Look at all you've accomplished."

"I haven't accomplished anything, though. I've constructed the idea, and planned and budgeted for this center, but that doesn't mean anything if it doesn't get built."

When I wasn't trying to scout for support and funding for this new center, I was spending most of my time sending out e-mails and making phone calls, trying to get volunteers to help with some of the programs we offered at our existing facilities. Important, yes. But enough to set me apart from the other employees? No. And definitely not enough to get a blink of an eye from my parents.

If this Arbor Hill center got up and running, maybe then my parents would see me. See how much I loved them, and how much I loved and still missed Lauren. How I never meant to hurt her . . .

I couldn't fix the past. Couldn't change that night. God knows how much I wish I could go back, make different choices, and have her still be alive. But I couldn't, and I had no idea when—or if—my parents would ever forgive me for Lauren's death.

All I could do now was try to make the present better. Make this center happen. Then maybe Lauren's overdose would spark awareness, and this rehab and prevention facility could give people a chance to get clean and heal before it was too late. If only one family was spared the pain my family had gone through, then it would be worth it.

"You're on the brink of a very important meeting," Paige said.

"Dinner," I amended, but she didn't bother with the correction.

Paige was a wonderful woman, but she had her own issues, and throwing herself into a bloodthirsty political world where she got to exercise her cutthroat needs was a good thing for her. It was how she thrived. However, emotional balance wasn't her strong point.

"Let me explain how this works." Paige held out her hands, palms up. "Here is the governor," she said, lifting one hand slightly. "Right now, he's drafting and finalizing the budget, then he's going to send it to the legislature." She lifted her other palm. "Once they get his proposed budget, they review, make changes to, and sign off on it. Then it becomes an appropriation bill." Her green eyes focused on me. "Amy, if you got your project put on the docket with the governor's support for state funding, you could get the New Beginnings Arbor Hill center its own bill, which would mean government funding for a lot longer than a single year."

"Whoa," Hazel said, taking the one word I wanted to use.

If Roman were to designate specific funding for New Beginnings with my rehab center as the head project, that would be a big step forward. But to actually secure the funds and get an appropriation bill? That would be a slam dunk, and would most likely mean long-term job security for me.

"You have a dinner date with the governor of New York," Paige reminded me. "How are you going to use it?"

Looking to the ceiling, I let out a loud breath.

Damn it. I wanted this to work. Was I comfortable in my current career? Not entirely. But I would be. In time. I wanted this rehab center built. And I wanted my job. But I needed the funding to make that happen. Still, one fact remained that I couldn't ignore.

"I know what it feels like to be used," I whispered, looking at Paige. "I can't do that to him."

Especially when tonight, there had definitely been something more behind those dark eyes. Politician or not, Roman Reese was different. He made me feel like all the greed and deceit that went with the rich and powerful didn't exist. Not with him. Going to dinner with ulterior motives was not something I wanted to do, or the kind of person I wanted to be. He had asked me for something true, and I had told him.

I just hoped that truth lasted until next week.

. . . • . . .

It had been several days since I'd kissed the governor, and I'd spent most of them thinking about him. Angelo's was a romantic, candlelit restaurant with red table linens. I tugged on the hem of my short black dress, clutched my small wallet, and walked toward the hostess.

"Is there a Mr. Reese already here?" I asked.

The woman smiled. "Right this way."

I followed her to the very back of the restaurant where, in the shadows of a dimly lit corner, sat Roman Reese. His eyes fixed on my face, and I felt like a mouse circling a watering hole while a hawk watched from above. He followed my every move.

Forcing myself not to fidget, or to cover the subtly low neckline of my dress, I sat down. The dress was another of Paige's, and a bit tighter than I preferred, but nicer than anything I owned. Roman, however, looked calm in a perfectly fitted steel-gray suit and black tie.

"Miss Underwood."

"Hi." I smiled.

He didn't return the gesture. In fact, he looked pissed. Pins pricked along my forearms and the hair on the nape of my neck stood up. He didn't say anything. Merely kept that unnerving gaze on me until a waiter poured us wine and shuffled off.

"It's nice to see you again," I stated, not sounding convincing even to myself. The tremble in my voice was apparent.

All weekend I had been thinking about this man. About the heat he made me feel and the intensity of his presence. I didn't know how tonight would go, but so far, that intense presence had shifted to suffocating.

"Is it?" he asked. "I suppose it must be, considering you didn't get to pitch yourself to me the last time we *interacted*." He said the last word like he'd tasted something foul, and embarrassment instantly flooded through me. Heat inched across my face and I could hear every pulse of my heart thumping in my temples. "I know who you are, Amy. You work for New Beginnings and are apparently quite ambitious."

I swallowed hard. He didn't stop his assertions.

"For the past three years, your *federally funded*—" he over-enunciated the words, "organization has begged me for special consideration and state funding on top of what it already receives." He folded his hands on top of the table. "But I see that my rejection has only spurred the notion of more direct tactics."

His hot, black gaze skated over my breasts, and I couldn't get my lungs to function right.

"I . . . I didn't . . ."

"You didn't sneak into a private gala, violate security measures, and trespass with the intent to harass and sway political leaders, myself included?"

"No!" I shot out. "I mean . . . yes. I went to the party to talk to some people. To show them why this rehab center would be a good thing and deserves funding."

"You have federal funding."

"That's to keep the programs we already have going. This is for building and staffing a brand-new facility."

His jaw clenched and I bit my lip because, damn it, this wasn't the reason I'd come tonight. I'd wanted to see him. To have a nice dinner, and maybe get a glimpse of the first man who'd made me feel real in a very big world that didn't seem to have space for me.

"I know who snuck you in, Miss Underwood." My eyes shot to his. "It's a shame. Bill really liked Paige. She was a good assistant. Rising fast, I'm told."

"Was?" I choked out.

"Once I inform Bill of Paige's indiscretion, he'll obviously have to let her go. She disregarded policy and went against security measures."

"Wait, please don't fire Paige. This is my fault, not hers."

He sat back in his chair. "Those big, blue eyes are so wide that I could almost believe you."

His smile was so guarded I could feel it like a physical force, weighing me down. I remembered how just a week ago, that mouth had looked very different. Felt different. Hot and gentle. Hard and consuming. The man before me was all power and politics and I couldn't win. Didn't even have a chance.

"Perhaps we can come to an arrangement," he said. "You came here tonight, like last week, because you want something from me."

What I wanted was to argue, to tell him that wasn't the case, but the look in his eyes told me it wouldn't do any good. He'd made up his mind about me. While I couldn't entirely blame him, it stung that whatever emotions could have grown from that kiss were long gone.

"I want something from you too, Miss Underwood."

"What could you possibly need from me?"

He grinned, and didn't bother hiding his insistent gaze as it dropped from my mouth to my cleavage, then back up.

"Several things," he said. "But I'll start with the blue-collar vote."

"You want me to vote for you?"

He scoffed like I was a moron, and I wanted to slap him right in his way too handsome face. The entitled asshole attitude I hated so much was gushing from him like he was a busted faucet. Reminding me again that this was not the man I'd met last week.

"I'm up for reelection in November. My team has been running a good campaign, but with my background, the blue-collar vote is always a struggle. Polls show that it is lower than last election, and the race between my opponent and me is tight. That's where you come in."

I sat there, my hands in my lap, completely lost. "I don't know what you think I can do, but politics aren't my thing. I have no desire—"

"I disagree. In fact, if memory serves correctly . . ." he ran two fingers along his jaw, "you have quite a desire for politics. Or perhaps just politicians?"

My skin couldn't have been hotter if it had actually been on fire. There was a flicker in those dark eyes that reminded me of the honesty from that night. How his mouth had worked mine, and all that strength wrapped around me. But the flicker disappeared quickly.

"Your mother is a school teacher, your father an Army vet turned electrician, and your only sister died of a drug overdose her senior year of high school." He spoke as if he were reading a dossier on my life, which he probably had. Because this kind of information took a bit of digging. "You were brought up in a solid middle-class family and now work for a nonprofit nobly providing the lower class with addiction rehabilitation programs."

That's when it hit me. It was the truth, just as he'd promised a week ago. But the truth hurt.

"You want to use me to boost your numbers, your reputation," I breathed.

"The arrangement I propose isn't just to benefit me."

"What arrangement would that be?" I snapped, hating every-thing about this moment. Tonight was supposed to be so different. Roman was supposed to be different.

"A relationship arrangement," he said.

My throat closed up a little. "You can't be serious."

He nodded. "You want that rehab built and your little Midwest name all over it, and I want the blue-collar vote. You on my arm at various events will elicit that. Show I am a man of the people."

"But you're not," I grated between my teeth.

Something dark flashed in his eyes. "Don't assume you know who I am or what has molded me. I understand more than you think, Miss Underwood."

There! A glimmer of the man I'd seen last week—sadness and darkness behind his eyes showing just a hint of vulnerability. But it was washed away with his next rough words.

"I can put your project on the budget proposal, and you can be with me for the next two months. When I win the election, I'll launch an anti-drug campaign with New Beginnings as the spearhead organization."

"You mean, *if* you win."

His jaw tightened. "All the more incentive for you to help me do so. Because *if* I don't, then I guarantee no other governor, or any other state official, will push to get funding or exposure for your little center."

Remembering how House Representative Miller had treated me at the gala made the rough truth of Roman's words sting. Breathing was nothing more than a wish at this point. Every time I tried, air just stuck to the inside of my mouth, refusing to come out. His offer was a good one, in theory, but an arrangement all the same. The kind that is surface based, breaks hearts, and uses others. Could I really put myself through that again? This time knowingly?

"After the election," he continued, "we go our separate ways, with the residual benefits to be had by both parties involved."

"Why me?" I asked, grasping at any loophole in this scheme. "There are other women with spotless backgrounds who I'm sure you can call on."

He nodded. "Yes. But you have an innocence."

The words cut me deep. It wasn't a compliment, it was the recognition of a trait. Something that he, like Warren, could exploit. It didn't matter that I felt used, discarded, and about as far removed from innocent as possible. Innocence was what he perceived.

"Besides," he shrugged. "You fooled me. If you can do that, you should have no problem fooling the people of New York."

I shook my head. In his mind, I was trapped somewhere between ingenue and liar.

"I won't sleep with you," I stated.

"Rest assured, sweetheart, that if you and I end up in bed, we'll be fucking, not sleeping." He tugged at his cuffs. "But this is not a sexual arrangement." His penetrating gaze slid over me. "Unless you want it to be."

He paused to flash a megawatt smile that nearly made me lose my mind and my panties in one swoop. Gritting my teeth, I internally cursed my body for responding to him. "To the world beyond us, we will appear as a couple. This is an upfront, honest exchange of services. We're using our strengths to gain better access to what we want. Sex isn't part of this agreement. That is a situation that, should it happen, will be because you want it to, and it will have no bearing on this disposition."

Tingling warmth shot up my back. There was something about Roman that had me so off-kilter. Just the thought of sex with him made part of me tremble, wondering what it'd be like. Wanting to find out. The other part of me didn't give too much weight to this notion, because in the end, he assumed I was using him.

I glanced at my lap and refused to think of Warren. How he had used me in this same way, and how little it had mattered—how little I had mattered. At least Roman was upfront with his intentions, instead of blindsiding me. Fooling me into thinking I was more than a convenience.

When I looked up, his gaze was locked on my face, his brows drawn tight, as if trying to read small print along my forehead. I would not make the mistake of taking that to be a look of concern.

I cleared my throat, a burst of pain ricocheting through my chest like a spiked boomerang. This man clearly thought something very specific about me. I just couldn't figure out if being part of a lie hurt more when it was done behind my back, or face-to-face.

Either way, the pain in my sternum and the thought of losing something with this man before I'd ever gained it hurt more than I liked. But that didn't matter now. At least I could salvage Paige's job, my career, and Lauren's memory.

Emptiness clawed its way up my spine, but I pushed it down. Like I always did. Skyscrapers and open fields didn't compare to how small I felt sitting before Roman Reese, governor of New York.

Paige had told me that when dealing with any kind of offer, get it on paper. I lifted my chin and with all the courage I had, looked him dead in the eye.

"I'm going to need something in writing."

He smirked and pulled a pen from his inside jacket pocket. "This," he said, writing on the white cloth napkin, "is all the documentation you get."

He tossed it across the table to me. Staring at the cloth, I read the words written in bold black ink:

You consider my interests and I'll consider yours.

"What happens between us is private. Everything. Always. You breathe a word of our discussion tonight to anyone, I'll pull my generous offer and crush your request for funding before it even sees the light of day. Do you understand?"

Swallowing hard, I glanced up from the napkin and nodded. It was no secret that politicians played their hands close to the vest, but the warning in Roman's voice and the fierceness in his eyes hammered home the notion.

"You have twenty-four hours to give me an answer, Miss Underwood."

Chapter Three

· · · • · · ··

"Hi, Mom." Pressing my cell against my ear, I walked from the bus stop to my office building. Between the fall breeze and the other commuters, it wasn't an ideal time to talk, but this was the first time my mother had actually answered the phone after five failed attempts I'd made, so I'd take what I could get.

"Hello, Amy." Her voice was low and kind of soft. It would have been soothing if not for the bitter undertone that always seemed to lace it.

"How are you? I haven't talked to you in a while." I wove through the crowd and turned down another street. The brick building that housed New Beginnings was only a few more blocks up. Though the center I wanted to build would be in Arbor Hill, near my home, New Beginnings was located in West Albany.

"I'm alright."

I nodded, wondering for a moment if the line had gone dead, but a quick check of the phone screen showed that all was fine. It was my mother's silence that was real.

"I'm good too. On my way to work. Things are really moving along."

"Did you build that counseling center you've been talking about?" My mother always called it a "counseling center." While yes, there would be counseling and prevention services, she never acknowledged what it would really be—what Lauren had needed—a rehab facility.

"Not yet, but it's looking really good that I'll get the funding, and hopefully get it up and running in the near future."

"What does near future mean? Tomorrow?"

My lungs hurt from both the chilly autumn air and my mother's even chillier voice. The jostling of the passersby wasn't helping either. "No, not that soon. These things take time."

If I'd thought the silence on the line was bad, the exasperated sigh my mother gave was worse. Like nothing I was doing mattered or could make a difference.

"You should have taken her to the hospital, Amy," she whispered, just loud enough for me to hear despite the bustling.

Every time I talked to my mother, I expected the conversation to somehow bring joy or happiness. But prying warm feelings from her was impossible. Because instead of making an effort to care about anything other than Lauren's death, she always took time to once again remind me of my fault in the matter.

"You knew she was . . ." My mother trailed off, unable to say what came next. The truth.

"Using," I mumbled. "Lauren was using." Yes, I had known.

That night flashed through my mind. Lauren had been prescription popping for a couple of months. I hadn't known how bad it was. Our parents were out of town for the weekend when Lauren called me to come get her from a party. I went. And when she begged me to not tell Mom and Dad, I agreed. She was my big sister, the strong one, and I loved her.

"I didn't know how much she'd taken, Mom. If I had—"

"It doesn't matter anymore, does it?"

Tears stung my eyes. The last thing I'd gotten to say to my sister

28

was that I loved her, right after putting her into her own bed. She was warm, sleeping. But the next morning, her lips were blue and her skin was cold. While I was busy covering for my sister, she'd died in her sleep of an overdose.

"I'm sorry." I had lost count how many times I had said it over the years, but it still wasn't enough. Not for me, and certainly not for my mother.

Another bout of silence on the line was the only response. It was all I needed to know that my debt wasn't even close to paid off. And probably never would be.

Walking up the steps to my building, I willed the burning behind my eyes to stop. Lauren had been their golden child. She had been special and kind, and you couldn't help but love her. I knew this because every day I thought of her, and every day I mulled over my mother's comments until I believed the same thing she did: *I could have saved her.*

Redemption was impossible, but this center was as close as I could get. My second chance to make it right. Since Lauren had died, my life had been spent with my mother's sour words ringing in my ears. She'd made it more than clear how she felt—that the wrong child had died that night. And that it was my fault.

"I've got to head into work, Mom, but there are some really great things coming." I thought of Roman's offer. "Maybe sooner than I expected."

"Good for you. Bye-bye." Not an ounce of love could be squeezed from her voice. Yet I still tried.

"I love—" I began, but the line went dead before I could say more.

The burning spread from my face to my chest. Pushing that feeling aside, I opened the glass doors of the building, stuffed my phone into my coat pocket, and tried to focus on what I could control.

Roman's face came to mind again, and something in my stomach tightened. Would an anti-drug campaign make a difference to the community? Yes. But would it make a difference to my parents? Maybe. Maybe not. My mother had spoken to me more since I'd taken on this project than at any time since Lauren's funeral. Mostly because whoever headed up the project got to name it. My choice? Lauren's House.

That had made my mother's ears perk. But with no results, the conversations were getting shorter and her tone, shriller.

I felt my phone buzz in my jacket. It was probably another text from Paige or Hazel asking what had happened last night. I'd made it a point to sneak in late and, thankfully, they had both been asleep. Paige and Hazel had early mornings. I was always an hour behind them, so I had successfully avoided the topic of Governor Reese for a good twelve hours now. But that wouldn't last much longer.

"Heard you bombed with House Rep Miller," Silas said, just as I hung my coat on the back of my chair and booted up my computer. "Shot you down hard, huh?"

He leaned against the opening of my cubical and smiled his wide, jackass smile, which matched his asshole glare.

"How do you even know about that?" I tried to sound unaffected, but it was a little late for that. It was creepy that he not only knew I'd been at the gala, but that I had "bombed" with Miller.

"You're not the only one going for the job, Indiana." He winked.

Ew. I had no idea how his gangly frame supported all that arrogance. Silas was my main competition at New Beginnings. He couldn't have been more than five-foot-seven and one hundred and fifty pounds, most of which seemed to be attitude.

"I'm aware of that, Silas. But I do seem to be the only one trying to get a new center built for the people of New York, rather than stalking people on the weekend."

He ran a hand through his light brown hair. "Don't flatter your-self. I'm trying to get funding for this center too. It's such a worthy cause, after all." Sarcasm dripped from every syllable and by God, I wanted to punch him.

Between the call with my mother and this guy encroaching on something that actually mattered to me, my bottled rage was enough to warm me up after my chilly walk.

I had spent my first month at New Beginnings taking calls on the crisis line. Listening to a teenage girl cry and threaten to kill herself because she couldn't get a fix. Or a boy, who couldn't be more than sixteen, asking for help, only to start gasping and gargling from the delayed effects of a lethal ingestion of meth he'd taken hours earlier. Just like Lauren. Addiction was heartbreaking. Lauren was gone, but there were kids still out there who needed help.

This new center could provide that. And getting funding for it was the one project I'd personally launched in my time here. It was also, apparently, the quickest way to get the bosses' attention, which was why Silas had jumped on board the moment our boss, Marcy, had shown genuine enthusiasm.

He didn't care about helping people; he just wanted the promo-tion, better pay, and benefits. Then he could be a project lead, sitting behind his desk and telling people what to do, while he did nothing and took the credit—kind of like what he was doing now.

"Project meeting in ten minutes," Marcy said, weaving through the cubicles, her short red hair bobbing around her face with each step in her sensible heels.

Every Thursday, Marcy gathered her employees to hear what we'd been working on and what progress we'd made. I knew that the other five Level Ones were working on operations and support for New Beginnings' already-established rehab center, which was overflowing with people who needed help. The wait time for admission to our current center was more than nine months, which was why we needed this new center desperately. And we needed it in Arbor Hill.

Silas and I both had degrees and backgrounds in nonprofit work, and we were the only two taking on the task of acquiring funds and local support for this new center. Marcy had let it slip last month that the available Level Two position would, most likely, come down to either him or me.

"I'm excited to hear about the headway you've made, Amy." She smiled, approaching me and Silas.

Marcy was nice, supportive, and one of the best bosses I could have asked for. She was in her early forties, and had been at New Beginnings for twenty years.

With a nervous smile, I nodded. She was excited to hear about the headway I'd made? A cold sweat broke out on my forehead as I recalled exactly what I had accomplished lately. Did a make out session with the governor of New York, followed by a proposed verbal agreement to play the role of his small-town girlfriend, count as headway?

"Looking squeamish there, Indiana." Silas smirked. "Something you wanna share?"

"Wait for the meeting," Marcy said, patting my shoulder before continuing her walk around the office.

Last week, I had made some pretty big promises on the topic of funding for this new center. Of course, that had been when Paige had just told me she'd be able to sneak me in: I'd been riding high on the idea of face time with important people who had a say over the state budget. Speculation was a bitch, and it was about to slap me in the face.

Damn it. I just wanted this center, my life, the governor . . . all of it, to just work out.

"See you in there, Indiana." Silas winked. "Hope you have something up your sleeve." Ugh. It was barely past nine a.m. and I was already annoyed, edgy, and ready to snap—likely at Silas.

My phone buzzed again. I grabbed it quickly and read the newest text message from Paige:

Girls Night Out 7 PM! Be prepared to spill the details about last night.

Chapter Four

Y ou're going to see him again?" Paige asked from across the small, square table. Running one hand along the stressed wood, I palmed my sweating drink in the other. "Like another meeting? Or another date?"

Hazel's eyes went wide at Paige's question and she took a sip of her martini. The bar was loud, and I considered pretending I hadn't heard her question. But I had already made up my mind, and it was time to stick to my decision.

"Like another date," I admitted and took a swallow of liquor.

Paige leaned back in her chair. Her white blouse was slightly wrinkled from the twelve-hour day she had put in. Obviously, she had come straight from the office. Though the bar was dim, lit mostly by neon beer signs, I could tell Paige was tired.

Several people lined the bar, leaning over the counter to watch the football game currently playing on all three televisions, while others huddled around a few scattered tables, laughing and cheering. The smell of draft beer and jalapeno poppers drifted around us. With my back to the front door, a fresh dose of cold evening air and cigarette smoke burst against my shoulders every time more people came in.

"Amy, that's awesome!" Hazel smiled. "It's about time you started dating again." While Hazel did look genuinely happy for me, Paige looked like she had swallowed a thumbtack.

"Are you mad?" I asked.

"No," she said slowly, and frowned. Shaking her head slightly, she looked back at me with a smile. "I'm just surprised. I never expected that one event would lead to you dating my boss. Well, my boss's boss."

I nodded. This wasn't the most comfortable situation, but Paige had always been supportive. She was an amazing friend that way. Even right then, when I could tell that this was awkward for her.

From the beginning, she had helped me in every way possible in my mission to fund the rehab center. This surprising turn of events was still a shock to my system, let alone Paige's.

"This won't affect your job at all," I assured her. Actually, agreeing to Roman's arrangement was saving Paige's job—a tiny factoid I could never tell her. All I had to do now was to get in touch with Roman and let him know my answer.

"Um, actually I'm pretty sure it will." She smiled and took a sip of her beer. "It's election season, and it looks like the governor just got a new squeeze." She tipped her head in my direction. Paige was trying hard to be calm and cool about this, but I could hear the worry in her voice. As assistant to the communications officer, Paige's main job was what she called "media damage control."

"This won't be an issue for you, will it?" The last thing I wanted was to bring Paige more stress. She loved her job, which was why agreeing to the governor's proposal was important—so she could keep it.

"Now *is* the time for bold moves," she said in the analytical voice she used when mentally sorting out a problem. "But only if they ensure a win. The governor's personal life is already on display. As long as your relationship maintains an even keel, and no incriminating information comes out, this could be a good thing. It all depends on what occurs and how it gets spun."

I took a deep breath. Hopefully there would be no negative repercussions. As for skeletons in the closet, I kept all mine back home in Indiana, which was where I intended them to stay. The unflattering events of my past weren't documented or mainstream accessible. My sister's death was public record, but the details behind it, like me driving her home instead of to the hospital, weren't. That was a detail very few people knew about.

I swallowed the knot rising in my throat. I had never doubted that Paige was smart and good at her job. She had special X-ray vision that saw straight through bullshit. But I couldn't tell her the whole truth regarding my relationship with the governor. If I did, the job that she was so good at would disappear, and all the help and support she'd given me to get this center up and running would have been for nothing. Roman had made that quite clear.

"Not everything is a calculated move, Paige," Hazel said. "He obviously likes her and you like him, right, Amy?"

For some reason, my mouth refused to produce words. Being less than totally honest with my friends was incredibly difficult, and the question hit a chord deep in my gut. I thought of Roman's hands on me, the way he had pulled me to his body, his strong mouth working mine. Every encounter with him was taking me further from sanity. In his presence, I felt desperate and aggressive, small and feminine, all at the same time.

"Yes," I whispered. "I like him."

I also kind of hated him. Last evening's chat hadn't been particularly pleasant, but for some reason, when I thought of Roman, our first encounter always beat out our second. The feel of his mouth and his chest, the sound of his voice—my brain refused to let go of a single ounce of memory from that night. Instead, it held the leading slot under "Things I Thought of Hourly."

Hazel smiled. "I'm sure everything will work out fine, for everyone." She glanced at Paige, who obviously wasn't entirely sure. And I couldn't really blame her about that.

"It's a different world, Amy," Paige said. The flash of concern in her eyes and the low tone of her words said it all. She was scared. For me.

"I know." I looked at her and said the phrase I had been chanting to myself mentally all day. "I can handle it."

Because this time, I knew what I was getting into.

Warren had blindsided me. Roman was upfront. From here on out, he couldn't hurt me if I didn't let him. Or at least, that was my theory.

"Just out of curiosity, what do you two have in common, anyway?" Paige asked.

"We're both Giants fans," said a deep, roughened voice.

I spun in my seat and saw the tower that was Roman Reese standing behind me. Paige immediately stood and Hazel followed suit.

"I'm sorry, sir," Paige said, "I didn't know you were coming tonight."

"Neither did I," I said, choosing to stay in my seat and look up at him.

His dark hair was perfectly combed, but a shadow of stubble covered his strong jaw, and his black eyes shone like onyx. His presence was engulfing. His massive shoulders and confident stature were very apparent even beneath his jacket. The top two buttons of his white collared shirt were undone, and just the hint of tan skin exposed made me wonder if it felt as smooth as it looked.

"Forgive my interruption," he said, glancing between Paige and Hazel. "I just came to check in with Amy about a lingering question."

He smiled at me and slid two fingers down the column of my neck. The confident grin he unleashed along with his blazing touch made all the moderate nervousness I had been feeling lunge into full-force anticipation.

"We were just leaving anyway," Paige said, collecting her coat from the back of her chair.

"No, you don't have to." I swung back around to face my friends.

"We'll see you at home later." Hazel winked and gathered up her things.

She was supportive of me and the governor having alone time, but Paige's jerky movements and quick verbiage were a dead giveaway that she wasn't completely sold. Her concern came from a good place, but I hated myself for adding another item to her plate of things to worry about.

They both hustled out, and Roman wasted no time taking a seat next to me and pulling it close.

"Well, you sure know how to clear a room. How did you know I was here?"

"I passed Bill's office this afternoon and overheard Paige making plans." He grinned, gently taking the drink from my hand and savoring a long swallow before handing it back to me.

"Mmm." He leaned in and whispered in my ear, "I've been craving blueberries all day."

A shiver ran over my skin as the subtle scent of tart blueberries from the vodka he'd just tasted fanned over my jaw. I turned slightly, bringing our lips inches apart. My lungs struggled to process oxygen.

"I can't believe you eavesdropped on Paige to find me."

He rested one forearm on the table and gripped the back of my chair with his other hand, effectively boxing me in. If I wanted to leave, I'd have to go through him.

"I was walking by the office of *my* communications officer in *my* place of business. Hardly eavesdropping." His words, accompanied by that sly upturn of his lips, were heartstopping.

I did my best to hide how he affected me. Opting to roll my eyes, I muttered, "Uh-huh."

"You left me little choice. If you won't come to me, I'll come to you."

I glanced at my watch. "I still have eight minutes of my twenty-four hours left."

He lifted his chin slightly and looked down at me. "So you do. Is it your intention to make me wait?"

"Absolutely." I smiled widely.

"Very well. I'm a patient man, especially when the odds are in my favor."

"You're so sure I've made up my mind?" I asked, hoping my bluff wasn't written all over my face. Maintaining some kind of pride would be useful. The last thing Roman needed was an easy victory over me to further inflate his ego.

"I think you made up your mind last night before you left the table," he said, his voice so low that only I could hear him.

He trailed his fingertip from my chin down my neck. The urge to break into a full shiver and wrap my arms around him became overwhelming.

Raw need buzzed through me so hard, it felt like an active bee hive had taken up residence in my chest. It was hard to remember that this was the same man who'd sat opposite me last night, harsh and demanding. This was the side of Roman that my body instantly recognized. He'd only touched me briefly, kissed me once, but it had apparently been enough to bury a seed of lust that was blooming into a full-blown craving.

"What if I need more?"

He frowned. "More of what?"

You. Despite that being the truth, I didn't say it out loud. The other night at dinner, he had been upset with me, and I understood why. He had thought I was meeting him with an agenda, and the idea of being used didn't tend to sit well with people. Hence, the emotional rollercoaster I'd been on for the past twenty-four hours.

I hadn't shown up at that restaurant to talk about the center or its funding. I had shown up to see the man who'd carried my shoes and made me feel like the wealthy world around me didn't matter. The man who'd kissed me with no reservation.

"I want more of that night," I whispered.

He looked at me for a long moment. "The night we met," he stated. Maybe he felt something too. Something beyond the proposed arrangement. Or maybe I was fooling myself . . .

"That was a good evening," he finally admitted.

Something inside my chest relaxed, and breathing became a bit easier. Just his acknowledgment sparked an ounce of hope that there existed the potential for something greater than what I was about to agree to.

"I saw you."

His frowned deepened. "What do you mean 'saw'? You don't see me now?"

"Not in the same way. I only get glimpses. That night you were . . ." A tremor rolled up my spine. He had been intense, engaging, consuming. But of all the things he'd been, only one word seemed to fit what I was trying to say. "You were real."

"And you want more of this man you think me to be? This man you saw at the gala?"

"I know I saw him," I said with all the confidence I felt, because *that man* was the one thing I was clinging to. The one who was honest and real, and seemed connected to a deeper part of me that I couldn't explain. "And yes. I want more of that man."

His fingers gently trailed behind my earlobe, then down to my collarbone. "Alright, Miss Underwood, I'll see what I can do." His mouth was so close I could feel the hum of his words vibrate my lips. "But I want something in return."

I knew right away what that something was: my answer.

"Do you always get what you want?" I breathed, completely aware that I was leaning into his touch and not caring at all.

"That depends."

"On?"

He palmed the side of my neck, and my gaze snapped from his mouth to his eyes. "On what the next word you say is."

Holding that piercing black stare, I whispered the only thing that felt right. "Yes."

He gave a quick nod. "Good."

Just when I thought he'd kiss me, a loud cheer erupted through the bar as the patrons celebrated a touchdown.

I pulled back, breaking the trance, and looked around. Six men in matching black suits were stationed around the bar. All with earpieces. How had I not noticed them? Maybe because every time Roman invaded my personal space, the world outside of his shadow didn't seem to exist.

Several mumbles and questioning eyes zeroed in on us. Then a flash of light. Cell phones were out and pointing in our direction. Roman's security detail flocked around us, like shadows coming out of nowhere.

Paige's words from earlier began to sink in. The governor's personal life was, and would be now more than ever, on display.

"Aren't you worried someone will see us?" I asked. "See you . . ."

"See me what?"

"You know." I looked around again. Though people kept their distance, many called out to the governor, cheered, or waved. "Getting cozy with a random girl in a bar?"

He arched a brow and grinned. "Getting cozy?"

"You know what I mean," I huffed quickly. Awkwardness enveloped me quicker than I could process it. Thank God I had remembered to take my anxiety pill this afternoon.

"I do." He tucked a lock of hair behind my ear. "And no, I'm not worried. Because you're not a random girl. You're my girlfriend now, remember? There is nothing wrong with me enjoying a night out with you."

The word "girlfriend" made my heart skip. "At a sports bar in Arbor Hill?"

"Especially at a sports bar in Arbor Hill." He wound his arm around me and palmed the small of my back, pulling me closer. "Now, make it look good, sweetheart. People are watching."

His lips landed on mine in a consuming kiss. Quick and hard, it was like a brand, telling me what I was and showing everyone else.

More flashes of light went off, and comprehension flooded my brain. This was what Roman was going for: being a "man of the people," hanging out on a Thursday night with his small-town girlfriend, watching the Giants game.

He drew away and smiled. The shouts continued. Questions of who I was and requests for autographs rolled through the crowd. There were even some catcalls and whistles.

I sat up straight, determined to put some distance between us and remind myself that this was, in fact, an arrangement. Titles like "girlfriend" didn't really matter, because they were based on a verbal contract.

He stood and helped me to my feet. Facing the crowd, he pulled me close and waved, then nodded to a member of his security. They began patting down a few people—the first of what would likely be many—and letting them come closer. People were still holding out their cell phones, asking for a picture with the governor.

"What's the next step, then?" I asked quietly.

As the patrons approached, he kept his hold on me and said in a low voice, "Dinner tomorrow night at my place. We have some rules to cover."

Chapter Five

· · · • · ··

The next night, Roman sent a car for me, which wouldn't have been that bad except that it meant questioning stares from both Hazel and Paige before leaving. The ride to his house wasn't long, but my thoughts, most of which weren't good, had more than enough time to take over my entire brain.

"Good evening, Miss Underwood," said a man in a—big shocker—black suit, opening my car door. "Governor Reese is waiting."

He escorted me up the steps and into the governor's mansion. It was massive, but held a homey quality. The red brick facade accented by white pillars and trim reminded me of something you might see in the country. Small fir trees lined the walk leading to the front door, and the fresh scent of pine wafted in the cool air. The large maple tree in the middle of the lawn was starting to lose its leaves, raining bits of yellow and orange on the trimmed green grass, like paint splatter. September was one of my favorite months in New York, because it was when autumn really started to show its true colors.

The guard ushered me through the front door, then stopped me in the foyer.

"Forgive me, but I need to check your purse."

"Of course." I handed it to him. He went through it quickly and thoroughly and handed it back.

"Amy," Roman said as he entered the room and walked toward me. He wore a white, form-fitting button-down shirt, rolled at the sleeves and tucked into dark pants. The black belt that lined his hips completed the look, making the governor positively drool worthy.

His eyes were fixed on mine, and the powerful, graceful way his body moved was enchanting. When he was toe-to-toe with me, he cupped my face in his palms and kissed me softly on the lips. I jumped, startled that he'd be so bold in front of one of his security men.

"You look beautiful," he said against my lips, ignoring my surprise.

"Thank you." My voice was a poor excuse for a choked whisper.

He smiled and, with his hand on my lower back, guided me to walk with him, leaving the security guy, and the bulk of my sanity, behind.

"Why did you kiss me?"

"Shh," he said and squeezed my hip.

I clamped my mouth shut and tamped down everything that was going through my mind. We didn't head toward the dining room like I'd expected. Instead, he led me down a more private hallway.

The high arches were lined with crown molding, and soft hues of cream and butterscotch accented the walls. Several winding turns later, we arrived at a large, wooden door with two men standing on either side.

"Gentlemen," Roman acknowledged as he opened the door.

"Good evening, sir. Ma'am," said the one I remember as Andrew.

"Hi," I muttered, feeling like I was walking into a special ops meeting or something.

There was no further exchange. Roman simply opened the door and led me in. Based on the security, I expected to enter an office or a secret meeting, but no. It was a bedroom. And it was intimidating.

"Is this your room?"

He nodded.

"Wow," I breathed, half impressed and half shocked. My whole apartment could fit inside this one room.

A massive fireplace was in the center of the wall across from us, giving off small pops and crackles, and making the room smell like pine trees and autumn. Two doors, which I assumed led to other rooms, were to the left of where I stood.

To the far right, there was a large sleigh bed made up in blue sheets, blankets, and pillows of varying hues. A little sitting area, complete with a small table and plush chairs, was situated in front of the stone-lined fireplace.

"I thought we were going to have dinner?"

"We are," he said and took my purse, setting it on the little table. "Food will be sent up."

"I . . ." My words were dying fast as I looked around.

This was a bad idea. Playing girlfriend was one thing, but I remembered the promise Roman had made about us being in close proximity to a bed—that if anything happened, it would be because I wanted it. Problem was, I trusted him more than myself when it came to that subject. I tended to lose my mind where he was concerned, and the closer he came, the more I lost.

"I don't think this is a good idea."

He didn't acknowledge my words. Instead, he invaded my space in one stride, eating up the distance between us.

"We need to talk," he rasped. His large palms cupped my neck, then trailed to my shoulders.

The moment his hands touched me, I shivered like a neglected kitten desperate for affection. I tried to hang on to my gumption, to broach the topics we needed to discuss, but he ran those warm palms over my back in a soft, sweeping caress, and my stupid body instantly arched into his touch. When he wove around to my front, sliding over my stomach and up to cup my breasts, I jumped back.

"What are you doing?"

"Frisking you."

He stepped closer, closing the distance again, seeming completely unaffected. Kneeling, he clasped my thigh between his hands and slid down past my calf, all the way to the ankle. The other leg received the same attention The entire surface of my skin was flushed and tingling from his touch, and I hoped he couldn't hear my heart, which was about ready to beat its way out of my ribs.

"What is it you're looking for?"

"Wires."

"I'm wearing a skirt. You'd see them if there were any." The statement came out a bit harsh, either from the absurdity of the situation, or the fact that his bare hands were on my bare thighs, and the only thing I could think about was being more bare.

He stood and shrugged, obviously pleased and not at all ashamed about copping a feel.

"You can't be too careful."

While my whole body was buzzing from that rather thorough frisk, Roman seemed as calm as ever. He simply motioned for me to sit in one of the chairs, which I did.

The fire's warmth heated my shins and face. I had opted for a skirt and blouse that were simple, but hugged my curves without giving too much away. I had let my hair fall casually and gone with minimal makeup. I'd had no idea how to dress for a briefing about a manufactured relationship, but this had seemed good enough.

He sat in the opposite chair and faced me.

"We need to discuss a few things before we eat."

"Alright." I folded my hands in my lap.

"This is not a game. What goes on between us is very real. I meant what I said, Amy. The moment you agreed to this, we became a couple to the outside world. That means no more questions or shocked reactions to my affections. Especially in public."

"Did you just put regulations on my feelings?"

He grinned. "Yes. Of course, if my attentions are shocking, then we can remedy that."

I frowned. "What do you mean?"

"The best way to adapt to something is through repetition."

The heat of his gaze burned more than the fire as those sweltering obsidian pools dropped from my mouth to my breasts, and back up.

Blinking a few times, I tried to break the spell before I fell too far under its power. To remind myself to maintain my sanity above all else, and not be sucked into the magnetic presence that was Roman Reese.

"But what if I have questions?" The tremble in my voice was apparent. Now I was certain he could hear my erratic heartbeat from where he was sitting. It was getting harder and harder to calm the pounding in my chest.

This didn't feel like an approaching panic attack. I was familiar with those. No, this was much different. It was anticipation on a level that nearly had me shaking.

"If you insist on speaking of our arrangement after today, or have a question, then we can discuss it in a location of my choosing, and you will be naked."

I laughed, then choked when I realized he was serious. "Excuse me?"

"Those are my terms."

"Why?"

"Wires."

"Is that your answer to everything?"

"No."

Take soothing breaths, I reminded myself. "You honestly think I'd be wired?"

He shrugged. "Could be. Which is why you'll be naked." A hot shiver broke over my skin, as if his words had already stripped me of my clothes.

"What about your security detail?"

He frowned. "I have no desire to see them naked."

I rolled my eyes while he grinned, clearly loving this. "No, I mean that they're obviously wired, and they're around you all the time."

"They don't know about this arrangement. *Everyone* other than you and me view us as a couple."

The fact that Roman was willing to go to such an extent to keep this a secret from everyone, including those literally closest to him, was staggering. Could he really not a trust a soul? Granted, if this kind of scandal got out, it would definitely be damning. His reasons made sense, but were still a little on the crazy side.

"Why can't you just frisk me again?"

"Naked, Amy. Those are my terms."

His face was hard with a steely expression. So stark and mysterious, yet slight laugh lines and a shadow of dimples were present. The contrast was beautiful.

"Can something like this really be kept a secret?"

He leaned forward and skimmed the inside of my knee with his hand, stopping right when he hit the hem of my skirt.

"You tell me, Amy."

I bit my lip because I was ready to surrender anything. I had already agreed to his wishes. But he was wrong about one thing. Last night when he'd found me at the bar, he'd said he'd thought I'd made up my mind about him the night he proposed this arrangement. In fact, I'd made up my mind about him the moment he'd first kissed me at the gala. Governor Roman Reese was more than a hardened politician, and the darkness flickering behind his eyes was only the beginning.

"Is there anything else we need to go over?" I said.

"You understand that my privacy is sacred to me. I'm trusting you with much of it, and we—"

"Are together," I said.

He nodded.

"I understand."

"And you agree?"

I thought of Lauren. Thought of all the kids who had called the crisis line. Thought of how many were out there now, suffering in silence with nowhere to go, their family members having no idea where to take them for help. My stomach instantly hurt.

"Yes. But I want your word that you'll help me with this center, and that sex isn't an expectation and won't affect any part of this arrangement. Whether I'm talking to you naked or not."

He looked almost . . . impressed. "The only time you'd have to disrobe to speak with me would be if you chose to discuss this arrangement. Unless you'd prefer to talk to me naked regularly, in which case, I have no objection." His gaze zeroed in on my mouth, and I zeroed right back in on his. "I have already drafted a proposal in the state budget stipulating funding for New Beginnings. I will also support the anti-drug campaign and introduce you to people with a lot of influence and money who are looking to donate." His gaze ran the length of my body. "And as I said before, sex isn't part of this deal in any way. It's a choice."

"Okay, then." I breathed. "What about my terms?"

"Your terms? Didn't you just state them?" Before I could answer he unleashed a sexy grin. "You mean your terms regarding more of this 'real me' you saw at the gala."

I nodded.

"You'll have to give me specifics, Miss Underwood. Because I'm happy to give you more . . ." His fingers, which had been drawing small circles around my knee, slowly trailed higher, disappearing beneath my skirt. My breath hitched.

My eyes drifted shut; I couldn't stop them. The fire's warmth licked my skin while Roman's touch seared me in an entirely different way. It made me want to strip down and feel the heat of both over my entire body.

"There is something about you, Amy," he said musingly. "I won't deny that. Won't tell you this is purely a game, because I think about that night too. Think about you. How you clung to me. From your sexy mouth to your sweet little moans. I replay our kiss. Over and over."

"How do you do this?" I whispered.

"Do what?" His voice was a growl and while my eyes were still closed, I felt him move closer.

"Enthrall people."

I heard him shift his weight and felt his breath skate across my lips. He must have been kneeling in front of me now, but his fingers never relinquished their station on my inner thigh. I refused to open my eyes. Couldn't. Because once I did, I wouldn't be able to look away.

"It's part of the job," he whispered. "Making you want me above others."

His mouth brushed slightly over mine, barely making contact. I wanted more. Needed it. Instinct took over and I did the only thing

I could. Snaking my tongue out, I tasted the seam of his lips. A low growl came from him, but he didn't pull away.

"You're good at your job, Governor."

"And you are not what you seem, Miss Underwood." He nipped my bottom lip, and a zing of pleasure shot through my entire body. "Open your eyes."

I instantly obeyed, as if helpless not to. Cupping my neck in both palms, he leaned back to look at me. "Do you feel forced to be here?"

There was something so vulnerable in his eyes, it made my ribs suddenly feel like they were crushing my lungs. He was asking me. Considering my feelings, my comfort . . . my interests.

There was so much power behind Roman Reese but there he was, on his knees, asking.

"No. I'm here because I want to be." And right then, in that moment, was exactly where I wanted to stay.

His gaze didn't leave mine. But he didn't move. Didn't push for more, as if waiting to make sure I was certain. His hard torso pressed against my knees as he once again overwhelmed my space—and it felt good. So good that I was already drowning in him.

It had been so long since I'd been with a man, and I'd never noticed how badly my body was crying out until I'd met Roman. There was a draw, a need to feel him, because I knew whatever he delivered would be mind-shattering in its intensity.

He had the power, but I had control over myself. Sort of. Unfortunately, I was losing what little restraint I had left.

My chest rose and fell with easy breaths, like it knew I was surrendering to the man before me. The one with the dark eyes, eyes that held the same wicked promise I'd seen the night I'd met him at the gala. The same man who'd flashed a look of vulnerability and rawness that I was desperate to see again.

"I want to know something true," I whispered. "About you."

"Why?"

"Can't a girl want to have a conversation with someone who interests her?" Throwing his words from that first night back at him felt kind of good. But the truth was, I did want to know him. Something. Anything. While this arrangement was new, he had never once revealed a single detail about himself.

"You want truth?"

I nodded.

"I am partial to the color blue," he grated, glancing down at my skirt.

Refusing to let go of his stare, my knees parted just a little. His hands slid from my neck down to the swell of my breasts, his thumbs barely skimming my nipples before continuing lower to span my waist.

"I'm competitive." His fingertip ran along the waistband of my skirt. "I love a good challenge."

My knees spread farther, allowing him access between them, which he took. Grabbing my ass, he pulled me against him. I gasped as my core pressed against his lower torso, his erection prodding me.

"You told me that you felt small in the world. I've never had that problem." He shifted his hips, rubbing the steel rod against my most sensitive area. "But sometimes, I wish I did. Wish I could just get lost."

His mouth seized mine. Plunging his tongue inside, he drank me in, consuming everything in one kiss. Holding me tightly, he ground his hips against mine again, sending sparks from my center to every limb.

I wrapped my legs around him, locking my heels, and hugged him closer. I just wanted to feel him. To have him stay here this time, with me, instead of being interrupted and walking away.

He worked my mouth like he owned it. Like every part of me was open to his exploration. There was nothing slow or sweet about his kiss. It was commanding and dominant. Rough and consuming. I let him do it: taste me however he wanted.

"I've thought of you, Amy," he growled, then delved his tongue between my lips again. "Every damn day since I met you."

He gently bit my chin, then moved along my jaw to my pulse point. When he ran his tongue along the shell of my ear, a violent shiver raced over my skin.

"I've thought of what you'd feel like . . . taste like . . . everywhere."

My whole body was bursting into flames, and all I wanted was more. To be the center of his attention. To latch on to his need and let it take me as far as it could. Because for the first time, getting lost didn't seem so bad.

"I've thought of you too," I groaned, my head falling back as he licked and sucked his way from my earlobe to my neck.

"Tell me," he growled against my skin. "Tell me what you thought of."

I buried my fingers in his hair as he moved lower, kissing my collarbone. He snaked one hand up and started unbuttoning my shirt.

"I thought about the way you treated me," I admitted. "How you kissed me. How you change."

"Change?" His fingers traveled lower, popping the last button free. He pushed the fabric open.

"There are different sides to you. You're a tough man to keep up with."

With his fingers on the front clasp of my bra, he looked up at me. "You don't have to keep up tonight, sweetheart."

A flick of his wrist, and the lace covering me fell open, exposing my breasts.

"Jesus," he whispered.

The air that wafted over my flesh was warm, but left tingles in its wake. The governor of New York was on his knees before me, staring like a man on the brink of devouring his last meal. Heat raced through my veins like freshly lit sparklers. Every cell was flooded with an achy desperation.

But as the moment lengthened, and he continued to simply stare, that tingle turned into a buzz of unease and anticipation. Did he like what he saw? Dislike? I wasn't tall or overly thin. I took care of myself, but no matter how hard I exercised, my breasts, hips, and backside had always been on the large side.

I unwove my fingers from his hair and went to cover myself.

"Don't you dare," he growled. "You can hold on to either me or the chair, but you're not covering up."

He gripped my sides, his palms heavy against my ribcage, and lifted me so that my back arched, pushing my breasts out farther. My hands flew to the armrests for balance. With his eyes on mine, he leaned in and slowly sucked my right nipple into his mouth.

I groaned, digging my fingernails into the chair.

"Fucking incredible," he grated.

He circled his tongue around my breast, leaving a trail of goose bumps before taking the peak between his lips again. This time, he sucked *hard*.

"Oh!" I flinched from the odd sensation that was a mix of pleasure and pain. So much intensity stung, but I didn't want him to stop.

Maintaining his hold and keeping me positioned like an offering, he moved to the other breast. All I could do was throw my head back, and let him sample whatever he wanted, however he wanted.

"Do you like this, Amy?" He slowly licked around my nipple, softly flicking the sensitive skin until my breasts felt heavy and achy. The gentle teases made my need smolder hotter, demanding more.

"Or do you like this?" He bit the tip, causing my hips to jolt out, ramming against his hard cock.

He didn't let up, instead pulling more of my breast into his mouth and sucking so hard, an orgasm threatened to unleash from just the promptings of his wicked mouth.

"That! I like that," I moaned to the ceiling.

Keeping his mouth on me, he threw my skirt up to my hips and tugged at my panties. I rose enough so that he could slide them down my legs and off. His fingers instantly circled my opening, and my hips moved to meet him, begging for deeper contact.

"Want more?"

"Yes," I breathed.

He plunged a finger inside and I cried out.

"Fuck, you're wet," he grated between laves of my nipple.

He withdrew, then ran the same finger over my clit, moistening it with my own cream. He did this again and again, delving inside only to retreat and tease, until my entire core was drenched.

"I didn't realize how hungry I was until just now," he said, releasing my breast and staring between my spread thighs.

Gripping the backs of my knees, he placed my legs over the armrests of the chair and bent down. I was spread to him, more vulnerable than I'd ever been. The first slide of his tongue against my hot flesh nearly made me explode.

"Mmm, better than my imagination." In one long stroke, he tasted the entire length of me. Then without warning, he thrust his stiffened tongue inside.

"Oh, God!" I moaned.

Keeping my legs where they were, I wove my fingers into his hair again and pulled. He growled and tongued my clit so fast and hard it felt like a vibrator. "Yes, Roman. Right . . . there . . ."

He devoured the sensitive bundle of nerves, sending my body higher and higher, reaching for the pleasure that was so close. When he thrust two fingers inside, I was shoved over the edge.

"Yes!"

My orgasm raced out of control. Burning every surface inside and out, until I felt like I'd just taken on a new body. A new soul. Every vein beneath my skin felt like dried kindling, splitting in half. It went on and on. My lungs struggled to keep up with my need for air.

After what seemed like an eternity, he slowed his assault, bringing me down gently.

Slumping against the back of the chair, I eased my grip on him.

"That was—" I began, but stopped when he suddenly rose to his feet and walked away.

I instantly closed my legs, but shock weighted my shoulders down.

I heard what sounded like a drawer opening and closing. Before I had time to right my clothing or look behind me to see what he was doing, he was back—standing before me with the fire behind him, glowing like a god.

He tugged open his belt with one hand. The other held a condom, which he ripped open with his teeth. He didn't bother taking off his shirt or his pants, just opened them enough to grip his cock, and roll the latex on.

I didn't even get a chance to really see it before he said, "Stand up and turn around."

My body was shaking, more confused than my mind. Intensity burned behind his eyes. He'd just spent a significant amount of time attending to my body. Praising me. But now there'd been a shift toward something animalistic.

I did as he asked. My skirt righted itself as I stood, covering me once more. His breath fanned over my ear, and he palmed the back of my thigh.

"You want this, Amy?" he asked.

I nodded.

"Say it."

"Yes, I want this . . . I want to be with you."

His hand slid up my thigh and cupped my hip, bringing my skirt with it. He nudged me to bend over. "Put your hands on the chair."

I did. With my skirt pulled up, my whole ass was bared to him as I held on to the armrests of the chair once more.

Though part of me didn't know whether to expect kindness or roughness, I was shocked to find that either option sounded amazingly desirable. There was so much of him that I didn't understand. But I wanted to. Wanted to be in his sights. Wanted to affect him the way he did me.

"Fucking gorgeous." He placed a hand on one of my cheeks and positioned himself at my entrance. When just the tip nudged inside, he gripped my hips in both hands. "Now hold on, sweetheart."

In one hard thrust, he sheathed himself inside of me.

"Roman!" The fit was difficult, despite how ready he'd made me. I hadn't been able to fully see him earlier, but he felt big. Almost overly so.

"Shit," he choked out, clinging to my waist and stilling his movements. "You okay?"

"Y-yes," I breathed.

Could he tell how long it had been? Somehow feel that I wasn't very experienced? It had been more than two years since I'd had sex, and that had only been a few times with Warren toward the end of our relationship. It had never been like this.

"You sure? You feel . . ." He slowly stirred himself within me, making me moan. "So fucking tight." He sounded on the verge, just like I was.

I pushed my hips back against him slightly, causing the crown to rub against that sensitive spot inside me.

"You feel so big," I gasped.

He gently pulled out, and I wanted to cry at the withdrawal and loss of connection.

"I'll go slowly this time," he rasped, pushing back inside at a steady pace.

I savored every moment. The feel of him, surrounded by me. My emotions were short-circuiting, senses fraying like the end of freshly cut rope. I was coming apart around him.

I was no longer alone. In this moment, I didn't have to hate myself for being the bad daughter who'd destroyed her family. Instead, I was part of something better—part of *him*.

It brought tears to my eyes. The intensity bordered on confused, amazed anguish. I wanted to bottle this feeling and keep it with me always. Roman wanted me. And I wanted him so much.

My heart beat wildly, pulsing through every nerve from the tips of my fingers to the base of my spine, and everywhere in between.

He leaned forward, rocking over my body. "You want more?" he grated into my ear.

"Yes."

Straightening once more, he gathered my hair in one fist while the other gripped my hip.

"Amy," was all he said before hammering inside of me.

My body jolted forward, but his hold on my hair kept me flush against him. My scalp burned slightly, the tingles spurring my already-aching body into a frenzy.

He thrust in and out, harder and faster. Pumping deeper every time. His grip kept me close, and his body moved fluidly with mine. He hit that spot inside over and over until I begged to come.

Releasing his grip on my hip, he wrapped his arm around me, delved between my slick folds, and rubbed my clit. I couldn't hold on anymore.

"Roman," I sobbed, shattering into a million pieces, his hold the only thing keeping me up.

He groaned and sank, if possible, even deeper. I clenched around him, over and over, bathing him in my orgasm. He stilled, buried to the hilt, as if simply enjoying the feeling of my body's spasms. His cock twitched inside of me, and his heavy breaths echoed through the room.

"Fuck, Amy," he growled, and I felt him tense with his own release.

He slowly withdrew, relaxing his grip on my hair. The strands fell from his fist and landed against my back as he pulled out.

I instantly felt chilly and achy. My body missed him already.

"I'll be right back." He headed toward one of the doors I had seen when I'd first walked in. Turned out it was a bathroom.

I took a moment to right myself. Standing up straight was almost painful, and the throbbing between my legs was one of total satisfaction and a little discomfort.

Had this been another situation with another man, maybe I would have felt different. But between my lack of experience and having no idea how to bounce back from what had just happened, anxiety rushed through me.

I felt confused. Like something had been taken from me, and all I could think of was how to get it back. But I couldn't. It was done. Over. The previously clear line of this arrangement had been irrevocably blurred, and I had no idea how to react.

I refastened my bra, my breasts screaming at the lace for scraping over my swollen nipples, and quickly buttoned up my shirt. Righting my skirt, I looked around for my panties, but didn't see them.

Roman returned from the bathroom looking more put together than he had when I'd first arrived. No sign of what had just happened. His hair was smooth, his white shirt tucked into his black slacks, his belt in place. Polished perfection. While I felt disheveled . . . cheap.

"Are you hungry?" He stood several feet in front of me, the fire shadowing his handsome face and making those eyes burn like the pits of a volcano.

"No." I looked at my hands, which were fidgeting, and tried to ignore the roiling in my stomach.

What had happened? More importantly, how? In one conversation, at the sound of his voice and the persuasive look of his eyes, I had melted. Just like I had the first night I'd met him. He'd walked up, out of nowhere, and put himself in my world. But he was right—he never forced me.

From the beginning, this had been my doing. I just didn't know how to handle the aftermath. The emotions of the last few days were like a rollercoaster in my chest. Up and down and up again, until I didn't know if I was reaching for the sky or clawing at the ground.

"I think you should eat something," he said, taking a step toward me.

"I want to go," I whispered.

"Amy, look at me." Another step.

I backed away.

"Amy," he said again. "Look at me. Now." The edge in his voice startled me, and I glanced up to meet his eyes. "I'm sorry. I didn't mean to hurt you."

I shook my head. "You didn't. I just . . . I need some time to think about this."

"Talk to me."

I bit the inside of my cheek to keep the tears from my eyes. "I can't."

That was what had gotten me here in the first place. Roman was good with words, pulling you in before you knew what to expect. Tonight was the first time in a long time I'd felt alive. Like every mistake I'd made in my life didn't matter. I was just a woman. A woman he wanted.

But that moment was over.

His energy had changed. Whatever ground we'd just gained didn't matter, because we were back at the starting line now. I could feel it. The dynamic between us had shifted, all the intensity of the last few moments dissipating.

Standing before him, knowing what it felt like to have him inside me, was too much distance to handle. The need for him wasn't fading, it was growing. It was pathetic how badly I wanted to just disappear in his arms. I hadn't realized how hollow I truly was until right then. And I couldn't face him.

"I don't want you to go," he said.

"Are you planning on making me stay?"

"No," he growled. The way he said it tore something inside of my chest. He looked angry. But I couldn't deal with that right then. I just needed space. Quickly. Emotions were flooding, and every insecurity, every ounce of doubt I had about myself and this arrangement, was rushing in on me. I refused to break down in front of him.

"You're different . . . I didn't expect this," I whispered.

Because the truth was, every time I crossed paths with Roman Reese, I seemed to see a different facet of him. At the gala he'd been charming. At dinner he'd been demanding. And tonight, he was intensely consuming.

"I didn't either," he said, his steely gaze boring down on me.

I couldn't take anymore. His looks and dominating presence were too much. I grabbed my purse from the table, walked to the door, and opened it.

"Let my driver take you home," he called after me.

I glanced over my shoulder. "Thank you."

"Amy—"

"Good night, Governor," I said, and shut the door behind me.

Chapter Six

H ey," Paige said, looking up from her laptop. She was in the middle of the living room floor, surrounded by crumpled papers, a legal pad on her knee. She closed the screen.

I locked the door behind me and took off my jacket. "Hi."

"You okay?" Her tone was soft. We hadn't spoken much since Roman had interrupted girls' night yesterday. I kicked off my shoes and crossed my arms.

"I don't know, Paige."

She set the legal pad on the floor and stood, approaching me. "Did something happen? Are you hurt?"

"No," I smiled a little. If there was a mama bear of our little den, it was Paige.

She cared—she just didn't do emotions well. Logic first, questions later was her thought process. I wanted to tell her everything—God knew I could use some advice right now—but there were pieces I couldn't share, not even with my best friend.

"We . . . Roman and I . . ." I glanced at my hands.

"You had sex?" she asked.

I nodded.

She sighed loudly, wrapped her arm around my shoulders, and sat me on the couch. "Want to talk about it?"

"That's just it, Paige, I don't even know where to begin, or what I'm feeling. I wanted to be there, but it was like once it was done, a fog cleared and it didn't seem . . . real. Any of it."

"They're a different breed, Amy."

"What do you mean?"

"Politicians. They're different. One of their strongest features is charisma. Not all of them." Paige rolled her eyes, as if mentally counting the people she knew to be otherwise. "But a lot of them. They have an ability to pull you in, consume your attention and focus, so all you can see is them. It's not just your vote they go for, it's your trust."

I nodded, knowing firsthand that Roman was good at what he did. I had said as much to him earlier. But hearing Paige say it made everything hit home. I craved Roman's attention, because when I had it, I felt special, a part of something. A part of his world.

"He treated me well," I whispered. I'd never had in-depth conversations about sex, not even with Paige, mostly because there hadn't been much to talk about. "But afterward, I couldn't figure out why I felt so cold and alone. I had to get out of there."

She nodded. "It's kind of like a drug."

"What is? Getting caught up in a politician's charm?"

"No, getting caught up in a man." Her voice was soft, like she was speaking from a place of real regret and sadness. If Paige had guy problems, she never spoke of them, or even showed an ounce of unease. "It's scary and consuming even on its own. But add the power and cunning that come with a man like Governor Reese, and you've got a combination that's hard to beat."

I knew that. Roman was beyond a typical man. Politician or not, his presence screamed dominance.

"Not to mention, if he 'treated you well'," Paige added, nudging my shoulder, "it added to your freak out. You only feel bad about losing something if it's worth missing."

I smiled. That was true. The few times I'd been with Warren had been, well, nothing worth missing. After tonight, I was painfully aware that I had been walking around with a soul-slicing void in my gut: a deep emptiness that I hadn't realized was so severe until I'd felt a connection with Roman.

"Did you tell him about your past?"

I shook my head.

"So he didn't know you'd only slept with one guy, and the last time was more than two years ago?"

Again, I shook my head. It wasn't a particularly awesome fact I enjoyed talking about. But apparently, not acknowledging it didn't make it any less true, a situation I was very familiar with. Paige squeezed my shoulder and her voice became even softer.

"Do you want some Tylenol?"

Though tonight had been confusing as hell with a backlash of emotional turmoil I couldn't quite sift through, it had been amazing and I didn't regret it. However, the soreness from earlier was creeping up a little.

"Yeah, thank you," I said.

Paige got up and walked to the kitchen cupboard where we kept the pills.

"Are you going to see him again?" she asked, handing me the medicine and a glass of water.

Her tone was a little different than it had been last night, when she'd asked me the same thing. Maybe she was coming around to the idea? I appreciated the kindness in her voice.

"Yes," I answered instantly, and realized it had nothing to do with our arrangement. The alternative of not seeing him didn't seem like an option. Already I was kind of wishing I hadn't left. I wanted to be back in his presence. "There's something about him, Paige."

She nodded. "Just be careful. In this business, there's always an angle. Find every ounce of strength you have and use it. All the time. Don't cower and don't back down. You control your world, okay?"

"You mean, power respects power."

She smiled. "Exactly. And you're stronger than you think."

"Thank you."

"You need anything else?"

"No, I'm good. Thanks for listening."

She nodded and bent to hug me.

"Paige, I really didn't mean for this to affect your job," I whispered.

"I know." She lightly patted the back of my head. "But it will." Deep down, I knew she was right. I was just hoping the effect wouldn't be major. "G'night, Amy."

"Good night."

It wasn't until after Paige had gone to her room and shut the door that I realized what she had said.

It's like a drug . . .

Only a few samples of Roman Reese had me wanting more. While I was with him, it was amazing, but coming down was a hard thing to deal with. I just wanted that next high. That next time to be with him.

My life's work was helping people battle addictions, but maybe I was no better than the thing I was fighting.

. . . • . . .

After a weekend of not hearing from Roman, I'd spent my Monday morning on the phone being rejected by potential private donors, all of who were informing me that while drug rehabilitation was a good cause, a new center in Arbor Hill was basically useless. Even if it did receive state funding, I didn't know how much money would come in, and I still needed to do my job in the meantime.

I was about to throw my work phone, otherwise known as the ringing spawn of Satan, through the window when my cell rang.

I didn't recognize the number.

"Hello?" I barked, a little more rudely than intended.

"Tough day, sweetheart?"

For a split second, my heart stopped pumping and my lungs stilled. I didn't know what to say to him. Partly because after I had left Friday night, I wasn't sure if I would hear from him again. I hadn't even known he had my number—I didn't have his—though it shouldn't have been surprising. He'd found me in a bar, after all.

Clinging to Paige's advice and my own will to stay strong, I spoke the truth.

"Just frustrating being rejected."

"I know the feeling," Roman countered.

Heat rushed to my face and, once again, I wondered if I had made a terrible mistake by leaving Friday night without talking to him.

"How's your day?" I asked, a little shaky because really, how the hell should I handle this? *We're together in the eyes of everyone around us.* I had repeated this to myself over and over, and a normal girlfriend would ask about her boyfriend's day, right?

"My day has been busy. Which is why I'm calling. There's a fundraiser this weekend, and I need you to come by my office so my staff can get you prepped."

"Right now?"

"Yes. I'll send a car for you."

I looked at my still-full inbox and the memos piled on my desk, and leaned back in my chair. "I can't, Roman. I can't just leave work in the middle of the day."

"Amy." The way he said my name—half growl, half stern warning—made me flash to Friday night, when he'd used the same tone right before thrusting himself inside me.

A hot flush broke over my skin, and my palms suddenly felt clammy.

"I need you to be here today. I've blocked out time, and this is an important fundraiser for my campaign that you are accompanying me to."

I could almost smile because he was telling me my duty, based on our arrangement, without actually bringing up the arrangement. Clever man.

Stay strong, I reminded myself. This wasn't a battle of wills, it was a battle of reality. He wanted this to be considered a relationship?

"Well, Roman, I can't leave my job on a whim to do my boyfriend's bidding."

"I thought your job was contingent upon securing funding for your Arbor Hill center," he countered.

Oh, he was good. Damn him.

"And if I get fired before I get a chance to secure that funding because I randomly take off in the middle of the work day, then our discussion is moot."

He was silent for a moment, but I could feel his angry energy buzzing through the phone.

"I wouldn't want that to happen, Miss Underwood."

The line went dead and so did my pulse.

Shit!

What was I doing? Everything was so tightly entwined together that no move seemed like the right one. If I jumped whenever he said, even if it interfered with work, that was bad for my job. If I didn't, that was bad for my "relationship," which directly correlated with my job. Now I really wanted to throw my phone.

Taking a deep breath, I stuck to my principle that I was right. It wasn't wise to take off whenever he called. Yes, pride was an issue, though I couldn't find much of it at the moment. This job was important to me. But had I just cost myself a fake relationship and gotten fired from my other "job"?

I tossed my cell on my desk and put my forehead between my hands. Today sucked.

Twenty minutes, fourteen e-mails, and three annoying visits from Silas, who gloated that he'd just landed a several-thousand-dollar donation, later, I was ready for a late lunch and maybe even an early happy hour.

"She's right this way," I heard Marcy say with a slight giggle. She had to be several cubicles away, but her giddy voice carried all the way down the aisle.

I opened my e-mail, determined to send out just one more before lunch and—

"Amy, someone is here to see you," Marcy said.

I turned in my chair to see her beaming from ear to ear, and realized right away that her obvious joy stemmed from the fact that the governor of New York stood directly behind her, a victorious look marring his handsome face.

"What are you doing here?" I snapped.

Marcy's eyes went wide at my reaction.

I tried to backpedal with a smile. "It's just . . . I'm so surprised!" My newly elated tone seemed to calm Marcy but only made Roman's grin widen.

"That's what I was going for, sweetheart." He turned to Marcy and glanced around the room. "I know how hard you all work, and I think New Beginnings does such a magnificent job for the state of New York and all her citizens."

"Why, thank you," Marcy preened, running a hand through her hair.

Glad to see I wasn't the only one susceptible to Roman's charm.

"I am going to be doing a lot of running around over the next couple of months, gearing up for the election," Roman started. "I was hoping to have my girlfriend on my arm for certain occasions, especially since one of the key issues I'm tackling this year is drug prevention. I must admit, Amy has sold me on New Beginnings, and I think your organization would be perfect to spearhead this campaign."

"Oh my," Marcy breathed. "That's wonderful!" She looked between me and Roman, so happy it practically radiated off of her. "Forgive me, but I didn't know you two were together."

"Please don't apologize," Roman said, clasping her hand in his two. "Amy talks all the time about the importance of her commitment to New Beginnings and what it means to her. I'd never want to cause an issue."

"No! No, of course not! Amy, anytime you need to go, please do." Marcy smiled.

I sat there, mouth hanging open, watching what was happening like I was on a different planet. Governor Roman Reese was in full swing, negotiating for what he wanted. And there wasn't a damn thing I could do about it.

"Thank you so much, Marcy." He patted her hand. "You're doing an amazing job here. Keep it up."

"Thank you, sir." The woman practically swooned. I couldn't blame her.

Roman's dark eyes locked on mine. The crisp navy-blue suit and steel-gray tie he wore made him look like he belonged in the pages of GQ, rather than in the middle of my cubicle.

"Amy," he said in that way that made my whole body respond. "Care to join me for lunch?"

"Just lunch?"

"And a meeting. We need to go over this weekend's fundraiser with my staff."

"I can't," I said through clenched teeth. "I have a lot to do around here."

"Oh no, it's okay." Marcy clapped her hands together. "Don't worry about coming back today. You just worry about the governor's fundraiser. We have everything covered here."

I tried really hard not to glare at Roman in front of my boss. She was all too happy to concede to his every wish, which was obviously why he'd come down here in the first place.

"Thank you, Marcy. I'll have my secretary send over my itinerary for Amy so you'll know which days she'll be absent."

"Perfect," Marcy smiled.

"Are you sure?" I asked her.

"Absolutely," she said.

There was something genuine in her eyes that made it hard for me to fight with her. Of course, Roman had just fought a battle for me, one I hadn't wanted in the first place. I liked my job. I wanted to be here.

I grabbed my purse and jacket. Roman held his hand out to me and I took it, hating how warm and comforting it was. Hating how my mind instantly shot to a few nights ago, remembering the way his touch had felt on my skin. How he'd gripped my hips . . . pulled my hair . . .

"Something on your mind?" Roman breathed in my ear as he steered me out of the office, everyone staring as we went.

"Yes," I mumbled, keeping my eyes down as we made our way out of the building.

"I'd love to hear what thoughts have you blushing."

I wanted to slap my hands over my cheeks, but it was too late. Instead, I went with, "Nothing I care to share."

"I see," he said.

We walked down the steps to a black car, and he opened the back passenger door for me.

"Perhaps you're thinking of something I've already had the pleasure of experiencing?"

My gaze shot to his. I was pretty certain his job description didn't include being a mind reader, but it was still hard to ward off the mortification.

"I . . . I wasn't—"

"Don't attempt to lie to my face, Miss Underwood." He moved closer, one hand still resting on the open car door. "Please."

He motioned for me to get in. I did, and he closed the door, then walked around the car and got in on the other side. There was privacy glass between us and the driver, and I suddenly felt too aware of, and too close to, the imposing governor.

I needed to find my strength. Tell him how I felt.

I swiveled to face him. "I can't believe you did that."

"I told you, Amy, if you won't come to me, then I'll come to you." He glanced over at me, but remained facing forward.

"But I can't just drop everything whenever you want. I have grant proposals to write and commitments to keep. Believe it or not, I work hard at my job."

"Entry-level job," he clarified.

Fire raged through every vein and my teeth nearly chipped from grinding so hard.

"Yes. Which is why I need to be at my *entry-level* job so that I can get the one promotion opening up soon."

"And my presence just sped that along. You're welcome." He still faced forward, casual and calm, as all his high-class entitlement suffocated me.

This was the side of Roman I didn't care for. But it was apparently something I had to get used to. The only good thing about his attitude was that it seemed to bring my strong side to the surface, because I wasn't feeling very shy, polite, or nice at the moment.

"What your presence did was basically start rumors that I'm sleeping my way to the top. I'm actually good at what I do," I emphasized the last word. "Now all of that doesn't matter, because I'll just be the governor's girlfriend. Not to mention the impression it gives when you waltz in and demand special privileges from my boss just so I can skip work."

"I didn't demand."

"Oh, yes, you did. Only you did it in your backwards, charming way so that it was hard to notice. Like she'd ever have said no to you."

He finally looked me in the eye and, with a way too sexy smile said, "You think I'm charming?"

I wanted to growl. Infuriating man! "I think you're irritating."

"Well, that's better than indifference." He faced forward again. "At least I know I get you hot."

My mouth hung open, again, which was becoming a common occurrence around Roman. He glanced at me again, daring me to lie and say he didn't have that effect.

I snapped my mouth shut. I was mad, raging mad, but my body was thrumming, and my heart racing. I wanted to claw at him as much as kiss him, and the fact that he knew just made it worse.

"The reason our relationship works is because we keep each other's needs at the forefront of our minds," he said.

My brows shot toward my hairline. "You mean, *I* keep *your* needs at the forefront of *my* mind. Because right now, you don't seem to give a damn about mine. Whatever happens between us is irrelevant to my present professional situation. I still have to prove I'm the best candidate for that job. I have to actually, you know, *work*, to get it."

"I just told your boss that your organization is going to play a major part in the anti-drug campaign."

"Which has nothing to do with me! You saying those things doesn't change the fact that I haven't secured funds. I haven't even gotten donors interested. All I have is a handful of maybes. When I agreed—"

His glare nearly burned my skin when it landed on me. I swallowed and regrouped. Having a conversation with this man was more work than I had ever thought just talking could involve.

"I want our relationship to work," I started slowly. Making sure I used the correct verbiage. "And I know that dating you comes with strings."

"You mean perks," he grinned.

Right now, it came with a sporadic heartbeat and trembling hands, but nevertheless, I forced myself to keep calm and continue.

"Roman, despite what happens between us, I still have a life I have to live. A job I have to go to. If I don't produce something by November, at the end of this election season, I won't get that job."

The position would have to be filled by then, and that person would likely be responsible for overseeing the management of the new facility's opening. If we got the funding, of course. Either way, Silas was ahead of me in terms of tangible progress. If I didn't get the Level Two position, there would be no reason for me to stay in New York. I was already tapping into my savings on a regular basis to supplement my income and pay bills. That would only last me a few more months. The thought of moving back home to Indiana, where my parents and all their misery waited, made me a little nauseous.

I needed to make this work, acquire a real income, and make Lauren's House a reality. The alternative would be to deal with another failure, and all the disappointment that came with it.

"Do you always wear skirts to work?"

I frowned. Where did that come from? "Most of the time."

"Why not pants?"

I shook my head. "I, ah . . . what does this have to do with anything?"

"I'm curious." His eyes left a trail of heat as his gaze skated over my knees, up my legs, and to my breasts before he looked forward again.

"The only pants I wear are jeans, and that goes against the dress code."

"Why don't you wear slacks?"

Holy cow, what was this? Wardrobe interrogation?

"Because I don't like the way they fit me, okay? Why don't you wear jeans?" I fired back.

"Because I rarely have the opportunity. Why don't they fit you?"

I looked around the car to see if I had somehow been transported to some alternate plane of existence where anything about this conversation made sense. Nope. Still the back of his car and beyond the point of irritation.

"Because I have a big ass. Happy?"

"Yes." He turned, openly eyeing my body like he had every right to do so. "Your ass makes me very happy, actually." His dark gaze paused on my mouth. "In fact, I was just recalling how you looked, bent over my chair, skirt up around your hips, while I fucked you from behind."

His lips twisted into a panty-melting smirk that nearly made my pulse flatline. I didn't know whether it was his words or his expression, but I was on the brink of cardiac arrest.

Before I could say anything, the car stopped and Roman got out. "We're here." He walked around and opened my door, helping me out. "Welcome to Capitol Hill, Miss Underwood."

Chapter Seven

· · · · ··

D resses or skirts for Miss Underwood, no pants," Roman said to a small woman in her fifties, who was waddling beside him and furiously taking notes.

I walked behind them, trying to keep up and definitely not looking at Roman's ass, or thinking about how perfectly *his* pants fit him.

"Get one of the assistants to bring up the wardrobe. I'm also going to need a draft of talking points drawn up, a schedule of engagements and events sent to Marcy Dunbay at New Beginnings, and all travel arrangements for the next eight weeks altered to include Miss Underwood."

"Yes, sir," the woman said, the beaded chain dangling from her glasses to her neck swaying as she peered through her bifocals.

She took an immediate right and sat behind the single desk in front of a massive mahogany door. The small bronze placard on her desk read JEAN POSY. Obviously Roman's secretary.

Roman opened the door and ushered me through.

"This is your office?"

He nodded.

I looked around at the intricate décor. Rich wood and soft creams contrasted nicely with the burgundy and hunter-green accents. A couch and two chairs faced each other in the middle of the room. Between them sat a massive rug, quite possibly the most beautiful I'd ever seen.

With floor-to-ceiling windows as a backdrop, the huge wooden desk faced the room like a king's throne. Cherrywood bookshelves lined one wall, while the opposite held a fireplace surrounded by extensive brickwork and art hanging above the mantel.

"You really like your fireplaces," I murmured.

"I've acquired a new appreciation for them recently."

He walked behind his desk, and I couldn't tell if he'd noticed how his mere words had made my face flush more than those damn glowing embers.

"Are you going to fill me in on what's going on?" I said.

He looked up from a few papers he was perusing at his desk. "I'm preparing for you to travel with me over the course of this campaign."

The only thing missing from that statement was a "duh," and I was in no mood for his obvious repetition.

"Yeah, I gathered that when you barged into my office—"

"Cubicle."

"And interrupted my day," I said.

"I thought my girlfriend would enjoy spending time with her man."

I folded my arms and walked toward him. "Maybe she would if that man wasn't being a gigantic prick."

He arched a brow, and I stifled the urge to throw a palm over my mouth. I didn't know where this forwardness was coming from, but I was so off-kilter at this point that anything was liable to come out of my mouth.

"What do you want from me, Roman?"

He slapped the paper he was reading down on his desk and walked toward me. "You know the answer to that already."

"Yes, I do. Which is why I can't figure out why you're acting this way."

"What way is that?" He put his hands in his pockets and leaned back against the front of his desk. A challenge.

In short, I was coming to realize that being with Roman was a game, and to win, I'd have to play by the rules, while daring the other person to break them.

I took a step closer, this time observing how his gaze skated from my heels to my shoulders, pausing at all the good parts in between. Maybe the governor struggled the same way I did.

Maybe he wasn't completely immune to me either. We were after all, a couple.

"You're being cold," I said, taking another step. "I don't like it. It makes me question why I'd be in a relationship with someone who treats me this way."

"I treat you well," he said in a low, deadly tone, clearly not liking where I was going with this.

He made the rules. No talking about the arrangement. Fine. Then I'd appeal to him as his significant other.

"Sometimes," I nodded. "But sometimes you don't." I shrugged a little and dropped my voice a single octave. "Other times you treat me *very* well." I looked up from beneath my lashes, trying that flirty eye thing I'd seen Hazel use on a man at a bar once. "I like that Roman." Step. "The one who is kind, makes me laugh, makes me . . ."

"Makes you run away," he cut in, obviously more upset about the other night than I had realized.

"I didn't know how to handle the other night," I admitted. "I just needed some space to regroup. But I don't regret being with you."

His eyes darkened, the nearby fire lighting them up like the eyes of some wicked, sexy demon from the underworld. "Did I scare you?"

I shook my head. "The only thing that scares me is how you make me feel."

"Excuse me, sir," Jean said, walking through the door. "I have most of the travel arrangements amended to accommodate Miss Underwood, but I wanted to know if you had solidified your arrangements for staying at your parents' estate next month when you travel upstate."

"No." His tone made the woman jump a bit. "We will not be staying there."

"Okay. And what sample size from the wardrobe should I have the assistant bring up for Miss Underwood?" Jean asked, as if I weren't standing right beside her.

Roman fired off my size, almost down to exact measurements, and I stared, astounded. The woman scribbled something down again, then hurried out, obviously picking up on Roman's mood and shutting the door behind her.

"You have a wardrobe standing by?"

"Yes, it was put together over the weekend. Various items." He lifted his shoulders slightly, like this was totally normal.

"How do you know what size I am?"

"I wasn't sure until I saw the tag on your skirt the other night." The rough edge of his voice made shivers slice down my spine. "And I still have your panties."

My mind slowed in shock.

"Now, you were telling me how I make you feel?" he said.

I opened my mouth to speak, but nothing came out. No matter how hard I tried, he always seemed to be one step ahead, and nothing, *nothing*, seemed to unnerve him. Meanwhile he had my panties, God knows where, and was discussing me like some farm animal, dressing me and putting me on show. And all while making my body smolder like I was having withdrawals from his touch. I wanted to scream at him. Shake him. Devour him. My mind and body were on the brink of operating on pure instinct.

"Not getting shy on me now, are you, Amy?"

"I thought that was a quality you liked in me."

"No. I said I liked your innocence."

"That doesn't really apply anymore, does it?"

He frowned. "I disagree. I'm more convinced than ever."

"But, Friday night . . ." I shook my head, having no idea where I was going with this.

It had been so raw. So wild and rash. There had been nothing slow, sweet, or pure about it. And when the moment had gone, I'd felt like we were back to business. A no-connection, emotion-free kind of business. Hazel once told me that sometimes, sex had nothing to do with feelings. Roman was obviously better at separating his. The question was, could I? All Friday night did was leave me wanting more while feeling vulnerable.

That word stuck in my head. It was the same feeling I'd had when I'd found out that Warren had used me. I felt like I had shown a private side of myself and now, in the light of day, it was being held against me.

"The other night was unexpected," Roman said. "You gave me a lot to think about."

"*I* gave *you* a lot to think about?"

"Yes. You left." He pushed his hip off the desk and stood up straight.

"What was I supposed to do?"

"Stay."

Uncertainty blistered until it felt like boils on my skin. I wasn't prepared for the sudden rush of adrenaline that spiraled through me. Adrenaline that left me feeling not innocent at all, but scandalous.

There were two raps on the door before it opened. A tall man with a receding hairline, and what looked to be a permanent frown on his face, walked in, swiping his fingers over his smartphone.

"We need to go over the major donors coming to the fundraiser Saturday, and what the hell is this rumor that you have a girlfriend?"

"Bill," Roman said, and the man looked up, catching my eye before looking at Roman. "This is Amy Underwood. My girlfriend."

Bill pursed his lips. Between the name and the fact that he obviously handled communications, I figured this must be Paige's boss. There was something kind of off-putting about him. His dim hazel eyes roamed over me, producing a very different shiver than when Roman did it. He was analyzing everything about me in a single look, and I didn't particularly care for the way his gaze paused on my breasts and hips.

"Can we have a word in private?" Bill said.

Roman casually adjusted his shoulders. "Just say what you need to say, Bill."

Bill glanced at me again. "I don't think that taking another person on your campaign tour is a good idea."

"It will be fine. I've done the preliminary background check and Amy, if anything, is an asset."

An asset? Again, it was like I wasn't there. And was this how Roman had talked about his past girlfriends? As assets?

"We can go over this more tomorrow," Roman continued. "Right now, I need to get Amy prepped for Saturday."

Bill obviously wasn't happy with that answer, and frankly, neither was I. Knowing Roman was going to discuss my worth with this guy, who obviously wasn't convinced I was a good thing, made me feel like I had just been fished out of the bargain bin.

"There are pictures floating around social media sites of you kissing someone, I assume her." Again Bill glared at me. "In a bar in Arbor Hill last Thursday."

"Yes."

"It doesn't look—"

"It looks like I was at a sports bar, not drinking, enjoying an evening in Arbor Hill—where low-income constituents hang out—like a normal human being with my girlfriend, who works for an anti-drug nonprofit. It looks like I was enjoying the state I love while interacting with the people of that state." Roman took a step toward Bill. "If that is not how it looks, then you have some spinning to do. However, I think the majority has seen this incident in a positive light, based on the research and report I received from your assistant this morning."

Bill grumbled something. I stared, wide-eyed, and Roman looked cool as ever. Was that what Paige had been doing the night I came home from Roman's? She'd said she was working this past weekend. Was that what she meant? Going over media for hours and "spinning" my relationship with the governor?

I never meant to affect your job . . . I know, but you will . . .

Those words made my stomach instantly clench. And yet, she'd still listened, still supported me, even though I was creating stress in her life.

"We'll talk about the rest tomorrow, Bill," Roman said with finality in his voice.

Bill nodded and left the room, not bothering to shut the door. I heard a sharp thump right outside the office, like something had been rammed into the wall, followed by Bill's annoyed curse.

"Roman, I can't—" I was about to tell him that involving Paige wasn't okay with me when another person walked in, pushing a wheeled rack of clothes.

"Here are all the samples . . ." Paige's words died when she saw me, and I about choked on air. She stood up straight and ran her palms down her pencil skirt, cleared her throat, and looked at Roman. "Anything else, sir?"

"Yes. We'll need shoes."

"No!" Both of them looked at me, but I didn't care that I had just yelled. "No, I can get my own shoes."

I didn't know exactly what I was supposed to be getting dressed for—maybe every event on Roman's calendar. All I knew was that Paige, who worked twelve-hour days and then some, didn't need hours of searching the Web for pictures and posts about Roman and me, *and* acquiring outfits for me. No, she was not going to be a gopher for these people, or for me.

"It's fine," she mumbled to me. "It's part of my job."

"No," I said again.

"Is there an issue here?" Roman asked, looking between the two of us.

"No, sir," Paige said, at the same time I said, "Yes."

"Will you excuse us, Miss Levine?" he said to Paige, but kept his eyes on me.

Paige left the room, shutting the door behind her, but not before I'd seen the look in her eyes. I couldn't tell if she was angry, embarrassed, or both, but she was right. I was affecting her job. And watching her bring a rack of clothes in when I knew she'd spent all week proofreading budget adjustments and documents was too much take. Whatever rubber band had been holding me together snapped.

"We need to talk," I said to Roman with all the guilt I felt. "About everything."

He lifted his chin. "You know the rules."

"Yes, I do. So name your place, Governor."

His nostrils flared and a muscle in his jaw twitched. "My house. Tonight."

"Fine."

Chapter Eight

I managed not to stomp through Roman's house on the way to his bedroom, but once he'd shut the door, I couldn't help it. Emotions had been bubbling since this morning, and I couldn't take it anymore.

"You can't just barge into people's lives and order them around whenever you feel like it," I said, pacing—not stomping—in front of the hearth. "When I signed up for this—"

"Ah-ah," Roman interrupted, motioning in my direction. "No chatting about that until you're undressed."

The gleam in his eyes and the smirk on his face made me hot. And he knew it. But in that moment, I didn't know if I was more on fire from anger, or the fact that this overbearing, domineering, incredibly sexy man was burning holes right through my skin and igniting something dark and needy in my core.

He sat down in the chair I had occupied last time I was here—the chair he'd bent me over—and casually leaned back.

"Proceed, Miss Underwood."

I froze. It was an odd reaction, considering the fire currently warming my shoulders. Looking at Roman and trying to keep my wits was difficult, because the man looked like he owned the world and everything in it. Including me. He sat back, comfortable and calm, resting his chin between his thumb and first finger, gazing at me as if awaiting a show. Those hot eyes daring me.

I lifted my chin and mustered every ounce of courage I had.

Dare accepted.

Gritting my teeth, I pulled at my shirt, untucking it from my skirt and yanking it over my head. The collar caught on the tight bun of my hair, so I reached up, undid the stupid thing, and let my hair fall.

Roman sat forward in his chair, resting his forearms on his knees, and watched. Perfectly still, yet completely engaged.

Something odd and new came over me. Control. Power. The governor was entranced by me for once. The feeling made me a little giddy. What had started out as anger, then rage, now felt a little edgy and hot . . . very hot.

Power respects power, I mentally repeated.

Gripping the small zipper on the side of my skirt, I slowly slid it down.

"I don't like Paige being involved," I said slowly.

With a little shimmy, my skirt fell to the floor, and I stepped out of it. Roman inhaled so roughly I heard it from where I was, five feet in front of him.

I should have been nervous, but there was something about the way he was looking at me. As though he was really seeing me, and liked what he saw. I placed a hand against the stone hearth and went to take off my heels.

"No," he bit out. "Those can stay on."

I stood up straight and looked at him. "I'm not wired."

His dark gaze slid over my body, and I felt it so acutely that it could have been his hands. "I'm still not convinced."

Taking a deep breath, which he really seemed to enjoy watching, I reached behind me for the clasp of my bra. I snapped it open and slowly let the straps slide down my arms, keeping the lacy cups in place with my hands until the very last moment.

"You can't come into my work and drag me out," I said softly, letting the material fall and land on the floor next to my skirt and shirt.

A full-fledged growl came from Roman, whose face was hard as he stared at my body. Every square inch all at once. I had no idea how he did it, but nothing went unnoticed. From my face to my lips to my breasts, he drank me in with a single look.

I ran my thumbs along the waistline of my panties. The action snatched his full attention.

"You can't expect me to come running every time you call," I whispered. "I know I'm not really your girlfriend." I pushed the flimsy material down to my thighs and let it fall from there. "But I'm not your slave either."

A tic worked in his jaw as he looked me up and down, pausing between my legs long enough to make me squirm.

"You are mistaken about several things," he rasped, and pushed to his feet. "First, Paige is good at her job. You interfering the way you did today only creates awkwardness for both of you."

I opened my mouth to retaliate, but he spoke again before I could.

"What we're doing will continue, and my team, which includes Paige, will deal with that. Second . . ."

He took a step toward me and I stifled the urge to cover myself, my confidence hanging by a thread. The fire at my back was hot, but nothing like the man with blazing black eyes coming toward me.

"I didn't drag you anywhere. I merely adjusted the situation to better fit my needs. And my needs included you." Another step. "Finally, you *are* my girlfriend. And I do expect you to come." His mouth quirked up at the side in a devilish expression. "Often."

I couldn't breathe. The faint essence of burning wood and Roman's masculine scent were too much. The closer he got, the further my thoughts strayed. I couldn't keep my mind on the issues. Couldn't think clearly enough to argue. A few syllables of his gravelly voice drained all the fight right out of my pores.

"I'm naked," I whispered, and glanced down at my body. I had been beaten. He'd won this match, and I couldn't maintain my false idea of power. I crossed my arms over my breasts.

Roman grazed his fingers along my forearm. "Yes, you are."

"Every time I get near you, alone with you, I . . ."

"Lose judgment."

I looked up at him, and he gently pulled my arm free, exposing me to his view.

"How do you know that?" I asked.

"Because I struggle with the same thing." There was a softness in his voice I was coming to recognize. Honesty. I wasn't going any-where, not even if I wanted to, which I didn't.

"I have yet to see you lose anything, Governor."

He lifted my chin with the crook of his finger. "You're witnessing it right now."

The idea that maybe he felt a fraction of what I did made him seem more . . . human. More like the man I'd met at the gala, who'd led me barefoot to the ledge of a giant city and made me feel worth-while for the first time in a long time.

My hands touched his chest softly. He was so hard and strong. So approachable, yet untouchable. A total and utter conundrum I couldn't figure out. And my body was in worse shape than my mind, because everything in me was screaming for more.

Of him.

Pining for a single touch, a single ounce of attention. A stron-ger woman would have admitted to that kind of weakness. Not me. Not at that moment. I was too busy being consumed by the addiction.

Addiction to *him*.

"You're free to go anytime, Amy. But never again with that look on your face." His fingers trailed from my chin to my jaw and down my neck.

"What look?"

"Fear," he growled.

I swallowed hard. I had no idea what expression he'd seen on my face the night we were together, but I could assume it hadn't been pretty.

"Are you putting regulations on my feelings again?"

"That depends." His thumb brushed the column of my throat. "Are you afraid of me?"

I swallowed and felt my throat bob against his gentle caress.

"Yes," I whispered. "But not in the way you think."

He frowned. "Explain."

I focused on his chest, the small buttons of his shirt. Before I lost my nerve, I started unfastening them.

"I'm afraid of the way you make me feel sometimes."

One button undone. I moved down to the next one, getting little peeks of that mocha skin and strong stomach. I had to lick my lips to keep from drooling.

"Sometimes?"

I nodded. What I felt was not a simple fear, but a confusing terror that this man had some kind of hold on me. The kind that made me forget logic, forget what I was doing here and how this whole thing had started. Forget how badly someone could hurt you.

Getting caught up was stupid. Too bad I couldn't get the better part of my brain to understand that right now. The only thing I could do was try to explain it.

"Being with you—" I started.

"The other night." It wasn't a question. He wanted me to say it. Acknowledge what had happened between us. All of it.

"Yes." I said. "It was like a haze. When it cleared, I didn't know how to act . . . what to do."

"What have you normally done in the past?"

I shrugged, unable to look him in the eye. He didn't need to know the details of my past relationships—or rather, relationship— but there was no reason to hide the basics.

"I haven't had a lot of experience dealing with things like this."

"You mean sex?"

I nodded. My face instantly heated, and I felt just a hint of anxiety. He spoke so bluntly sometimes. Untucking his shirt, I freed the final button.

"How much experience are you talking about, Amy?" His hands ensnared mine, stilling them before I could open his shirt fully.

"I've had one boyfriend. We were intimate . . . but only a few times . . ." I mumbled, all the heat I'd been feeling turning chilly as unwanted memories suddenly invaded.

"How long ago?" Roman's voice was low, like he really wanted to know, cared to know.

"Two years."

"Jesus Christ." Keeping a grip on my hands, he ran his free palm down his face.

"I liked the other night . . . with you," I said, cutting him off.

He was on the brink of saying something, most likely something along the lines of me leaving. Which was not happening. I was standing in front of him naked. I wanted to take advantage of that fact while I still had the good sense not to have sense. He was finally showing the real side of him that I was desperate to know more of. Maybe we could be more than an arrangement. Maybe sex and emotions did go together, because right then, I saw it on Roman's face. Emotion.

"I just didn't know how to react. But now I have a guideline." I tried to tug my hands free, but he kept a tight hold.

"Amy." The way he said my name wasn't like the other night. And it wasn't like at the office. He wasn't demanding, commanding, or asking. He was unsure. Again, the tone of his voice allowed that tiny sliver of softness to come through.

"You said it's my choice," I whispered. "I want to be here, Roman."

He shook his head and backed away. Wait. Why was he pulling away from me? I tried to hold on, but he just took another step back, making me release my grip. As my hands dropped, they snagged the edge of his shirt, opening it just enough to see his torso.

"Oh my," I breathed, lost in his presence.

Roman was pure strength. I knew this. But the sight of him—slightly disheveled, his perfectly pressed shirt hanging open, revealing flank after flank of lean, cut abs—was dizzying. A small line of dark hair trailed from his navel to the waist of his low-slung pants. I wanted to see the rest of him. Wanted to experience him. Because right now, he didn't look like the governor. He looked like a man.

Clarity hit me. Without fully understanding it, I knew this moment was important. Something very consuming and very rare washed over me.

Pride.

I had an opportunity to see Roman in a way not many did. For the first time, I felt like we were close to the same level. He wasn't tiers above me, polished to perfection. He was a man. An incredibly built, complex, endearing man, who I wanted to know. Wanted to feel in more ways than I could even fathom in that single second.

"I think we should call it a night, Amy."

My gaze snapped to his, surprise and terror enveloping me when I saw his face. It was like he'd fastened a mask back into place—the glimpse of softness I'd seen in his expression was gone, replaced by a cool indifference. Nothing, not even the fire at my back, could have warmed the chill that raced through me.

"Why?"

He looked me over, but not like before. There was a sorrowful expression, like pity, in every rove of his stare.

"I just think our expectations don't match up." There was no sugar in his voice.

"What do you mean? I thought we were going to—"

"Fuck?" The single word was like a shot to the stomach: hard and brutal. "We can. And I'd like that," he went on, his eyes roaming over me once more, "but I don't think you can detach yourself."

"And you can?"

He nodded.

My blood turned to ice in my veins, and I couldn't form a sentence. Couldn't figure out how in a matter of milliseconds, I'd gone from desperation for this man to utter embarrassment. How was he able to make me feel the very ends of the emotional spectrum with so little effort? He built me up with a series of hot gazes and erotic promises, then shot me down with a single cold glare and look of pity. It was as though the truth of my past relationship—what little there was of it—had changed his perception of me.

Did I want meaningless sex? No. I wanted something meaningful. With Roman. He'd given me a taste of that, so I knew it existed. Now, though, he didn't seem to care to explore that option, so he was pulling back.

I was a fool. A naïve fool.

"You expect honesty from me." It was the only thing I could think to say as I quickly bent to grab my skirt and put it on.

"I'm being honest with you."

"You make me stand in front of you naked when I speak," I continued, my tone louder than I had expected.

Recapping the moment wasn't helping, but it was the only handle I could grasp. Why did he do this? To purposefully hurt me? Humiliate me? Remind me that he was beyond anything I could ever be?

"Amy," he said, reaching out, but I jerked back.

"No."

My mind was jumping like a cut telephone wire crackling in a puddle. In light of my thwarted desire, complete humiliation, and the sheer vulnerability of this moment, my entire being mustered up the only defense mechanisms it could.

Fight or flight. I chose both.

"You wonder why I left? Why I feel the way I do?" I snatched up my shirt and pulled it over my head quickly, not caring to bother with a bra. I just needed enough to cover my body. "You! Everything about you unnerves me. I get these small glimpses of the man I thought you were, and all other thoughts go out the window. I trusted you, like an idiot. Answered your questions. Went along with this whole thing—"

"And that was your decision to make," he said, throwing my admission in my face.

"Well, it looks like maybe I made the wrong the one."

"Amy," he said slowly, as though trying to soothe a spooked animal. His tone only made my fury and tears rise. "I think we should talk and reevaluate a few areas of this arrangement."

"Now?" I looked down at my poor excuse for an outfit, feeling similarly messy and frayed. "What is it you want to reevaluate? The fact that you'll *fuck* me so long as I don't get clingy? So long as I promise not to actually feel something?"

His jaw clenched, but he didn't say a word. The look on his face spoke volumes, an expression of "poor-damaged-confused-girl" mixed with some kind of anger. I wouldn't take it from him, sad looks and exasperated words. I might not have been experienced, but that was the least of my problems at the moment. Roman had made me feel more like a competent woman than I ever had, and now he was taking that away. Right in front of my face. Telling me what I could and couldn't handle.

I clutched the fabric of my shirt against my stomach and tried not to cry. "I don't need you to feel sorry for me," I said.

"I don't. I just think that my behavior the other night was over-zealous."

My chest struggled to take in breaths. His words were so clinical. I wanted him to look at me like he had previously, with fire and intensity. Not like something he was trying to contain.

"Your behavior was intense. It left me feeling several things, but weak wasn't one of them," I said.

"I don't think you're weak."

"Then stop looking at me like that!"

He raised his chin. "I'm trying to have a discussion with you so that we're clear on this relationship."

"Oh, I'm clear. We are together in the eyes of everyone, right? We need to behave the way a real couple does. We can behave the way a real couple does in private too, so long as I understand that no real sentiment or feelings are involved. Is that correct?"

"It is not my intention to cause you pain or discomfort in any sense."

"You are right now," I whispered.

Something in his expression changed. An awful look laced his entire face, and I hated myself for causing it. What was happening? I couldn't read him. He looked almost sick, like my admission that he was hurting me truly bothered him. And suddenly I felt the need to apologize.

"Roman, what's happening? Are you messing with me on purpose? Playing mind games?"

"No," he said roughly.

"Then why are you treating me this way?" I said, unable to hold back my confusion and shame any longer.

"Because I don't know how the fuck *to* treat you, Amy," he said, running a hand through his hair. He paced a few steps and mumbled something that sounded like, "I didn't plan for this."

"Well, if your plan was stomping on my sanity for fun, then congratulations, Governor, you've won that race."

He stared at me, zeroing in on my expression. I honestly had no idea what was visible on my face at that moment, but whatever it was, he didn't like it.

"I'm done playing," I said, and walked toward the door.

"Amy," he called after me. "Let me at least take you home."

I was clenching my jaw so hard, it hurt. I couldn't look at him or say anything to him. Keeping my head down, the last thing I saw before leaving was my undergarments, still lying on the floor.

Grabbing my coat off the rack by the door, I wondered how things had gone so wrong.

Chapter Nine

......

I tugged my jacket tighter and crossed my arms, trying to seal in the warmth. It was late and cold and, in theory, not a good time or place to take a walk, but I had to get out of there.

I just couldn't handle Roman's presence any more. Couldn't take the idea of his chauffer driving me home. Couldn't have another discussion about our twisted "relationship." I had to clear my head before this spiral of shame became inescapable.

My heels clicking on the pavement sent tiny shocks up my calves, reminding me that it had been a long day and my feet hurt.

"The bus stop is just right around the corner," I said aloud, mostly to create the illusion that I wasn't alone on a dark street. As my nerves grew and my body cooled off from the encounter with Roman, a dose of adrenaline coursed through me.

Fear.

I was alone.

Every little sound echoed. Every shift of the breeze sounded like a whisper.

Paige had taught me to carry my keys in my hand so that if someone attacked me, I could hit them with the jagged edges. I reached into my pocket to grab my keys—

Empty.

"Shit," I whispered. I started going through my pockets. No keys, no phone, no wallet. Closing my eyes, I let out a long breath. I had left my purse at Roman's.

I looked around quickly. The night felt like it was closing in as the street lights illuminated my every insecurity. I couldn't even leave right.

Headlights approached and I picked up my pace.

The car sped up, then screeched to a halt. I didn't look behind me, not even when I heard the door open and close, then quick footsteps. My pulse pounded in my throat, and my nose and lips were turning to ice from breathing the cold night air too quickly.

"Amy!"

My entire body froze as if commanded to do so. It was like the pavement beneath me had snatched my ankles and wouldn't allow me to walk away.

"Amy!"

I turned and saw a dark figure striding toward me. The deep rasp of his voice and those bright obsidian eyes were recognizable anywhere.

"Roman."

The relief that burned through me was quickly replaced by embarrassment. I had nothing left: I was out of fight, out of reasons and gumption to argue, out of the will to defend myself—to do anything.

"I forgot my purse—" I started, but my sentence was cut off when Roman charged at me and wrapped me in his arms.

With my face pressed against his chest, I could hear his wild heartbeat. He hugged me so tightly I could barely breathe, but I liked it: I felt safe and wanted. So much so I wanted to cry, but I forced myself to maintain my composure.

He took a deep breath, my cheek rising and falling with his chest. Then he stood back, gripping my arms and looking at me.

"Are you alright?" he asked, examining the entire surface area of my body.

"Yes."

As I said it, his face morphed into sheer anger and his brow sliced into a scowl so deep, it looked painful.

"What the fuck were you thinking?" he yelled.

Whoa, what? He was just—I'd thought—happy to see me. Or relieved. At least, not mad.

"I was thinking that I wanted to leave," I retorted.

"By ditching my driver and walking half naked across town?"

I looked down at myself. "I'm not half naked." True, I wasn't wearing any undergarments, but it wasn't obvious.

"You can't do that, Amy!" He gently shook my shoulders, and I saw a look of utter terror behind his normally steely stare. "You can't just take off. I had no idea where you were. What had happened to you." His tone was harsh, but there was that familiar glimpse of pain behind his words and expression. Like I had truly scared him.

"I'm an adult, Roman."

"You're mine, Amy," he said, and a tremor slid over my skin. "If we disagree, fine. I'll take you home. But don't run off and disappear. Do you understand?"

Water danced on the rims of my eyes, and my shoulders slumped from the weight of tonight. Too much. It was all too much, and I had no idea how to process it all.

"No, Roman. I don't understand."

He glanced at the ground and gently rubbed my shoulders. Pulling me into another hug, he kissed my forehead and whispered, "I don't either."

His warmth and scent surrounded me. I gave myself up to the moment, to him, because there was nowhere left to run and nothing else to do. Roman seemed just as confused as I was. Earlier, when he had been trying to create distance between sex and feelings, he'd been upset when I'd left. In light of that, his behavior now didn't make much sense. Whatever was going through his mind, whatever he was feeling, I didn't know. But right then, I felt like he truly cared. Maybe that was something.

Or maybe I was once again being naïve.

"Not many people scare me," he said against my brow. "Don't do it again."

I nodded, resigned to letting go for tonight. I needed time, space, rest. I needed my nerves to calm and my perception of reality to right itself before tackling this issue that was Roman Reese. I needed a clear head.

"Will you please take me home?" I asked.

He looked down at me, and that slight flame of vulnerability flickered across his face. Whatever thoughts caused that hurt, that unease, I wanted to know. To help him. I was sure that this time, he was going to say something. Something to give me a glimpse into the darkness he kept bottled up.

Instead, the only word he uttered was, "Yes."

· · · · ● · · ·

"Thank you for coming," Roman said close to my ear.

They were the first words Roman had spoken directly to me since Monday night's disaster. It was now Saturday, and while I had gotten a few text messages and e-mails, there had been no verbal communication until now. I had heard the phrase "leaving with your panties in your purse" before, but I'd had no idea how humiliating it could be. To say my emotions had been tumultuous would be an understatement. It had been days, but my body was still humming with confusion and achy from the amount of stress and adrenaline endured that night.

Now, standing in the governor's mansion and getting ready for the fundraiser, I worked on taking calming breaths and focusing on the external environment. I had no desire to be inside my head right now, or to overthink how to handle the spiral staircase of feelings I was currently treading. Besides, every time I tried, I came up with no solution. I liked Roman, but the situation was tricky. Nope. I would tackle that later. Right now, I needed to prepare for tonight's fundraiser.

Between the setup and the people bustling around, it didn't look like the subtly lit, quiet home I'd visited just a few days earlier. The organized chaos was a welcome distraction.

I looked up at Roman, my heels squeaking as I adjusted to the brand-new stilettos.

"You're welcome," I said.

I didn't know where we stood after Monday's fiasco. But there was something in his eyes: a softness. The thing I was now calling "The Real Roman" burned in those charcoal depths.

I turned to face him as people continued to rush by, setting up chairs and coordinating where the orchestra would be staged. I simply focused on Roman.

"I shouldn't have left the way I did the other night," I said.

He lifted his chin slightly and gave me a look that was wary and cautious, as though I was luring him to his doom.

"You were right," I continued. "It wasn't smart. It could have been dangerous, and," I shrugged, "it was definitely kind of stupid to leave without any money, house keys, or cell phone."

He scoffed, but I caught sight of a small smile. Roman wasn't offering to share any of his own thoughts, so I was doing the only thing I could to move on: taking responsibility for my part.

"I usually don't get so upset. I felt like you were toying with me. But I'll be more prepared in the future."

He frowned. "I wasn't toying with you."

I pursed my lips because I didn't want to argue, not here and now. I didn't think Roman had meant to mess with me, but he had. I had been too confused to sleep well the last few days. Yet, despite all that, my mind was consumed with thoughts of Roman's body. The small glimpse I had gotten kept me buzzing, wanting another look. Maybe a taste. I wanted to tap into all that power and confidence and devour him.

"I pushed you too far," he rasped. His fingers brushed a lock of hair behind my ear. It was the first sweet gesture he'd made all day, and I found myself arching into it. "You seemed like you could use some space."

In some ways, yes, he had pushed too far. But in others, he hadn't pushed far enough. There was no way for me to explain this to him, especially now. Based on his behavior and change in attitude since finding out about my sexual history, I assumed he thought he'd crossed a physical line, but all I wanted was to get back there. To him dominating me, taking me, consuming me.

Yes, I needed time to think, reflect. But it wasn't space I was looking for, it was him. The wall he'd put up, the delineation between intimacy and physical contact, was a barrier that posed a lot of problems.

Later, I reminded myself. I'd tackle that later. First I needed to find out what my hard limits were. What I was willing to give up, or give in to. What I was willing to concede. But one thing was certain—intimacy wouldn't be one of them.

"Can we just chalk it up to the fact that both of us were caught off guard and got a little emotional?" I said.

He grinned. "Politicians don't get emotional."

I raised my brows. "Seriously? That's what you're going with?"

He shrugged. "Depends. Are you buying it?"

I smiled and shook my head. "Nope."

Warmth bloomed through my belly. This was the Roman I craved. The one I'd been missing. Though the more I thought about it, the more I realized how the different pieces of him blended together, creating a potent dose of strong, seductive male I couldn't resist. This is what I needed, what we needed. The casual, sweet conversation of a couple.

I glanced around. "I haven't seen Paige today."

She had been gone when I'd gotten up this morning, and I'd figured she was working. Every time there was a function, she typically worked from dawn until late at night.

"She and Bill are taking care of media issues. She'll be here tonight."

I nodded. The idea of having Paige close by made me feel better.

"You nervous?" he asked.

"Of course I am."

He grinned and looked down. "Are your shoes more comfortable at least?"

I thought of that night, his hands on my calves and how easy things had been with him. How he'd made me feel like I was acceptable just as I was. "Yes, thank you."

"There are dresses to choose from in my room, and Selena will do your hair and makeup. She'll be here in about an hour."

Yikes. This was getting more and more real, and my nerves were rising.

"I've got a few things to take care of, but I'll come get you when it's time so we can walk down and greet everyone together."

I nodded. He cupped my face in both hands, his palms covering the majority of my cheeks and neck, and brushed his lips over mine. The feel of his soft mouth swept over me while his hands remained steady and strong, holding me close. Hard and soft. Intense and controlled.

Against my lips he whispered, "Wear your hair down tonight."

Chapter Ten

· · · • · ··

I watched Paige hold court with a few men and women on the other side of the ballroom. The band was playing softly, and everyone had a glass of champagne. Aside from the night I'd met Roman, I'd never felt so out of place, especially since a few pictures had been snapped of me and the residual effect of the flashing light was still burning my retinas.

Clinking my fingernails against the crystal glass, I glanced between Paige and Roman. He was near the middle of the room, smiling and chatting. The man looked good in a tux, and people were all but shoving checks into his pocket in support of his campaign.

Roman had introduced me to various people earlier, and while Selena had done a great job on my makeup and hair, I'd still felt transparent. Like everyone could see right through me. I was sipping my champagne, happy to be lost in the crowd, when I felt a tap on my shoulder. Smile in place, I turned around.

My gut plummeted and I almost wretched.

"W-warren?"

He smiled, way too sinister and happy to see me.

"Look at you, moving up in the world." He took my champagne glass and drained the contents. "And here I thought you were just a simple girl from Indiana."

His breath smelled of something much stronger than champagne, and suddenly finding myself in his presence again made me want to bolt out the door.

"It's been a long time." His blue eyes skated over me, leaving me feeling cheap in their wake. "You look good."

It wasn't a compliment; it was a pity statement. Boredom and condescension dripped from every word.

"What are you doing here?" I asked, trying to keep the shock from my voice.

"I could ask you the same thing."

"I'm here with the governor," I said, straightening my posture a little.

Pretending to be confident had never been so hard, mostly because the last time I'd seen Warren was when I'd walked in on him with another woman. He'd only laughed, and explained he'd been using me to maintain his grades and his standing in his family. Then he'd asked me to let myself out. I hadn't seen him since.

"The governor, huh? I saw you on his arm earlier and thought he was doing some kind of charity work."

Okay, that dig really smarted. But Warren had never been one to walk away unless he'd fully demolished you.

"That's nice for you though, Amy," he snickered.

My pulse beat in my temples. "Is there something you want, Warren?"

"No, just being polite to an old friend." He grabbed another flute from a passing tray. "And I'm here to support my mother. Assemblywoman Cunningham. She's retiring this year."

I nodded and looked around, trying to find anything to save me from this conversation. Paige was still talking, but I caught Roman's eye from across the room. He was still engaged in conversation, but his gaze darted from me to Warren and back, darkening with every sweep.

"So." Warren stepped closer and pointedly looked down on me from his superior height. "How's the family?"

I swallowed hard. "My family is fine."

He nodded. "You still obsessed with saving the world?"

At any other time, with any other person, I would have called him out on his disrespect and walked away. But my feet were frozen, my pulse was rising, and every awful memory from my past was playing before me.

There was nothing I could say. In college, I'd talked constantly about what I was going to do when I graduated. How I was going to make a difference: preserve Lauren's memory. And then, just like now, Warren had only mocked me, making it clear he wasn't interested in my dreams. But to defend myself now would be giving him information I didn't want him to have, like where I worked and what I did.

"I'm still passionate about the anti-drug cause." I knew he didn't care and was really making fun of me. I just wanted to get out of this conversation.

"Really? Well, that would be a change. You passionate about something." He laughed and took another drink.

Water rushed to my eyes. He used to tell me how frigid I was . . . in every area of our relationship. Which was why we'd only explored those areas a few times, and I'd always walked away with tears and insecurity.

"You really are a terrible man, aren't you?" I whispered.

"Excuse me?"

I stared at him, which I hated, because everything about him—from his dull blue eyes to his sandy hair and rude expression—made me want to crawl into a hole and never come out.

I looked around again, my glance resting on Roman for a few moments. I tried to think of good things, to grasp to the fact that a lot had changed since I'd seen Warren last, and I was older and smarter now. But despite that, he had all my dark secrets, all my insecurities, wrapped in a perfect package that he could unleash at any moment.

"You want to talk about terrible people?" he snarled, glaring at me.

He leaned in way too close for comfort.

"We should be talking about you then. Shouldn't we, Amy?" He grinned, and my windpipe closed.

Pulling back, he took another drink, and I felt the urge to cross my arms over my chest and become as small as possible, as small as I felt at that moment.

Years ago, after a particularly horrible talk with my mother, I'd broken down and told Warren everything. My part in Lauren's death, and how I could have saved her. How I should have taken her to the hospital instead of home.

That it was my fault she had died . . .

Instead of consoling me, he'd affirmed what my mother already thought and what I was fighting:

I'm a terrible person.

"Having a nice time?" Roman's deep voice asked from behind me. His palm rested on the curve between my neck and shoulder, and I felt instantly comforted, as though my muscles had received a fresh dose of strength.

"Yes, sir." Warren smiled and shook Roman's free hand. "Looking forward to next term."

I glanced up at Roman, who pulled me a little closer. "Indeed."

"I hear you have a strong campaign going this year, but the competition seems pretty solid. Going to be a tight race, eh, Governor?" Warren said, all cocky attitude.

Roman didn't seem impressed, and I couldn't blame him. There was nothing impressive about Warren other than his bank account, and frankly, that only mattered to some. I wasn't one of them.

"I see you've met my girlfriend," Roman said, and gave me a gentle yet possessive squeeze.

Warren's eyes widened. Apparently he either hadn't believed me, or had figured I was just a one night date, and the word girlfriend caught him off guard.

"Wow." He took a step back. "Girlfriend? That's . . ." Warren frowned. Either the liquor or his lack of brain cells was getting to him.

"How do you two know each other?" A rough edge tinted Roman's question.

"We went to college together," I offered quickly, not interested in explaining the embarrassing details. Warren, however, managed to gather his wits and correct me in typical asshole fashion.

"*Dated* in college," he amended with a disgusting smile.

Roman's entire body tensed, and the energy crackling between him and Warren instantly shifted to something very unnerving. My blood pressure was high and my skin felt too tight for my bones. I forced myself to take calming breaths, trying to ward off the anxiety.

"Is that right?" Roman looked at me. "Small world."

"We were just catching up," Warren continued. "Chatting about her family. Her sister."

I swallowed hard and folded my lips together briefly, trying to keep the nervousness and discomfort down. A cold sweat lined my brow, but my cheeks were so hot I was afraid I might pass out. My pulse was increasing, getting louder and louder, until I could barely hear anything else. I was on the brink of having a panic attack—I felt it rising in me, like a hungry monster rousing from sleep.

I tried again to take a steady breath through my nose, but it wasn't helping. Roman's arm encircled my waist, and it wasn't until I felt his strong hold that I realized I'd been swaying.

"Are you alright, sweetheart?" he said softly.

I blinked several times, but the blur wouldn't clear.

"I just need a moment," I breathed, barely hearing my own words over the crashing blood in my head.

Roman didn't bother with niceties or pretend to acknowledge Warren any further. He just ushered me through the crowd quickly, until we reached a quiet hallway. As soon as I saw the stairs that led to Roman's room, the dam broke. I couldn't hold back the panic anymore.

My breath shot from my lungs and intense heaving knocked me forward. Roman caught me just has my knees buckled, saving me from hitting the floor. I squeezed my eyes shut, trying to keep from hyperventilating.

Tears spilled from my eyes. My legs shook, and I clung to Roman's arm.

"Amy . . . Amy, sweetheart, look at me."

I heard Roman, but he sounded so far away. The world was spinning and all that remained was darkness. I couldn't open my eyes, couldn't breathe. I didn't want to see Warren, his beady eyes judging me, damning me, spilling my secrets.

I needed to get out of here. Away from everyone.

I tried to stand, but it didn't work. There was still a voice close by. Roman.

I heaved again, but couldn't get enough oxygen. Roman said something, but I couldn't understand him.

Suddenly I was weightless, floating, supported by a wall of muscle. I clung to that wall. Clung to Roman. He was carrying me. I didn't know where to, but I didn't want to risk opening my eyes. I buried my face in his neck and held on, inhaling his scent, his warmth. I felt small again, but this time, it didn't feel like a bad thing.

A door opened and shut. I took another breath, and another, focusing on Roman's scent: spicy, divine, powerful. Focusing on how his heart thumped in his chest, steady and smooth. I let its rhythm move through me, hoping my own heart would take a hint.

"We're alone now, Amy." I felt him sit, his grip remaining tight, keeping me on his lap. "Open your eyes. Look at me."

My heart was still racing and my breaths were quicker than normal, but I was backing away from the brink. I opened my eyes, slowly. When the blur started to fade, dark eyes came into view just inches from my own.

"Deep breath," he said. "Good girl, just like that."

I was sprawled over his lap while he sat on his bed. He cupped my neck in both hands, keeping my face near his. The tips of our noses touched. He breathed deeply, slowly.

"Good. Just like I'm doing. In," he inhaled and I followed. "And out." He exhaled, his lips so close that I breathed his sweetness into my lungs.

I could taste him already. Crisp and hot.

When my breathing had slowed, he leaned back enough to look at me. With my neck still clasped in his hands, he swept his thumbs along my cheekbones, wiping away the wetness left by my tears.

"I'm sorry," I said, but it came out more like a croak.

"Don't be. Are you okay? Do you have anxiety pills?"

I frowned. "How do you know I take medication?" It was only on occasion but the fact that he knew was surprising.

"I know what a panic attack looks like." He wiped my cheeks again. "And I've researched you, remember?" He grinned a little, and I mirrored it.

"Right."

"Do you want to tell me what that was about?"

The instant need to run enveloped me. It must have showed, because his arms tightened.

"You don't have to tell me now," he clarified. "But you're not going anywhere just yet."

I calmed a little. "I just . . . I have an issue with Warren Cunningham."

He scoffed and smiled, those damn dimples disarming me and making the last of my nerves fade away.

"Yeah, I gathered that. Is he the one ex-boyfriend you were telling me about?"

I looked down and nodded.

"I see."

Roman's whole body tensed, and I felt anger radiating from him. Was he mad at me? Almost everyone had at least one ex, and I didn't think he knew how Warren had used me. Something like that wouldn't be in a "file." It was a personal tidbit that no one except Paige knew, and she'd never tell. The only other person who knew my darkest secrets was Warren. Because like an idiot, I had trusted him.

"It didn't end well," I murmured, hoping that was enough.

Roman inhaled deeply and I felt his chest flex farther. I didn't want to talk about Warren or relive the past. A change of subject was the best I could do.

"How did you know I was having a panic attack? Have you seen them before?"

He nodded, but his face remained hard and his eyes like black steel. "Something like that."

I searched his face. Something that looked like shame flicked across his expression so quickly, I almost missed it.

"Do you have them?" I asked softly.

"Not anymore," he said. "I did a few times when I was a kid."

My hands started to fist his shirt, but I held back, not wanting to wrinkle his tux any more than I already had by sitting on him. I remembered the hard muscles and tan skin beneath the formal attire.

The open, raw energy currently pouring from him was such a contradiction to his usual composure.

"Do you want to tell me about it?" I asked.

"No." The word was quick and definite. No room for questions. Which I could understand. I would respect his boundaries in this, just like he was respecting mine. The other night had shown how far each of us could be pushed. Roman liked control, especially over himself and his world. That much was perfectly clear. Why he kept such a tight grip on situations and people, I didn't know. But I didn't want to go there, or poke too much only to have him close up completely.

Something was hidden deep within Roman. Maybe I would see it in time. Maybe not. But whatever it was, it was dark. That much I could feel.

"Thank you for getting me out of there. I hope I didn't cause a scene."

His thumb trailed from my cheek to my bottom lip. "No one noticed."

"Won't they notice you're gone?" I breathed, as his thumb kept up a slow sweep along my mouth.

"We have time." His voice was gravelly and low, and held the same tone I'd heard Monday night before things went to hell. "Why don't I take you home?"

And again, like Monday night, it was as if some kind of "helpless" sign had flashed across my forehead. That was not what I'd been expecting—hoping—he would say next.

"But this fundraiser is important. I can handle it." Even as the words came out, the thought of going back down and facing everyone, mostly Warren, made my stomach churn.

"It's getting late and guests are already leaving. I think we should call it a night for you."

"Oh." I glanced at my hands, suddenly feeling like a child. Then I looked him in the eye one more time. He leaned in slightly, his mouth so close I could almost taste him. But he didn't close the distance. Instead, he pulled back again. My hands itched with the need to reach out and cling to him. To bring him close. Instead, I got up and stood on shaky legs.

He rose as well and buttoned his tux jacket. I ran my hands over my dress, trying to straighten it. I didn't even want to think about how my face looked after that mess.

"I'm not going to kiss you," he said, standing before me. "Because if I do, a whole hell of a lot more will happen."

My breath caught, but he didn't let me speak. He just grabbed my hand and tugged me toward the door.

"Andrew," he called as soon as we hit the hallway. Andrew appeared as if from thin air.

"Yes, sir."

"Bring the car around back. We're taking Miss Underwood home."

"Yes, sir." Andrew disappeared down a hallway while Roman led me to a different part of the house I hadn't seen before. Private and quiet, you'd never know a full-blown gala was happening in the same building on the bottom floor.

We passed a set of closed metal doors. "I didn't know you had an elevator. Do you ever use it?"

"No."

"Why not?"

We came to a small stairwell at the back of the house, descended, and went to the back door.

"Because I don't like them," he said plainly.

When the crisp night air hit my face, I took a deep breath. The familiar black town car I had gotten used to was already running at the curb.

"You don't need to come with me," I said. "You have guests and—"

"I want to make sure you get home safely."

He opened the car door for me. I felt bad that he was leaving his party because of me. Some of his reasons probably had to do with the other night. He seemed legitimately worried about me, an idea that made my heart do weird flips, but I wasn't interested in chasing that feeling if it meant being an imposition on Roman.

"It's not something you need to witness. I'm not going to tuck and roll out of a moving vehicle. I'll be fine."

"I want to ensure that," he said, the look on his face daring me to challenge him further.

I swallowed hard and got in. He came around the other side to join me. The privacy glass was up. The leather seat was cool against my thighs as we made the short trek from Albany to Arbor Hill.

My whole body buzzed with tension. It had been another stressful day of crazy emotions and adrenaline, and I was coming down so hard I could barely keep my footing. It was enough to drive a girl insane.

"Still feeling anxious?" he asked, glancing at my slightly twitching knee.

"Yes. But not because of earlier."

"Then why?"

I waited until his eyes landed, and stayed, on my face. For a moment I simply watched him, wondering if I could extract anything from of his expression. Read him somehow and know what to do, what to say. There was a sophisticated way to play this game, I was sure of it. The problem was, I was neither sophisticated nor interested in games. I wanted the real Roman. Not the politician, the man.

"I want you," I said honestly, voicing my inner thoughts. "All the time. Even when I'm angry at you. Even right now."

Each word came out softer than the last, until I almost looked away in mortification. But it was the truth. Perhaps I'd been blunt, but whatever hold Roman had over me wasn't lessening, or even becoming more understandable.

"I feel like I'm in a constant battle with myself, and I never know what you're thinking or what to do. It's . . ." I let out a loud breath, "confusing."

His jaw shifted enough to show that he'd clenched his teeth, once again refraining from saying something.

"Can you just speak? Say whatever it is going through your mind right now?"

"No," he said.

"You're always thinking through your words. I can tell. I can see it on your face. Can't you just say what you want? No one is listening but me."

"It's wise to think before speaking."

"Even if it's the truth?" I said.

"Especially if it's the truth."

My heart sank a little. "Why?"

His throat bobbed, as if he were swallowing a bit of resolve. "Because the truth is a dangerous thing to admit."

"Yet you've given me some."

He nodded. "And so have you."

The mutual acknowledgment somehow made me feel a little better. Like we were on some kind of track in the right direction. While Roman kept many things to himself, he did offer up some details, share some thoughts with me. Yes, I wanted to know him better, wanted him to let me in, but it had to start somewhere. A simple foundation from which we could build.

"I want *you*," I whispered again. Whatever he'd allow, that was what I wanted. A starting point. "Please, say something to that."

"'Want' doesn't describe it, sweetheart."

The edge in his voice cut through all my pent up emotions from the last four days. My skin zinged to life. My fingertips ached to touch him, and my mouth watered for a single taste of his skin.

Without further thought, I gave into instinct.

Quickly, I crawled across the backseat and hiked my dress up so that I could straddle Roman's lap.

"Amy . . ." Again, his voice held both warning and dare.

I chose to only hear the dare.

Winding my fingers in his hair, I gripped him hard and pressed my lips against his. All the heat and angst poured out, and I couldn't stop. I was calling his bluff on emotion-free sex. At the moment, he didn't seem to have his feelings in check, and neither did I. When I bit his bottom lip, he growled and gripped my ass.

"I warned you," he said against my mouth before plunging his tongue inside.

I moaned and returned his attentions. Dueling and tasting each other like our lives depended on it. With a firm grip, he ground me against him. His thick erection pressed against me, making me groan again. He felt so good. So strong and safe.

Holding on to his shoulders, I twisted my hips and rocked against him, harder, faster. Even with our clothing between us, the pressure of him against me sent shivers of pleasure along every inch of my skin.

"Shit, Amy." His fingers dug into the backs of my thighs. He was close, I could feel it. Because I was right there with him. It didn't take much—all our pent up need was on the brink of bursting.

I rolled my hips again and swallowed his growling response with an even deeper kiss.

He not only wanted me, he cared about me. I was sure about that because, try though he had to convince me otherwise last night, this wasn't just physical for him. It couldn't be. He could have let me walk home the other night, but he came after me. He could have let me get swept up in a panic attack, but he brought me back from the abyss.

Maybe I was grasping at straws—or maybe I was right. Maybe Roman didn't separate sex from feelings as well as either of us had thought. Whatever he was attempting to accomplish by keeping a distance between us wasn't working. When we were together, there was a connection.

I wanted to feel that connection again and apparently, so did Roman, because he wasn't pushing me away, he was pulling me closer.

"Take me," I begged, reaching between us to unfasten his pants.

"You sure you're ready?" he said, kissing my neck while his fingers disappeared beneath my dress to toy with my panties, pushing them aside.

"Yes, I'm very ready."

He retrieved a condom from his inside jacket pocket and lifted his hips enough so that I could tug his pants down and free his hard cock. With my dress falling around us, I couldn't see it, but I felt it brushing against my inner thighs.

He rolled the latex on. I was already arching into him, seeking him. With one hand on my hip, he gripped himself with the other. My panties still pushed aside, I rose enough to take the head of his cock into my depths, then slowly sank down.

"Fuck," he rasped. When sheathed to the hilt, he began moving me.

I kissed him, pausing only to whisper his name.

He moved me faster. Harder. In and out several times, only to slam me down while pumping his hips up, forcing his entire length as deep as possible.

Holding on to the back of his neck, I threw my head back. He sucked and bit along the column of my throat. Hot and savage, he worked my body closer to the edge only he could bring me to.

"Come, Amy," he said against my collarbone. "Come for me."

We moved back and forth, up and down, until I was helpless against his demand.

With a strangled gasp, my body pricked as if wasps had been unleashed beneath my skin. The intensity of my orgasm was shocking. I held on to Roman tighter as he thrust hard, his body quaking from his own release.

I kissed the top of his head, his temple, his ear. Loving how he felt, enveloping me even as I melted into him. We had each other. This was the moment I'd been craving. The reason I knew this was more. We were more. What had just happened had held more emotion than the last seven years of my life put together.

The car came to a stop, but I didn't move off of him. "Roman." I kissed him softly on the lips and whispered. "Come inside with me."

He instantly stilled, and as though my skin had turned to dry ice beneath his fingers, he yanked them away.

I pulled back enough to see his eyes smoldering with a very different kind of intensity than they'd held a few moments ago. His eyes remained on mine, but he didn't say a word. Perhaps this was one of those moments when the truth was so dangerous, he had to think before speaking.

"Look," I ran my palms down his chest, "I know I have some issues, but there's something here, something more than . . ." I wanted to say "the arrangement," but couldn't.

I wanted to escape the cloud that had been hanging over us since Monday night, when he'd explained that for us, sex and feelings weren't to be intertwined.

"I can't go inside with you, Amy."

I smoothed my hands through his hair, hoping he'd return some affection. He didn't, and the reality of the situation hit me. He couldn't come in because there were loose ends to tie up, like his fundraiser back at the mansion.

"I know you have to go back to your place first. But come back later. After everyone leaves."

The heat between us was cooling quicker than it had crept up.

"That's not a good idea."

I was about to ask why when a soft yellow glow caught my attention. My porch light was on.

"Paige is still at the gala, and Hazel had plans tonight. No one is home," I offered, thinking that was his concern.

He scooted me off of him. Feeling him leave my body was like losing the last of the warmth he'd offered. I felt instantly empty. He didn't look at me as he grabbed his pocket square, took care of the condom, and refastened his pants.

I didn't even have time to ask what the problem was before he opened his door and got out.

My door opened soon after, and Roman was waiting to help me out. Andrew, also standing outside the car, handed Roman my purse, which I'd completely forgotten about. Their every move was fluid, like the passing of a baton, reminding me of the practiced actions I'd seen the first night I'd met Roman. He was indicating the night, and his time with me, was over.

Shards of ice spearing my ribs would have been more comfortable than my feelings then. When I had agreed to this arrangement, everything had, in theory, sounded fairly simple. In practice, it had the potential to shatter me. Still, I needed to hear him admit to certain things. Explain his reasons out loud.

"Why won't you come in?" I asked. It wasn't until Andrew got back in the car that he spoke.

"It's just not a good idea," he said and gave me my purse.

"Not a good idea," I shot back. "Why?"

His eyes took on that hard, challenging look, but I wasn't backing down. Roman Reese would answer me.

"Because it doesn't look good."

His statement jarred me and once again, I felt stupid for not even considering appearances. My thought process just didn't work that way. But there it was. The truth. And he had been right, it was tough to take.

"I warned you about this, Amy. Told you where I stood on this matter."

"About screwing me, you mean? Can you honestly stand there and tell me you feel nothing when we're together?"

"I didn't say that. I just think you hold a different caliber of feelings than I do."

Wow. That really hit home. And by hit, I meant punched: a swift, straight strike to the gut. I told myself that I wanted The Real Roman. I had just seen him, felt him. Now this Roman, the one with the mask, was pulling back. Telling me I was wrong.

Maybe I was. Maybe The Real Roman was an illusion.

"I suppose you're right," I said, grabbing all the dignity I had before it flew away. "The governor of New York entering a small apartment in the middle of a crappy part of town—"

"I'm more concerned about leaving said apartment, and at what hour."

If words had arms, Roman's would have backhanded me a few times now.

"It's not just that," he added, a bit softer.

Oh boy, there was more! I honestly didn't think I could handle whatever else he was going to hit me with.

"You apartment hasn't been swept."

Was that supposed to make me feel better? "You think there are bugs? Are you that paranoid? Who would even think to do that?"

"Someone with something to gain from certain situations or admissions."

I frowned. "Who would stand to gain something like that?" The moment the words left my mouth, I wished I could take them back.

Roman's stare bore down on me. A blast of fire shot through my stomach so fast, I thought I might be sick. It turned out he didn't have to explain further. The look on his face made it quite clear.

Roman didn't trust *me*.

He didn't even let me talk about our arrangement unless under his roof and stripped bare, for goodness' sake. He'd never spend time with me in my home, a place that hadn't been dusted, searched, and secured.

There was nothing more to say, so I tried to give my best fake smile. Rejection hurt, and I'd had plenty tonight. Actually, I'd had plenty the last couple of weeks. Feeling like a world-class fool was becoming my signature style. I was throwing myself at a man who was obviously uninterested in sharing any real part of himself, and I was suffering all the damage.

"Have a good night," I said, trying to sound collected, praying he wouldn't call after me, but wishing he would.

Walking up my steps, I fished my keys out and opened the front door, never once looking back at the governor or all the baggage that came with him.

Chapter Eleven

. . . . . .

Sunday mornings were usually my favorite. They were a chance to hang out, be mellow, and just relax. Of course, after being dropped off last night by Roman, relaxed was the furthest thing from what I was feeling.

I was the only one awake, and I didn't want to turn on the television and disturb my sleeping roommates, so I opened Paige's laptop and huddled on the couch. She let me borrow it whenever I liked, and today I needed simple entertainment to take my mind off the drama of my real life. Maybe some kind of sneezing panda video would cheer me up. As Paige's computer fired up and took me to the browser she had left open, I realized that escaping drama was impossible.

"Oh. My. God." My eyes went wide as I looked at the blog site with my picture slapped at the top of the page. The headline blared:

Governor's Girlfriend Drunk at Fundraiser?

The only photos that were supposed to have been taken had been during the meet and greet. Not throughout the evening. I didn't even remember seeing someone click a camera in my direction after the initial onslaught at the beginning of the night.

But there I was, holding a glass of champagne, eyes squeezed shut, with an unflattering expression on my face that made it look like I was hammered. Roman was cropped out of the photo, but I saw his hand on my hip. It had been taken when I was dizzy and on the brink of having a panic attack, right before he'd gotten me out of there.

I looked up to see Paige, with tangled hair and tired eyes, walk into the living room.

"I wasn't drunk, Paige. I didn't even finish a whole glass of anything last night."

She nodded. "I know. Don't worry, it's being dealt with."

I scanned the blog. "Dealt with? This whole piece is speculating that I was intoxicated, and asking how I can be a good role model in my profession when I'm a lush." I scrolled down and read a blurb. "The governor disappeared with Underwood for almost an hour, only to return to his guests without the blonde activist on his arm." Even the tone sounded snippy.

It went on, but I couldn't bear to read anymore. I knew the media had a part in every politician's world. Until now, it hadn't been overwhelming. Glancing back at the screen, I realized that whatever role the press played, I had no idea how to handle it.

"You said it just right. This is *speculation*. It's what people, especially the media, do. And I promise, it's being addressed." Paige sat down next to me. Gently taking the laptop, she closed the screen. "Governor Reese has already authorized a statement saying that you had to leave due to illness, you were not drunk, and the photo was unflattering and unfortunate."

I scoffed. "Isn't that nice."

"Would you rather he came out and said you panicked because you saw your ex-boyfriend at the fundraiser?"

I let out a long sigh. Of course Paige was up to date on what had happened, at least while I had been downstairs.

"This just feels awful," I said.

She nodded and gave me a one-arm hug. "I know. Why don't you leave the media to me? There's no reason you need to see this stuff. The moment you start Googling yourself and Roman, it will turn into a black hole and affect your relationship with him. It's just not worth it, and it will only upset you. In the end, there's nothing you can do about it anyway."

"I hate that idea. It's like I'm completely powerless."

"It's just not worth getting upset over." She rose and headed to the kitchen. "Why don't I make us some coffee and we'll try to salvage the day?

Smiling as best I could, I nodded and hugged my knees to my chest. I felt very alone and very noticed, all at the same time.

. . . • . . .

"I thought you said you were making hot chocolate with whipped cream," I said, my eyes watering and throat burning from the generous gulp I'd just taken. And it had nothing to do with the temperature of the liquid. The rest of the weekend had been uneventful, aside from me wallowing, and Hazel had suggested greeting the new week with a sweet drink.

"It is," Hazel said over the rim of her mug. "Hot chocolate with whipped cream flavored vodka."

I nodded and took another, smaller sip because wow, Hazel seemed to really like "whipped cream."

"Thanks for staying in with me tonight," I said.

I set the mug down on the coffee table and grabbed a string of red, yellow, and orange lights shaped like leaves. Stepping on the couch, I placed one end of the strand at the corner of the window.

"Of course. I'm glad we finally get to spend some relaxy time together." She took a sip of cocoa and handed me a tack.

"Does relaxy time include using me as manual labor to hang all your fall decorations?" I moved along the couch, holding the string as I went, and Hazel handed me another tack to secure the next length along the top of the window.

"Hey, you're taller than I am, and tell me these aren't adorable." She held up what was, I assumed, a turkey. It was made out of papier-mâché, sequins, and twine, and looked as if it had suffered a stroke.

"It's still September. A little early for Thanksgiving decorations, isn't it?"

"They're not Thanksgiving decorations, they're autumn décor," Hazel clarified, accenting the last word a bit.

A slice of dread ran through me as I realized these things would be up for the next few months.

"Where did you get that thing?" I asked, trying to find something positive to say.

"The farmers market. Isn't it unique?" She smiled at stroke turkey—which I was now mentally calling Stroky—and I just nodded.

"It's something, alright."

"So," she said, handing me another tack, "how's everything going with Hottie McGovernor?"

I wished I could reach my cocoa just then because I needed a distraction from the question. I had no idea how it was going with Roman. Mostly because I hadn't heard from him in two days, not since our wham-bam-can't-come-inside-cuz-I-don't-trust-you-but-I'll-have-sex-with-you-in-the-car-thank-you-ma'am incident.

I didn't realize I hadn't answered her question until she followed up with, "Are you worried about your busy schedule coming up?"

"Yeah," I said, though that wasn't entirely true. The traveling was just the tip of the iceberg.

Roman's secretary had sent me an e-mail this morning, outlining the itinerary for the next month. October was right around the corner, and most of it would be spent campaigning in various cities, with only a few days in between to pop into work.

However, since the fundraiser, I hadn't actually talked to Roman. The one follow-up text he'd sent me, informing me of my required appearances, didn't count as an actual conversation. He hadn't mentioned the blog post, so I hadn't bothered asking. I was trying to take Paige's advice and not worry about it.

I leaned down and Hazel handed me another tack. Two more, and the leaves would line the whole window.

"Everything will be okay," Hazel assured me. "I bet you won't ever run into Warren again."

I sighed. It was a logical conclusion to draw, from her perspective. After the panic attack at the fundraiser, Paige had apparently texted Hazel to rush home and check on me, since she couldn't leave the mansion. I had amazing friends. Even though I was inarguably making Paige's life harder, she was still supporting me.

Because of the agreement, I hadn't gone into the details of what had happened that night. Problem was, I could really use some advice.

"I think I spooked Roman," I admitted.

"What do you mean?"

"After seeing Warren, I sort of had that mini-attack, but Roman calmed me down before it got really bad."

Hazel's eyes went wide. "That's great! Well, not great you had an attack, but it's great how he helped you."

Exactly what I thought. He'd been so amazing. Calming. Comforting. Which was why I was convinced there was something real between us. Why I had let myself get caught up in the backseat of his car. None of that mattered at the end of the night, though, because once we were done, the masked man had returned.

"I'm pretty sure it changed Roman's perception of me. He's been different." I didn't know how else to describe it without going into all sorts of details.

Hazel just looked up at me like what I'd said made no sense.

"Don't let him," she stated simply, and handed me the last tack.

"Don't let him what?"

"Think of you in any other way than the one you want."

I smiled, and after making sure the string of lights was supported, I hopped down. "You make it sound so easy."

"Oh, it's hard as hell. But if you want to be respected or viewed a certain way, you have to *be* that woman before you can project it. Know what you want and don't settle for less."

That actually made a lot of sense. I knew what I wanted professionally: funding for the Arbor Hill center, the Level Two job opening, and a career helping people. Emotionally though, I wanted strength. Peace. Roman. I was just struggling with how to go about getting those things. But Hazel did an amazing job of owning herself and her world. She was barely five feet tall, a tiny thing, but her presence took up the entire room and made her appear as big as her personality.

"You're right," I said. I needed to get it together. But one major issue danced around inside my skull. "I can't seem to kick my anxiety problem, though. It's like, when I'm caught off guard, I spiral down into all my fears."

"Except with Roman," Hazel said and handed me my cocoa.

I took it and sat on the couch. "Yeah. Except with Roman."

He caught me off guard in a totally different way. A way that made me want to tap into the edgy need he brought out in me. Made me want to reach for the rising heat, instead of run from it. When I was with him, I felt free and powerful, like I could feed off of his capability and match it. Like I could be a good counterpart.

"I know you struggle with anxiety and your past, but it's not all you are. Warren's a douche and just happens to bring out the worst in you, no shocker there," Hazel said. She started arranging Stroky and his equally sad-looking flock on our coffee table.

I smiled, loving her more by the minute. She didn't know the details surrounding my sister's death, how my choices that night had been the wrong ones, or how they ate at me every day. And I was glad for that.

It wasn't because I didn't trust her. I just didn't want one more person looking at me with disgust or pity. My issues were my own, and even though I had a hard time dealing with some of them, others I could handle. Like Roman. And it was time I started doing that.

"But are you weak, Amy?" Hazel said, jolting me back to the present.

"No," I said, suddenly feeling like I needed a megaphone.

"That's right. And my guess is, Roman's a guy."

I laughed. "I can confirm that."

Hazel glanced up from Stroky and smiled. "What I mean is, guys are stupid sometimes. He's either tiptoeing around you because he doesn't want to hurt you, or he doesn't know how to deal with his big scary man feelings, so he just pretends they don't exist. But if he didn't like you, or you weren't worth the trouble, he'd just dump you."

"Don't sugarcoat it or anything," I mumbled, and she smiled.

Roman wouldn't dump me during the campaign because of our arrangement . . . then again, maybe he would. If I wasn't providing him with any "value," why keep the deal going? Maybe he did like me beyond our secret pact. If so, I needed to bring out that side of him. Because it was no secret how I felt . . . and my poor body was damn near shaking from withdrawals already. I needed his touch.

"Time to start taking control and going after what you want," Hazel said, lifting her mug and gently bumping it against mine.

I smiled, because I knew exactly what, rather who, that entailed. Roman had his agenda: to keep a firm line between the physical part of our relationship and the rest of it. Fine. But my goals were different. I wanted The Real Roman. And I knew now that I couldn't separate my feelings the way he seemed to. Therefore, I wouldn't give into one aspect of our relationship without the other. This would be either a business deal, cut and dry and completely emotion free, or it would be more—on every level.

Arrangement or not, I had a feeling I'd still want him after the election, which gave me a little more than a month to show Roman what I saw: that there was something real between us.

"You've got an ambitious look on your face there," Hazel said with a grin.

"Just thinking of how to go after what I want."

"Good." She beamed at me. "Now open that box and help me with the rest of the decorations."

I pulled the box toward me and removed the lid, revealing a bright pink crocheted cornucopia and a set of antlers.

"Oh! Those would look great in the kitchen."

It was going to take a few more cups of cocoa before Hazel and I saw eye to eye on that.

· · · • · · ·

"You've traveled around New York with the governor for his campaign the last couple weeks, right?"

"Yes, that's correct." I acknowledged quickly.

"And you work at a nonprofit rehabilitation facility?"

"New Beginnings," I answered, mentally double-checking my posture and keeping my eyes on the interviewer, just like I had been taught.

"Is your personal relationship with the governor the reason he has turned up the heat on anti-drug policies, and is pushing for more funding for facilities like the one you work for?"

"The governor supports New York and all her citizens. Drugs are a serious problem that needs to be addressed. The solutions he is putting forth are for the good of New York."

"Do you stay in separate hotel rooms when you travel?"

"I . . . ah . . ."

"No!" Bill slapped his papers down. "That pause is the same thing you did last week. Respond quickly and clearly, or you look guilty of something."

I pinched the bridge of my nose. "I'm sorry. I can do better," I promised. Yes, I could do better—if I could just get a handle on my freaking brain, and get it to think about something else other than Roman's body and all the things I wanted to do to it.

The last couple of weeks had passed so quickly. Between traveling around New York with Roman and attempting to keep some kind of work schedule, I could count on one hand how many nights I'd slept in my own bed. Which was still more than I'd slept in Roman's.

I'd made a commitment to myself that I wouldn't sleep with Roman again until there was a real exchange of honesty and emotion between us. Unfortunately, the lack of connection, in every sense, was taking its toll.

Because the truth was, not only were we *not* sleeping together, we were staying in separate rooms. Ever since the night I'd had the panic attack and Roman had reiterated that his feelings weren't tied to sex, he'd kept everything surface level between us. He wouldn't talk about that night, and until he did, I wouldn't give in, a fact I had made very clear. But that hadn't stopped him from trying to lure me to the dark side . . .

"Maybe you're stressed out, sweetheart," Roman said, leaning over the back of my chair so his lips were right by my ear. "Maybe you need to blow off some steam." He nipped my earlobe, and I stifled a moan. Lowering his voice so that only I could hear him, he finished with, "Say the word and I can help with that."

I glanced up. Damn him. This wasn't the first time he'd tried to bring me around to his way of seeing things. Roman thought we were "real enough" without him actually sharing some piece of himself or talking about what had happened between us. The sly glances he threw me, the way he would whisper naughty phrases, had me constantly wet. But I stayed strong. He had his terms, and I had mine.

I wanted more.

He wanted more.

We just had different definitions of what that word meant.

I didn't think anyone had noticed a difference, except for me. I knew the difference between being seen by Roman and being looked over. And the lack of connection with him was chipping away at me, making my plan to achieve what I wanted all the more difficult.

"That's enough for today, Bill," Roman said, standing to his full height.

Bill rose and gathered his files.

"Practice." Bill handed me the list of questions he had been grilling me on for the last two weeks.

I nodded and took a deep breath. Roman showed him out, shut the door, and walked toward me.

"You okay?" He had been asking me that a lot lately, and frankly, I was feeling more like a porcelain doll than a human being.

"No, I'm not okay." I gathered my nerve, stood, and stepped toward him. "I need to practice my replies."

I handed him the paper, and he cleared his throat and leaned against his desk.

"I only have a few minutes," he said.

Of course. Keeping it quick, like he had been doing for the past two weeks. Tempting me one moment with his sexual innuendo, only to hustle me out the door if we were on the brink of actually talking. That's when he suddenly became busy. He was probably worried that if he was near me too long I'd . . . what? Freak out? Insist that he talk to me?

I was already not thrilled by my behavior at the fundraiser. But at the time, he had been supportive, calming me down, not making me feel like some kind of unhinged female. There had been a moment when something in his eyes had told me he understood. Knew what panic, lack of control over your emotions, your body, felt like. But whatever piece of Roman had related to me in that moment was gone now, because there was one thing I was certain of: Roman was in control of his world and himself. All the time.

"Why don't you start where Bill left off?" I suggested.

"Do you and the governor stay in separate rooms?"

"Yes." Quick and concise. Bill would be proud. But why not elaborate? "And we do so because lately, the governor doesn't seem interested in being in *any* room with me for too long."

His jaw ticked. "That doesn't sound like something Bill would have advised you to say, nor is it accurate."

"It's not?" I shrugged. "Because it's an accurate observation."

"I enjoy being in any room with you, so long as we both understand that what happens in that room means something different to me than it does to you."

"And why is that?" I lifted my chin. "What I want and what I can handle are two different things. Shutting down completely is impossible, especially when we're together." I enunciated the last word so he would know what kind of "together" I meant. "I'm not going to break down or go overboard, but it's just stupid for you to deny everything emotional between us. And I don't know why you do it."

"Is that what you think?"

"What else am I supposed to think? We're in a relationship, are we not?" I raised my brows, challenging his own rules about our arrangement, and the fact that we weren't allowed to voice that reality unless he permitted it. He clearly didn't like that. Well, too bad. He'd gotten to play the "couple card," now it was my turn.

"We are together, right?" I asked again.

"We are. And my hope is that you'll trust me and know that my treatment of you comes from a place of concern."

"I don't need your concern. And it's ironic that you want my trust when you won't budge on doing the same. Believe it or not, I can handle more than you think."

"I'm very aware of that, Amy. But I pushed your limits before we were clear—"

"I like it when you push my limits," I cut in. "What I don't like is the aftermath, when you pretend that it meant absolutely nothing."

I took another step, closing in on him. Maybe some explanation and action would hammer home my point.

"I liked the night in your room, the way you felt . . . inside of me," I whispered. I'd never said such things out loud, but if I wanted to salvage this bond between us, it was time for honesty. "I miss that feeling, Roman. I miss you."

"Amy . . ." It was more of a croak than a voice.

But I was done pretending that I was okay with the distance growing between us.

For the last two weeks, I had been colder than I had since Lauren died. It was the kind of deep chill that creeps up and settles in your bones when you've lost something you're not ready to let go of.

I wasn't ready to lose Roman.

Not yet.

Not this way.

If there was one thing I did know, it was that having a choice was a powerful thing. And I had some to make. Either let others, including Roman, dismiss my worth, or show them otherwise.

I didn't know what Roman and I were, but whatever it was, while large parts of it were built on falsehoods, there was something very real at its heart. I'd felt it the night I met Roman at the gala. Though brief, there was an intense connection, an uncertain draw to one another.

There was something very wounded, very genuine about Roman Reese, and I had gotten a glimpse of it. I wasn't ready to toss that. It was that small part of him I held on to, the one real thing I identified with. It was simply *him*. When all the bullshit, swagger, and stature were peeled away, the titles, strategy, and politics pushed aside, I was left with Roman: The man. Which was what I wanted. Needed.

He felt real.

We felt real.

I took another step. I could reach out and touch him, but I didn't. Instead I said, "Next question."

He took a long moment to look at the paper before he finally asked it.

"Are you sleeping with the governor?"

"No," I grinned. "I was informed once that if I ever came close to a bed with him, we'd be fucking, not sleeping."

He took a deep breath, his impressive chest rising and falling while he took in my words. Bill had been harping on appropriate public behavior, talking points, and "prep-work" for the last few weeks, and as a result, I was getting better at responding quickly without showing my nerves. It was an ability that was helpful right now.

"You're playing with fire, Amy. You want something that I'm

more than willing to give you." His dark gaze dropped to my breasts, then lower, taking in my entire body before meeting my eyes again. "But I don't want you to misunderstand what it meant when we're through."

One more step, and I finally entered his space. Felt his breath fan over my forehead. Smelled his crisp Italian suit and spicy masculine scent. Heat radiated from every square inch of him. I'd been desperate to be near him again.

Over the past few weeks, I'd learned that Roman did, indeed, have big scary man feelings, just as Hazel had suspected. I was also certain, from the way he treated me in the moments that counted, that he was purposefully not acknowledging them.

I didn't know if it was the lack of touch, or that he'd foregone a jacket today and stood in black pants, vest, tie, and bright white button-down, but damn it, the man was chiseled, composed, and fine as freaking hell.

"I'm not playing with anything, I just want you to talk to me. And maybe kiss me," I whispered. "And I want you to mean it."

His gaze locked on my mouth.

"You want to kiss me, don't you?" I asked.

"Yes."

"But you don't want to mean it?"

He stayed still. Didn't shake his head, but didn't agree.

"Why is this hard for you?" I asked.

"Because you're . . ."

I swallowed, waiting for him to finish, understanding why quick responses were better: too much elapsed time led to thoughts. Bad thoughts. Like, does he not want to kiss me because I'm ugly? Annoying? Weak? Was I overplaying my hand?

"You're different than I expected," he finally said.

My heart pounded and defeat washed over me. I went to step back, but he dropped the paper and grabbed my hip, preventing me from stepping away.

"I mean that as a compliment."

And with that one admission, just like the night I'd met him, I felt whole. Like I wasn't some small, insignificant thing floating through life. I was grounded, if just for a moment, in his arms.

His lips brushed over mine. "You have been the only thing on my mind," he said. "Do you have any idea how hard it's been to keep my hands off of you?"

"Then don't. I want you so much." I couldn't get my mind and my hormones to agree. It was a big problem, because right now, I was on the brink of giving in. Closing my eyes briefly, hoping to gain some composure, I opened them only to be re-enthralled by that dazzling, dark gaze. I said the only thing I could, "We have to be on the same page with our emotions."

"I know," he said.

I wrapped my arms around his neck and flicked my tongue out to taste his lips. He growled and his hands landed heavily on my ass, clutching me closer. My belly pressed against the physical proof of just how hard it had been on him.

"I can't give you what you want," he said.

"You sure about that?" My tongue darted out again. "Because you already are." He was talking to me. Honestly.

"You drive me crazy," he said and consumed my mouth.

I gasped at the force of his kiss. Hard, demanding. Like he'd missed me. Like he really had been thinking of me.

Plunging his tongue between my lips over and over, he devoured me in a consuming rhythm that made my head swim and my knees weak.

"God damn it, Amy," he rasped between strong draws and nips at my bottom lip. "You confuse the hell out of me."

Another taste, another bite.

I wound my fingers into his hair, pulling him closer, needing more.

"You're so soft, so innocent."

He gripped my ass hard, his erection prodding, begging for attention, so I reached between our bodies to give it. He hissed as I gripped him through his pants.

"Then there's this other girl," he said, as he thrust into my hand, "bold and demanding and so fucking sexy." His words made my chest split with joy and my lust rise. "I want you so damn bad, but don't want to hurt you," he whispered. "If that means keeping a distance—"

"Don't you dare," I snapped. I leaned back just enough so I could see him, our breaths mingling and coming fast. "You've been staying away from me because you're concerned about me?"

He nodded.

"I'm going to ask you one thing," I said. Roman was battling his own feelings, and I was battling mine. The problem was, it was starting to sound like he did care about me, but didn't understand it. "What do you think will come of us after the election?"

He frowned and I rolled my eyes. "I mean, after you win the election, of course," I clarified with a smile.

He grinned and barely grazed my bottom lip. "I don't know. I figured we'd part."

"Is that what you want?"

His eyes searched mine as what looked like a minor epiphany hit his expression. "No. I'd like to keep seeing you."

That simple admission made me want to dance with triumph. Roman did want more, it was just a matter of him figuring it out.

And what I was finding was that if I held on long enough, Roman would come around. This was the first honest conversation we'd had since that night in his car. We were making progress.

Even though a big part of me knew I wasn't as strong as I'd like, I'd never before felt more alive. Maybe I could—and wanted to—deal with my world. Roman brought out the power, the confidence in me.

"What changed that night at the fundraiser?" I said against his mouth.

Was it finding out that Warren was my ex? Seeing my panic attack and deciding I was too fragile to cope with certain kinds of emotions? Whatever it was, that had been the night Roman had shifted and begun guarding himself against me.

He took another deep taste and I moaned, gripping him a little tighter. "That night after your panic attack, you looked at me like . . ."

He kissed me again, then shook his head.

"Like what?" I breathed.

"Like I was a goddamned hero." My heart sped up and I clung to him.

"You are." I wasn't sure if I'd actually spoken the words, or if he'd heard them, until he responded.

"And what if I'm not?"

His mouth was so forceful I could hardly breathe, but he didn't let up. Like a punishment or a warning. I saw something good in Roman, something I was willing to fight for, but it was the same thing he was running from.

"Excuse me, sir?"

I pulled back instantly at the sound of Jean calling from the door.

Roman grinned at me and looked over my shoulder to acknowledge her.

"Yes?"

"I just wanted to let you know that Mayor Stanton and his wife have confirmed for tomorrow night."

"Thank you, Jean."

She scuttled out, and Roman traced my bottom lip with his thumb.

"How do you feel about meeting the Mayor of Albany?"

Chapter Twelve

· · · · ···

"So what do you have in mind for tomorrow's dinner?" I asked Roman as we wound through the produce section.

"I have no idea. I wanted to call the caterer, remember?" He picked up an apple and put it in the basket he was carrying.

"Cooking dinner for him will be charming, though. Plus, I like to cook, and I'm happy to help. So I think the words you're looking for are 'thank you, Amy.'" I grinned at him while putting a few onions in a plastic bag.

"Thank you, Amy," he replied with his own smile. I had to admit, seeing him like this, in his pressed suit and polished persona, holding a little red grocery basket while browsing the fruit section, was so wonderfully . . . normal.

"What's your favorite thing to eat?" I asked across the display of potatoes.

He glanced up and met my gaze, a wicked smile splitting his lips.

My eyes shot wide. "I meant food."

He feigned a pout and heat rushed to my cheeks. The man was incorrigible and practically had me giggling like a teenager.

"Well . . ." He walked along the column of vegetables, perusing the artichokes. "There was this one dish my mother made. It was actually the only thing she made." His tone was sharp and his whole body was tense, but he continued. "It was a seared pork chop and some kind of cheese pasta."

I came to stand by him. He tossed a head of lettuce into the basket. "She only cooked it a few times when I was really young. I don't know how she made it, and I'm sure she doesn't remember anymore either."

I gently set the onions in the basket and ran a hand down his arm. Whatever the issue was between him and his mother, it was obviously touchy. Deep sadness and anger radiated from him, and I didn't want to push. I was just ecstatic he was sharing something real about himself.

"Well, I think I can figure out something close," I said.

He shrugged, then went to the section against the wall that held the berries and herbs. His expression had changed, just like after we were intimate. Closed off. It was as though he threw away whatever thoughts he was having and replaced them with indifference. Like he didn't want to feel whatever it was he was approaching.

It was right then that I silently reached a new level of understanding of Roman Reese. He stayed away from things he had no interest in remembering, handling, or controlling.

And I was lumped into that group.

Yet, he was still here with me.

There was hope.

"Make what you want for dinner," he said, grabbing a carton of blueberries and zeroing those dark eyes in on me. "So long as I get what I want for dessert."

. . . • . . .

"Now this is comfort food," Ken Stanton, the mayor of Albany, said. "You made this?"

He looked at me from across the big dining room table. He had to be in his late fifties. With his white hair and kind eyes, a certain jolliness radiated from him.

I smiled and nodded. "Yes, sir."

Though Roman had insisted that his staff help, I had gotten to make my version of Roman's mother's dish. Not to mention, using his kitchen was like working in a dream. There were state-of-the-art appliances and so much space that my entire apartment could have rested on the countertop like one of Hazel's creepy crafted turkeys.

"Wow." He took another bite, then pointed his fork at Roman. "I think you've got a keeper here, Reese."

Heat rushed to my cheeks, half from the mayor's praise and half from the way Roman looked at me. Like he was proud.

After grilling Roman about what he remembered of the dish, I had spent all afternoon trying to perfect what I was pretty sure was macaroni and cheese and a shake 'n bake pork chop. With a little engineering, I had made everything from scratch and added home-made apple sauce as another side. I just hoped it was everything Roman imagined.

"Indeed I do," Roman said and palmed my knee under the table.

Now my blush was turning into a full-body heat. Aside from the steamy kiss in his office yesterday, it had been weeks since Roman and I had been intimate. The smallest touch still set me off.

The mayor and Roman chatted about the state and various events coming up, while the mayor's wife and I mostly nodded and smiled. The couple seemed nice and genuine. But what was interesting was the way Roman looked at Mayor Stanton—with a certain respect.

"I hear your campaign is going well," Roman said.

Ken took a drink of his wine and nodded. "We'll see after his new ad comes out. Cunningham is running a tough campaign."

"I thought Mrs. Cunningham was retiring this year," I said. I was certain Warren had said that at the fundraiser.

"She is. It's her son who is going for her seat," Ken affirmed. "Young guy, mid-twenties I believe."

I accidentally dropped my fork, and it clanged against my plate. "Her son. As in, Warren Cunningham?"

Roman nodded, his jaw clenching tightly. I tried really hard to not look shocked, but this was definitely news to me. Roman returned to his conversation with Ken, for which I was grateful.

"Tough?" Roman asked. "It looks like Cunningham has launched a smear campaign against you. How are you going to retaliate?"

Ken took another bite of his pork chop and smiled at me before returning his attention to Roman.

"I'm not, son," he said, like he didn't have a care in the world. "What Cunningham is putting out there about me is baseless and without fact. The people of New York know I'm honest. I just have to trust that."

Roman looked at me for a long moment. Something was going on behind those eyes. Something I so badly wanted him to share with me. And in his own way, he was. Slowly. Dropping little hints here and there about the man he was, the man he wanted to be.

As if reading my mind, he smiled and wound his fingers with mine, holding my hand under the table, offering a glimpse of support.

Despite all that had happened over the past few weeks, tonight, for the most part, was a success. And I'd cling to that.

. . . • . . .

"What are you doing?" Roman asked from the doorway of the kitchen.

"Apparently nothing." I spun around and looked at the spotless kitchen. "I was going to help clean up, but it looks like your staff already did."

He nodded. "They left over an hour ago." He leaned against the doorjamb and stared me down. "Dinner was impressive."

"Thank you. I hope it was like you remember it." Taking a page from his book, I did my own leaning: a hip against the island in the middle of the massive kitchen.

"It was better."

His voice sent sparks along my nape. Running my fingertip along the cool granite counter, I kept my eyes locked on his, and my body language approachable, but strong. Another thing I was learning from him.

"Thank you for cooking, Amy. It really was incredible, and you didn't have to do it."

"You're welcome. And I wanted to."

He nodded slowly, his gaze going from my eyes to my toes, then back up again.

One thing Roman was good at was eliciting information using few words. Right now, he was testing how much I'd say. Seeing if I'd broach the subject of us not "sleeping" together, as I had earlier.

Instead, I took the opportunity to practice my method of "showing," rather than "telling."

"We are going to talk now," I informed him. Yeah, *informed.* The idea made me giggle internally a little.

He raised a brow. "Are we?"

I nodded, keeping my casual stance.

"And what would you like to talk about, Miss Underwood?"

"This afternoon and what you said."

He crossed his arms over his chest, making them look even wider and his sexy hips delectable. No one pulled off business casual like Governor Reese. His button-down had white cuffs and collar, while the rest was the same blue as the French Polynesian coastline. The color made his tan skin pop and his dark eyes shine.

I swallowed hard and adjusted my footing. Sensible heels or not, my simple dress suddenly felt too hot and constricting. Or maybe it was my skin.

"I said a lot of things. Including my thoughts on dessert."

"You asked for blueberry pie."

His gaze was hot. "I did. But I didn't enjoy it the way I wanted."

My breath stuck in my chest like cotton candy. If I didn't try now, I'd miss my chance, and I didn't think I could ward off Roman any longer. I was aching for him. But there was one thing we had to clear up first. One thing that he'd said that I couldn't let him go on believing.

"I just want to talk about what you said earlier. About you not being a good man. You don't honestly believe that, do you?"

"You have brought out certain traits that I'm forced to acknowledge."

Even though the house was quiet and we were alone, I knew there was no way Roman would let me talk about the arrangement. Once again, I had to speak like the girlfriend.

"What traits? After we had sex the first night, you changed. You said that you hadn't meant to hurt me. Was it something I did?"

He didn't say anything. Deny or defend. So I cast a wider net, looking for anything I could think of that may have caused his different reactions.

"Is it because of my experience level?" Or lack thereof. "Is it because of my panic attack? Do you think you have to handle me a certain way or something?"

His nostrils flared, and he pushed off the wall to stand up straight. "No."

"Then explain it to me." I tried to keep my voice level. "Please."

Though his arms were crossed, I could see his fists clench. His upper lip jerked up slightly, as if holding back a snarl. He was on the brink of admitting the truth. It was something I was desperate for, so I pushed a little harder.

"It doesn't make sense, Roman. You don't make sense. I won't just take your word for things, especially when you'll barely discuss them. Admit it. You think I'm some sad weakling who can't handle life or sex or something."

"No," he said between gritted teeth.

"Then what? What do you expect me to think if not that?"

"I wanted to kill him, Amy!" he snapped, and stepped toward me. "The moment I saw the effect that son of a bitch Cunningham was having on you—all the color drained from your face while he smiled and watched." Roman's dark eyes were like those of a wolf, and I'd never heard a more deadly voice than his when he said, "It took everything I had not to end him right there."

"What?" I breathed, unable to form any other word, much less thought.

Roman took another step toward me. There was so much more to him than he let anyone see. This whole time he'd been thinking of me? My welfare? He had used the word "concern" before, but that had been in a different context. I'd never tied it together this way.

"You think I enjoy staying away from you? You think it's easy?" He closed the remaining distance, crowding me, and when I arched my neck to look up at him, my chin skimmed across his sternum.

"It's not. But every time I get close to you," he pushed his body against mine, physically emphasizing his words, "I lose my better judgment."

My lower back pressed into the counter as a whole lot of intense male desire stared down at me.

"If you knew how many times I've replayed that night . . ." His hand ran up the inside of my thigh. The slight scratch of his rough palm made me shiver. "The firelight on your skin . . . being so deep inside you that I could feel you coming all over me."

He dove beneath my dress and cupped the warmth between my legs. I gasped, as much from his touch as from his words.

"I know you can handle sex, Amy. I know you can handle life. I just don't know how to handle you."

He trailed his finger along the edge of my panties, and I gripped the counter behind me for support.

"There are so many things I want to do to you." His mouth hovered over my forehead, down to my ear. "But I never want to scare you."

I met his gaze. "Then trust me when I tell you that the only time I've been frightened is these last two weeks. Not knowing where we stood or what you've been thinking. Wondering if you were done with me."

"Done with you?" He nipped my bottom lip and said, with a sexy smirk, "I haven't even started with you."

He seized my mouth in one consuming kiss. His dominating power poured over me like warm caramel, rich and smooth. My whole body was bathed in his presence. Gripping my hips, he lifted me and sat me atop the counter, instantly wedging himself between my thighs, rucking up my skirt.

I wrapped my arms around him and scooted closer until I felt his hard cock press against my core. The only thing between us was a few layers of fabric—which I was dying to rip away.

"Fuck, I've missed you," he said, and I wasn't sure if he realized he'd spoken aloud.

Something in my chest twisted like an invisible knife between my ribs. Had he really been trying to stay away from me for my own good? The fact that he cared that much both shocked and thrilled me. But his fight was coming to an end. I'd make sure of it, because he brought out feelings in me that I didn't want to deny.

Thrusting his tongue between my lips, he toyed with mine in such a delicious dance, it made my head spin until I couldn't find gravity. And I didn't care. I could stay in the clouds so long as his mouth was on mine, because my God, the man could kiss. Hard and powerful, consuming and giving. I felt everything he was in the way he kissed me.

Reaching around, he clutched my ass in both palms and yanked me closer, rubbing that steel rod along my folds. Though we had barriers between us, I still felt every glide of him against me.

"Oh, yes, Roman." The zing of pleasure shot from my core to the tips of my ears and toes, tingling everything in its wake.

He kissed his way down my neck, his five o'clock shadow gently scraping as he went. I wove my fingers in his hair and threw my head back, letting him devour me and loving every rough scratch of his jaw and hot sweep of his tongue.

"This dress has driven me crazy all night," he said against my collarbone, his mouth trailing lower.

He bit the hint of cleavage swelling over the bodice. My dress was classy but due to its décolletage, I'd had to skip a bra, a fact for which I was now very thankful.

"All through dinner I was thinking about how you'd taste." Bite. "About how I wanted to eat you."

He nipped my other breast and I jumped a little.

Gripping the neckline of my dress, he yanked it down, ripping the material enough to wedge it beneath my breasts, which were instantly lifted up like a plump offering. I couldn't finish a breath before he latched on to one aching nipple and took a deep draw.

Keeping one hand on his head, I balanced on the counter with the other, leaning farther back, silently begging him to take more.

"You like this, don't you?"

"Yes," I breathed.

Before Roman, I hadn't known that my breasts could be such a turn on. He laved at me, worshiping my flesh with his talented mouth, splitting my nerves and leaving me intoxicated with pleasure. He blew over my nipple and I squirmed.

"So sensitive," he smiled.

Goose bumps broke out over my skin and I arched my back farther. "Please . . . more."

He tongued the other breast, taking his time, tasting every inch of flesh, before circling around the tight point and finally biting down hard.

"Ah, yes!" My hips shot out, rubbing against his hard cock. My panties were so damp, I worried I was getting his pants wet.

There were too many layers between us. But Roman took his time, devouring my breasts until I couldn't breathe and was on the brink of release, just from his insistent oral torture.

Taking matters into my own hands, I reached between us and started unfastening his belt. The metallic clanking echoed through the dimly lit kitchen.

I couldn't control my hands. The smallest tasks, like removing his pants, became too difficult. So I started clawing at his shirt, the buttons too tricky to unfasten. When the sound of them hitting the floor reached my ears, I realized I was pulling apart the material.

Roman bit down hard on my nipple and growled, as if liking my forwardness and responding in kind. I ripped farther, not stopping until his shirt was hanging like tattered curtains around his impressive chest.

"You're so amazing," I whispered, my hands moving over his hard chest. His warm, soft skin was like a freshly brewed mocha, and he had the most incredible abs I'd ever seen.

He rose enough to kiss my lips. My fingers trailed down the defined swells of his stomach muscles. Just the feel of all that strength made me shudder, and damn it if he didn't notice.

When I came to the waist of his pants, I reached inside and gripped his erection.

He hissed.

"Oh, my God . . ." Shock came over me.

He pulled back enough to look at me, a questioning frown marring his face.

"I just . . ." I bit my lip and gave him a tentative stroke. "I haven't gotten to really touch you. You're . . . you're big."

He grinned. "And you're blushing."

I knew I must be, but I refused to give into my inexperience. Instead, I stuck to the new, emboldened side of me. Whenever Roman was involved, my instincts came out. I'd just have to trust those, because there was no way I was letting this end here.

"My purse is over there." I nodded just behind him, to where I'd hung it earlier. "There's a condom in it."

When he gave me a disbelieving look, I simply shrugged and said, "I've had a bit of wishful thinking lately."

"Me too."

He kissed me softly, then turned and got the condom from my purse. Within a few seconds, he was standing before me once more.

Just like last time, he opened his pants just enough to roll it on. I knew I wouldn't get to see more of him right now, even though I was desperate to see all that skin and muscle. He certainly had nothing to be ashamed of in the body department. No, with Roman, it was something else. Like keeping it quick and mostly clothed also kept it casual. Maintaining control over the situation was a driving goal for him. If he stayed mostly clothed, he could adjust quickly.

It was as if he didn't like getting too close to something without a barrier. As if he was afraid that if he really let his guard down, felt only the moment, he'd be vulnerable to the world around him. To me.

But now was not the time to push him. I didn't want to ruin the moment. So I watched him sheath himself, taking in every detail I could, while I could.

He stepped between my spread legs. Gripping his cock, he used the head to push my panties aside and position himself at my entrance. I cupped his face and kissed him hard, wiggling my hips so that the crown nudged inside. He groaned against my mouth, and the feel of his need running through him and into me was like a shot of adrenaline.

I flicked my heels, scraping their sharp edges across his ass to spur him. He moaned again and thrust hard inside of me.

My eyes shot open and all the air left my lungs. The sudden fullness of him inside of me burned a bit, but it felt so right. So necessary. If I'd had any doubt before, it was gone now. I needed him. So much. The connection I'd felt was back. Us. Together. We fit.

He nipped my chin, my jaw, my earlobe. Locking my ankles together, I pushed even harder against him, any distance suddenly unacceptable. I needed more. My bare breasts pressed against his heated chest, and the sensation made me moan. Skin against skin while he was deep within me was the most blessedly wonderful feeling I'd ever had.

"Don't leave me," I whispered between kisses.

I didn't think my words were coherent, and didn't care if I sounded needy. All I cared about was holding on to that moment. Holding on to him. Feeling him against me. In me.

He gave me what I wanted and stayed. Didn't withdraw. Didn't retreat and return. He remained buried, right where he was, and stirred me. Hitting that spot inside over and over, while his pelvis rubbed over my aching clit. It was amazing. Inside and out, touching, feeling, seeing everything I was.

He gripped behind my knees and pulled, sending himself another inch deeper, and that was all it took for my body to fly over the edge into the abyss. I hugged him close as my core, my skin, my soul, burned up and shattered. Over and over, I came undone around him. And like a spindle winding silk, he wrapped me up and caught me.

"I feel you, sweetheart." His voice held a hint of amazement, like he didn't want to leave either, even for the short time it would take to thrust back and forth. Instead, he remained right there, barely pumping his hips, staying deep, staying connected.

"You're incredible," he rasped.

If possible, I felt him grow even harder. His skin flushed a degree hotter against mine, and he pulled back enough to look me in the eyes. Cupping my face, he stared at me. Being consumed by those dark eyes was like being lost in midnight. And that's where we stayed, stranded together somewhere beyond reality, as his release took over.

It was so powerful I felt it, even through the latex barrier. Looking into my eyes, he came, and I was helpless not to follow. Never had I felt more vulnerable, and more understood, than right then.

"You're everything," I muttered, hoping that my words were too quiet for him to hear.

Roman Reese was, in a word, *everything*.

And I had no idea how to handle the truth of that.

Chapter Thirteen

A soft kiss fluttered along my forehead, and I opened my eyes to find Roman hovering over me.

"Good morning," he said.

I stretched and smiled, the softness of the sheets against my skin making it difficult to want to move.

"This is a vision I could get used to seeing." He smiled, staring at my breasts.

I looked down to find that the sheet had fallen enough to expose my nipples. My hard nipples. My desperate-for-Roman's-touch nipples.

Roman sat at the edge of the bed, looking as handsome and sexy as ever in his suit. I grabbed the sheet and pulled it over myself as I sat up to face him. He pretended to pout, which made me smile like a moron.

"Thank you for letting me spend the night," I said.

He tucked a lock of hair behind my ear. "Thank you for staying."

"I guess it wasn't so bad," I teased.

"Oh, really?" His hand trailed from my ear down my neck to my side. "You survived alright?"

I gave an exaggerated huff. "Barely."

He pinched my side, tickling me, and a throaty laugh escaped my lips.

"You're such a mouthy tease." Roman smiled and kept tickling.

"I'm sorry!" I laughed, squirming and kicking. The blankets were just for show at this point.

"What was that, Miss Underwood? I didn't hear you?" He tickled again, and I thrashed harder.

"I-I'm sorry!" I hollered, water spilling from my eyes from laughing so hard.

His wicked fingers ceased their torment, and I flopped on my back. With a hand on either side of my head, he leaned over and kissed me.

"Seriously, having you naked in my bed is about the hottest damn thing I've ever seen."

I tugged a little on his Windsor knot, my heartbeat still a bit hectic.

"But it doesn't look like you're coming back to bed," I said. It was my turn to pout, only mine was very real.

"Unfortunately, no. I have to go in early this morning." He kissed me again and against my lips said, "But you take as long as you'd like."

"Thanks."

He rose, a little reluctantly, and that made me feel good. I couldn't beg him to stay, though I desperately wanted to. He was an important man and I had a job to get to as well, but still, a day in bed with Roman would be a day well spent.

"I'll call you later," he said, walking toward the door.

I smiled, because after last night, I actually believed he would. Maybe the ignoring me thing was finally over.

I watched him walk out, and the room was suddenly cooler, empty. I already missed him.

My addiction to the governor was getting worse.

· · · • · ··

Clutching a paper bag in my hand, I was winding through the hallway of the state capitol toward Roman's office when, coming around a corner, I collided with another body.

"Ow!" I yelped as I ran right into—"Warren?"

He stepped back, a glare firmly in place.

"Still looking down when you walk?" He shook his head, not bothering to say the rest.

He had recited this bit of "constructive criticism," as he called it, at least a dozen times in the years we'd dated. But instead of nodding and complying like I would have when I was younger, I squared my shoulders and prepared to walk around him without sparing him a word.

"Here to see your boyfriend?" he snapped, then puffed out his chest. My pulse quickened a bit, but I focused on maintaining a steady presence.

"That's none of your business, Warren," I said coolly, happy that Bill's interview training was paying off.

Warren was obviously upset about something and ready to spit fire. I had enough experience with his temper to know that I wanted no part in that. Simply walking away, I left him to mutter whatever unflattering thing he was saying under his breath. It felt good.

When I got to Roman's office, the door was open and he and Bill were talking. I peeked in.

"Amy?" Roman said.

"Hi. I didn't mean to interrupt. I can go."

"No, come in." Roman seemed a little upset, and so did Bill. Something was going on with the men under this roof today.

"What's that?" Bill nodded at the paper bag in my hand.

"I made Roman a lunch." I'd shredded a left over pork chop from last night's dinner and made it into a sandwich.

I glanced at Roman and a smile split his face. Bill, however, looked confused.

"I've never seen you guys eat lunch around here," I offered.

This morning, after I had gotten out of Roman's bed and dressed, it had occurred to me that maybe bringing him something would be nice. I didn't know what he typically did with his afternoons, or if he even had time to eat. But the way Bill was glaring made me feel like an idiot for thinking such a thing.

"Thank you, sweetheart," Roman said. He kissed my forehead and took the bag, putting it on his desk. Then he looked at Bill. "We'll discuss this more later."

Bill leered at me for some reason, then returned his attention to Roman. "Don't let things that aren't important affect your campaign," Bill snapped, then stomped out.

Roman shut the door behind him and returned to me.

"What was that about?" I asked.

"Politics." There was a good deal of annoyance in his voice.

"I saw—well, ran into—Warren in the hallway," I admitted.

"He just left," Roman said and walked behind his desk. "He came to get my support in his bid for his mother's seat."

My mouth dropped open. I'd known Warren was running, but had had no idea he would ask Roman for support.

"Are you going to support him?"

"Most likely."

My heart did a summersault, and I felt instantly sick. "But he's . . . awful."

Not to mention, I'd seen how Roman looked up to Ken Stanton, Warren's competition.

"I'm aware," Roman said. "But believe it or not, this isn't about you. I can't base my decisions on what my girlfriend thinks."

That summersault came to a dead halt, and for a moment I thought my heart had actually burst. Gone was the carefree Roman of this morning, who smiled and was sweet. Instead, I got a hard look that chilled my skin so fast, the violent shiver made me sway on my feet.

"I just came to drop that off," I said, motioning to the stupid sack lunch and feeling very much like a child. "Have a good day," I managed and turned to leave.

I had a feeling that Roman wasn't going to call today after all.

. . . . . .

"So I was thinking," I said, balancing my cell between my shoulder and ear while filling the coffeepot. It was a double-caffeinated kind of morning. "I could fly in on the sixteenth, then spend a couple days with you and Dad."

"I don't know," my mother said. "The airport is quite a ways away, and your father doesn't like the drive."

The airport was an hour's drive, but like every year I went home for Lauren's anniversary, I didn't think the drive was the reason that my parents weren't thrilled to see me.

"Shit," I whispered when I spilled coffee grounds all over the front of me. Now I'd need to change before work, and at this rate, if I didn't hustle, I'd miss my bus.

"I can rent a car and drive myself from the airport to your place. I'd like to be there, Mom. Go to her grave with you guys."

"I just don't know," she said. "I thought you were working anyway."

"I am, but I can take a long weekend. I've already cleared it with my boss."

It was the one thing that wasn't on the schedule Roman had handed Marcy, because Roman didn't know about my travel plans. Not that it was a "need to know" thing. But Marcy had cleared it all the same.

"We don't really have the room, Amy," my mother added, all but telling me I wasn't welcome.

I pressed my lips together to keep the tears from rising and gave up on the coffee. More of it was on me than in the pot.

Channeling any strength I had left, I cleared my throat and said, "That's okay, Mom. I'll stay in a hotel. Why don't I call you when I'm in town? Because I *will* be there."

I heard her exhale long and low and in that moment, I didn't care that she didn't want me. Lauren was important to me and I wanted to be there, just like every other year. Maybe it was strange, but the anniversary of her death was when I felt closest to her. It was the only time I could tell her how sorry I was and feel like she could hear me.

"Do what you like," my mother said. "Bye-bye."

I listened to the line die and felt like a useless waste of skin, fighting for yet another situation that "wasn't about me."

And it hurt like hell.

. . . • . . .

The knock on the door jolted me out of a light nap. I sat up on the couch, feeling sore and horrible. It was past dinnertime and today had mostly sucked. Work had dragged by, Hazel was at a late class, and Paige still wasn't home.

Making my way to the door, I adjusted my sweatshirt and sweatpants. Then I opened the door, and about lost my stomach when I saw who stood on my porch.

Warren.

He had one hand on the doorjamb and was eyeing me with such venom, he could easily have passed for part snake.

"What are you doing here?"

"It took me a minute," he started, leaning in and making me really uncomfortable. "But after I saw you today, everything clicked."

I frowned and crossed my arms over my chest. "I don't know what you're trying to say, but I'm not interested."

"Oh, I think you will be. Because it's your fault the governor is flipping on me."

"Excuse me?"

Warren straightened to his full height, which, when paired with the glare in his hazy blues, was a little scary.

"Reese was set to support me, back my campaign to run for a house seat. Now all of a sudden, something has changed." He slid his foot forward just enough to technically be inside my home. "And that change is you."

I swallowed hard, and tried to back away slowly without looking like I was retreating. Realizing how very alone I was, I did my best not to let my fear affect my expression.

"I don't know what you're talking about, Warren. I didn't even know you were running until recently."

"I don't believe you!" He struck my door with the palm of his hand, and I winced a little at the sudden bang. "I think you've been talking shit about me and fucking the governor to get what you want."

Respond quickly, I reminded myself. Hoping a straight posture would camouflage my trembles, I lifted my chin and spoke the way I had been practicing.

"I don't have any say in his politics, Warren. You're not welcome here, and I'd like you to leave."

This was not a conversation I wanted to be having, but unfortunately, what I wanted didn't matter just then. The truth was, if I could sway the governor to oppose Warren, I would. He was an asshole. Now, hearing Warren whine about Roman flipping on him, I was half confused and half happy.

I didn't know what Roman's motives were, of course. Today, he'd made clear that his job wasn't my business. Warren, however, seemed to have his own theory.

"A Cunningham has sat in a house seat for the last five decades. I'll be damned if some small-town whore is going to fuck with that." That time when he snarled, I smelled the alcohol on his breath. "And you're going to fix what you've done, Amy."

"I haven't done anything," I said again in the calmest voice I could muster, hoping to defuse the situation so he would go away and I could lock my door.

"Reese is going to announce his support for that seat in a few weeks. If you don't convince him that I'm the man for the job, then I'll tell him what kind of person you really are."

My heart lurched in my chest, and every ounce of blood I had in my face drained away. The night I'd been stupid enough to open up to Warren all those years ago had returned to hit me.

"You think he'll still want you around when he finds out you let your sister die?" Warren tsk-tsked, and bile rose in my throat. "Won't look so good for his campaign to be dating someone like you. Hell, you can't even get your own parents to like you."

My entire ribcage was shaking from my efforts to exhale. Breathing was difficult, and I struggled for control because the moment I gave into panic, I would crash in a tailspin of self-loathing. And I would crash hard. I couldn't do that in front of him.

He tapped his chin. "I wonder what one would call what you did? Accessory to involuntary manslaughter?" He glanced at the sky. "You know, that has a nice ring to it." Stepping away with the most evil look I'd ever seen, he stared me down. "Think about what I said."

He turned and damn near skipped off my porch. "Have a nice night, Amy."

I immediately shut the door and locked the deadbolt. Pressing my back against the door, I sank to my knees and cried.

Chapter Fourteen

"What an asshole," Paige said, pacing in front of the coffee table with her hands on her hips.

I sat on the couch and watched her brow furrow while she thought, until finally she faced me.

"Okay, let's look at the facts," she started in true Paige fashion. "First of all, the governor never committed his support to Warren."

"Did you know he was running?" I asked.

"Not until recently. I didn't even know he was going to be at the fundraiser. He announced he would run right after that. I should have known though," Paige grumbled. "He's going for his mother's seat, and Bill is pushing for him to get it. He thinks another Cunningham on the house floor will keep the relationship in our favor. But from what I gather, Roman isn't so sure."

She started pacing again.

So Roman hadn't committed, but Bill was on Warren's team. No matter how hard my brain worked to find a solution, one fact kept rearing its head: This isn't my place.

I understood that Roman had to do what was right for his office and for New York. I just had a hard time believing Warren Cunningham was a right choice for anything, especially when blackmail came so easily to him.

"Maybe I should tell Roman about Warren's threats," I said out loud, not sure if I was asking Paige's permission or trying to convince myself this was a viable option.

"Then you'd have to tell him everything," Paige said, stopping and staring at me.

My hands instantly went clammy, and the need to cry, or throw something—preferably at Warren's face—rose to the surface.

"If Roman finds out what I did to Lauren . . ."

"Stop," Paige snapped. "You didn't hurt Lauren. She's the one who took the pills."

I rested my forehead in my palm. The world felt very heavy all of a sudden.

"Listen to me very carefully." Paige came and sat next to me. "I know you're a good person, and I know you deal with a lot of shit about Lauren from your parents and now this douche, Warren, but you have to remember: You didn't kill your sister." She grabbed my hand and gently shook it. "Do you hear me?"

I nodded, yet my chest still hurt. I wanted to argue that I'd had a responsibility to Lauren and I'd failed her, but Paige's stern look made me keep my mouth shut.

"Good, because what I'm going to say next is going to suck."

My eyes shot to hers as my entire body tensed in dread.

"I'm going to be honest with you, Amy. If Roman, or anyone else, finds out about that night, the media can, and probably will, spin it to reflect badly on you and Roman. This is a political race and there are a lot of assholes out there. Smear campaigns, and questions about your character *and* Roman's, will come into play. It won't look good."

I swallowed hard. "Could Roman lose because of this . . . because of me?"

"If it gets spun how Warren hopes it will, and your parents say one word to anyone about their thoughts on the matter?" Paige took a deep breath. "It could cause some serious damage to Roman's campaign."

Now my head really felt like it was going to implode. I'd never intended any of this, for Lauren or Roman. Now everyone was tangled together and I was the one in the middle, the one at fault. Roman was a good man and an honest one, which was hard to find in any situation, let alone politics. If he lost because of me . . .

"No," I whispered. "He can't lose."

"Then this can't leak." She patted my hand. "Does anyone else besides your parents, Warren, and me know the details about that night?"

I shook my head. "No. I've never told anyone else, and I don't think my parents have either."

"Okay. Then for now, it's contained. We just need to keep it that way."

"What do I do? I can't push for Warren's interests. Just the thought of him makes me sick. Plus, Roman would never believe I'd truly help my ex after the way he's treated me."

"That's true," Paige agreed. "All you can do right now is buy yourself time. Warren wants that seat, but he needs the governor's support to have a shot at winning it. The man he's going up against has more experience, a better track record, and a relationship with the governor. Warren won't rat you out until the governor has declared his support for one candidate or the other."

"And that's in a few weeks?"

Paige nodded.

"And Roman can't declare his support after he's won another term, because all offices are up for election on the same day, huh?"

"Yes, but again, this is all up to Roman. Let him decide who he's going to support, and pray to God that Warren keeps his mouth shut. Otherwise, we need to be prepared for the fallout."

Shit. I had three weeks to come up with a Plan B. Figure this out, come clean, or risk Roman's campaign.

"This blows, Paige," I mumbled into my hands.

"Yeah." She patted my back. "Unfortunately in this game, you go up against a lot of dicks."

. . . • . . .

Toweling my hair dry after a longer than usual shower, I looked through my closet for something to wear.

Sweatpants being my first choice.

I hadn't heard from Roman since I'd left his office three days ago, after the pork chop sandwich fiasco. Between Warren's icky threats, Lauren's impending anniversary, and an MIA "boyfriend," zippers just seemed like another complication I didn't want to deal with. Yep, sweatpants were a winner.

"Amy?" Hazel called from the living room. "Will you come here for a second?"

I threw on said sweats and a T-shirt. Still patting the ends of my hair with the towel, I opened my bedroom door and walked into the living room. I only made it two steps because I could barely see, being in the midst of a losing battle with tangles.

"What's up?"

"Oh, not much," Hazel said sweetly.

My hair was a wet, blonde wall over my eyes, so I bent over to gather it.

"Just entertaining the governor of New York."

My head snapped up and all my hair hit my back, sounding like muted firecrackers against cement.

Roman stood in the doorway holding two paper cups of coffee. He was in dark jeans and a black wool coat, looking tailored and casual all at the same time. Could the man ever not look hot?

"Hi," I said, a little shocked.

His eyes raked over me, the one look leaving me warmer than my recent shower. Hazel smiled at him, then at me, obviously happy to be witnessing this awkward exchange of silence.

"I stopped by to see if you'd like to go for a walk with me?" He held up his hands, "I brought coffee."

I let out a breath, one I'd been holding for the past two days and hadn't realized it.

"That'd be nice." I looked down at myself. "Let me just put on some jeans and get my coat."

"No, I can wait until you dry your hair."

"It's okay. I can just throw it up in a ponytail."

"I insist that you dry your hair," he said.

I stopped and looked at him. "Why?"

"It's really cold outside and wet hair can get you sick."

I swear I heard Hazel sigh, the way she did when she watched chick flicks, and clap her hands a little.

"That's so thoughtful," Hazel said. "Would you like to sit down, Governor?"

He unleashed one of those "I belong on the cover of *Forbes*" smiles, and Hazel got a little giddy.

"Thank you so much, and please call me Roman."

Did Hazel just flip her hair and giggle? Once again, the Roman Reese charm was in full effect.

"You sure you don't mind waiting?" I asked.

He sat on the couch and put the coffees on the end table. "For you? Not at all."

He smiled at me, and now I wanted to giggle. The law should require him to register that charm as a weapon.

There was so much to talk about, so much I wanted to say, but between Hazel and my frazzled nerves—I mean, Roman was actually sitting in my living room—I was a bit too frantic for small talk.

He'd entered my apartment when, a few weeks ago, he made a big deal about not doing so. I was learning quickly that Roman needed time to process, just like I did. Did I wish he'd gotten in touch at least once over the past few days? Yes. But this was progress, right? He was here. Taking literal steps toward me and my small little world in Arbor Hill.

I hopped into jeans and made quick work of my hair, blow-drying it, then plating it into a simple braid. Topped off with a warm hat, coat, and scarf, I was ready.

Emerging from my room, I found Hazel and Roman chatting. She was smiling and Roman was as sweet as ever. His thick voice carried though our tiny apartment and made everything feel more . . . full.

I liked having him here. A certain hope and relief spread through me. He'd actually come. I hadn't had to go to him this time. He'd ventured into enemy territory to see me.

"I'm ready." I smiled and he rose. He handed me the coffee he'd brought for me and opened the front door.

"It was very nice to meet you, Hazel."

"You too, Roman. Come back anytime."

He glanced at me and, with a smoldering heat, said, "I just might do that."

Tingles bloomed in my stomach. Like a small step had just been taken. And it had been a step initiated by Roman—toward me.

With his coffee in one hand, Roman clasped mine in the other, our fingers entwining, and walked us toward the nearby park. The sidewalk was slick with last night's rain and only a few people lined the street.

"I apologize for my tone the other day," he began.

I looked up at him, a cool breeze hitting my face. "I shouldn't have overstepped. It's your job, your life. You were right."

He stopped and looked at me, like this was some kind of trick. Which was cute, because I could see how a man like him would think that if conversations seemed too easy to be true, they probably were.

"Look, I just want you to know that I'm not going to interfere with you being governor and all," I said.

Warren's nasty face flashed through my mind. Ken Stanton, however, was a good guy, and I wouldn't try to sink him with Roman. I didn't have a plan yet for how all this would play out, but I had time. And in that time, I would stick to the truth, which was, "Roman, you're an amazing man and a great governor." I looked up at him, getting lost in his dark eyes. "Whatever needs to happen in relation to your office is your call. I know that certain matters don't concern me."

He gripped my hand a little tighter and that dark gaze grew hotter. "You matter to me."

His voice was rough, and as if he couldn't look at me too long, he kept walking, staring straight ahead. Something confused and almost angry plagued his face.

I laughed a little and sipped my coffee.

"Something funny?" he asked.

"Yeah. You say things like that, super sweet things that make me all . . ." I wiggled my shoulders, "warm and fuzzy. But then I see your face, and it looks like you're pissed as hell."

He grinned. "I'm realizing things that are surprising to me, and it's an adjustment."

I could understand that. Everything about Roman was an adjustment for me. But truth be told, I liked the way he pushed me, because I felt more alive, more connected to him, when he did it. I felt like a real human being when I was near him.

"So, certain realizations have you upset?" I nudged him a little.

"Politicians don't get upset." He grinned. I recognized the go-to answer, and knew Roman was thinking more than he was speaking.

"You matter to me too," I said. "And it is an adjustment, but I kind of like you, so . . ." I shrugged. "I guess I'll learn to deal with it."

"Well, I wouldn't dream of causing you distress, Miss Underwood," he said, smiling.

"Then learn how to use a damn phone."

The smile turned into a deep chuckle, and the sound of something so contented from Roman was amazing. For a moment, things didn't seem so hard. I could almost forget that Warren was threatening me, and that this "relationship" with Roman technically wasn't real. I could even almost look past the gut-wrenching emptiness I'd been carrying around for the past seven years.

Almost.

"Now you look like the one who's upset," he said.

I took a sip of coffee and took in the expanse of street before us. "Just warding off bad thoughts."

"Want to talk about these bad thoughts?" His tone was soft, not pushy, his words just an offer.

"No thanks. I don't want to ruin this moment when we're actually getting along."

"Hey." With my hand still intertwined with his, he reached for my side and pinched. I gasped with a short laugh. "If memory serves, we get along quite well."

Even the crisp fall breeze couldn't combat the heat that rushed to my cheeks.

"I have to admit though, I have an agenda," he said.

"Of course you do," I replied, taking another sip.

We came to a bench and he sat me down. The wood was cold but thankfully not overly damp. Roman took the spot next to me.

"As you know, we're traveling upstate next week," he started. "There will be a couple stops, one of which will be my parents' estate."

I nodded, remembering Roman's secretary saying something about this a couple of weeks ago.

"We won't be staying there," he said quickly, as though the thought made him sick inside. "But I should stop by. And I was hoping you'd come with me."

My brows shot up. "To meet your parents?"

"Isn't that what couples do?"

"Yeah, but . . ."

I was shocked. Mostly because it would be so easy for me *not* to meet them. I could go to the hotel and not even have to set foot on their property. But Roman was making an effort. Choosing to bring me, to share a part of himself with me. Like we were an honest to God couple, in every way.

"You sure that's what you want?" I didn't know how else to ask this. I couldn't say what I was really thinking, which was, "Hey, remember how this is supposed to be 'fake' until you win the election? So there's no real need for me to get too close, meet your family, and drag this thing out with complications." But of course, I couldn't say that.

His words from earlier hit me hard.

You matter . . .

Something was pulsing in the sore spot in my chest. It was the spot that been hollowed out when Lauren had died. The same spot that had been through a rollercoaster of emotions since I'd met Roman. But this time, the ache was different. This ache had a happy lining around it.

I mattered to someone.

Mattered to *him*.

He ran his fingers along my cheekbone. "I typically don't do things I'm not sure about."

I wanted to scoff—because boy, was that the truth—but something in his gaze, in his touch, seemed almost worried. Dear lord! Was the governor holding his breath?

"I'd love to go with you and meet them," I said.

A steady exhale came from that impressive chest. "Thank you. But don't get too excited. You may not feel the same once you meet them."

Something dark flashed across his face.

"You want to talk about it?" I asked.

He shook his head and brushed his lips over mine.

"No. Not when we're getting along so well."

With that, he consumed me in one intense kiss, and like every other time, I was lost in the power of Roman Reese, the only person in the world who seemed to want me.

"I have one more request," he said against my lips.

I tried to reply with, "Anything," but it came out more as a moan.

"Will you stay the night with me tonight?" he asked. He looked a little nervous waiting for my answer, and it made me want to kiss him all over again.

I wrapped my arms around him. "Yes."

He smiled and kissed me, like a real man might kiss his real woman.

. . . • . . .

I splashed some water on my face and looked in the mirror. It had been a good day, and Roman was waiting for me on the other side of the door. I looked around his master bathroom and wished I fit in a little better. My worn jeans and simple top were so plain against the marble counters and glossy fixtures. Still, he'd invited me. He wanted me here. I just had to keep reminding myself that.

Pulling off my clothes, I tugged the T-shirt I'd borrowed from Roman over my head. It hit mid-thigh and was as appropriate as anything for sleepwear.

All day he'd stolen kisses and touches, but now, it felt like something was changing. Like we were on the brink of a shift in our relationship, an important one. We had spent the day together, like a real couple, which was nice since we were in the homestretch of the campaign. It was one of his few days home before he would pick up traveling the state again. We were nearing the finish line.

Unbraiding my hair, I ran my fingers through it and opened the door. All thought, reason, and breath left me when I saw Roman standing by the bed, wearing gray pajama bottoms and a white shirt like mine.

"Wow," I breathed.

The thin cotton pants hugged his butt so perfectly, it made my mouth water. It'd be so easy to peel them down and off in two seconds flat. I could see the contours of his back muscles against the tight fabric of the shirt. He looked so casual. So sexy and . . . just . . . wow.

He turned and faced me. "See something you like?"

"Just admiring how your shirt fits you." I could almost see his chiseled stomach muscles through the fabric, which was pulled taut across his chest.

"I was just thinking the same thing," he said, and walked toward me.

His gaze swept me from head to toe, taking in everything, leaving me feeling exposed and hot. Needy. Ready. Was this how normal people in normal relationships felt? Did just the simple act of getting ready for bed feel like more? Like you were where you belonged?

"You look better in my clothes than I do," he said, cupping my hips.

My hands fisted the material covering his chest as he leaned in and kissed me. I craved that touch. The tiny moment right before our lips met was packed with so much anticipation, it could last two lifetimes. Because I knew what would follow once our skin touched. Warmth. Connection.

I lifted to my tiptoes for more, but he stepped back. He didn't look mad, just unsure. The last several weeks had been filled with ups and downs, emotional highs and lows. Every time we were together, he either pulled back or surged forward. There was no steady pace, only extremes. Maybe it was time to slow down a little. To enjoy each other a bit more.

I didn't know what Roman hid or carried with him. Didn't know his past, or why there was always a faint, dark cloud that seemed to hover over him. But I felt it in his movements, his actions. It was in the way he tried to control his world.

Tonight, I wanted it to be just us. Stripped of everything except each other. I wanted to know him, feel him. I just prayed he'd let me.

I said the only thing I could think of. "I've never seen you naked."

He smirked. "That's true, isn't it?"

I nodded and went for a casual smile. "Hardly seems fair." I stepped toward him. "I don't pretend to know everything about you, but I do know that it's hard for you to let go completely. To give up control and get lost in a moment."

"I don't care for surprises," he said, his eyes going vacant for a moment.

His words were so raw, it was as if someone else were speaking. That voice came from a deep, dark place. I opened my mouth to ask about it, but he shook his head, as if dislodging something from his mind.

"And in the past, we've been a bit too preoccupied with other things to fully undress."

"I'm not going anywhere unless you tell me to," I whispered. "No surprises tonight. Just us."

"Good."

"I just . . ." I gently tugged on his shirt, "I like it when our skin touches."

Something wild and black burned in his eyes and I thought, *This must be what the rim of a volcano looks like.* Hot, on the brink of smoldering out of control.

"So do I," he said.

He gently ran a lock of my hair through his fingers. His brows sliced down as he watched it, almost entranced.

"It's like touching sunshine," he whispered.

My heart broke right down the middle. Roman looked . . . sad. He let my hair fall and traced my neck.

"You look like perfection. Fresh. Innocent."

I was scared to breathe, to move. He was talking, his words churning out what his mind was thinking. I wanted to gather every syllable and clutch them close, because there was an important truth to his words. To how he saw me, responded to me.

"The thought of anything, or anyone, damaging you, including myself—" he clenched his teeth around the last word.

"Shh." I cupped his jaw. "I'm right here, in your arms, and all you make me feel is wanted."

My words seemed to stir something in him that looked like happiness mixed with despair.

"You keep going against my plan," he said.

Roman was a strong, capable man, there was no doubt about that. But the flash of vulnerability in his eyes called to me. Since the first night I'd seen him, I'd recognized the level of need, of pain, that he tried to keep hidden. And without knowing it, we'd bonded over common ground. We didn't know what the ground was, only that it existed—in both of us.

"Is that a bad thing?" I asked. I had pieces, but nothing was adding up.

I took a mental tally of everything I'd learned about Roman so far. His need for control. His kindness, softness, regard for my well-being. He understood me and my anxiety, because he knew what it felt like, but then stayed away from me for days on end.

It was like he was worried I would lose my innocence. Or rather, the idea of innocence he thought I radiated. Yet when we made love, it was hard, rough, consuming. What had happened to him to make him so closed off? Even when he sometimes seemed open, it was mostly a facade. There was nothing easy about understanding Roman Reese.

"What are you so afraid of?" I asked.

He leaned toward me, his thumb brushing across the seam of my mouth. "You."

He pulled my bottom lip between his two. Cupping my face with one palm, he snaked his tongue inside my mouth, and in one burst of crisp decadence, I tasted everything Roman was.

There were so many things I wanted to tell him. That I . . . what? Liked him? Needed him? And there was so much I desperately wanted from him in return. Opening up the way he had, though it had been slight, brought hope of progress. But it also brought more questions. I didn't know where to begin or how to end. I just wanted . . .

"More," I breathed against his mouth and kissed him hard. Slowing the pace, he gently pulled back, reached behind his neck, and pulled his shirt over his head. In one movement, the material was gone and Roman stood before me, shirtless, the firelight flickering on his tan skin.

I smiled, and took my time examining him. I had seen him before, but always in some kind of clothing. Some kind of visual obstruction. But not this time, and I fully intended to take advantage of that.

"You're flawless," I breathed, staring at everything from the curve of his shoulders to the taper of his waist, and the sexy way his hips formed a V that disappeared into his low-slung pants. So much hard muscle wrapped his chest and lower torso. Not an ounce of extra was on him, and when his stomach flexed on an uneasy breath, I all but drooled.

"Scrutiny can make a man uneasy," he said, a light note in his voice.

I shook my head dumbly, my eyes still taking in the expanse of his body. "Not scrutiny." I finally met his gaze. "Admiration."

Yet, I knew how it felt to stand before someone with all your vulner-abilities exposed. I took in his every expression, which was becoming more strained by the second. Though he was just shirtless, which wasn't typically a big deal for a man, Roman was obviously a bit nervous. Had he never been like this with anyone before? Exposed and open to their view? Again, I wondered why. But that would have to wait, because I didn't want him to think he was anything less than perfection.

I pulled my shirt off, leaving me in only my panties, and hoped this would put him a bit more at ease. I closed the distance between us. Roman looked shocked, and when I launched to my tiptoes and wrapped my arms around him, his body tensed slightly.

"You're beautiful," I said and hugged him closer.

My breasts pressed against his bare chest, and the feel of his hot skin against mine was like coming home. His body relaxed and he wrapped his arms around me, his big palms splaying over my back.

"What am I going to do with you, Amy?" he said into my ear. "Every damn time I think I've got a read on you," he kissed the top of my head, "how you're going to react, you throw me off."

I kissed his shoulder, then trailed little kisses to his chest over his heart. The strong beat was soothing. Gently releasing my hold, I skimmed my fingertips to his stomach and ran them down his side, feeling all that power beneath my touch.

Never taking my mouth from his skin, I slowly slid to my knees, kissing every ridge of his stomach as I went. He tensed again, those chiseled flanks of muscle jumping beneath my tongue.

"Amy . . ."

My name in *that* voice sent shivers down my spine.

I nipped his hip bone and looked up at him. Something fierce and stark simmered beneath his skin, so acutely I could almost see a glow surrounding him.

Whatever tore at Roman's mind on a regular basis was very much alive. I felt it. Felt his brain roil as the battle between what he wanted, needed, and what he didn't understand played out on his face. I wanted to chase away whatever awful memories came with such an expression. Because for the first time, I truly understood: Roman was at odds with himself. And in this moment, it was my fault.

It was time to make myself clear and alleviate the burden of thinking . . . for him.

On my knees before him, I licked my lips.

"I've been wanting to do this for a while," I said, looking up at him, my fingers trailing over the band of his pants.

He cupped my face and the tic in his jaw moved. He was over-thinking things again. I wanted to be something good for him. Something he enjoyed. Someone he respected.

He looked like he was about to back away. Probably revoice his previous notion that this wasn't as planned. I knew that being exposed this way was obviously outside of his comfort zone. But he'd pushed me beyond mine and only left me wanting more. It was time I did the same for him.

He said my name in that way that was a half question, half plea.

"I wasn't asking your permission," I said. I gripped the hem of his pants and looked up at him with my best sexy smile. "Unless you want me to stop? Get up and leave?"

"No," he said roughly.

I gave a quick kiss on his bellybutton. "Good, because I've thought about this . . ." I slowly pulled down his bottoms just enough to free the tip of his hard cock. "Thought about taking you with my mouth . . ."

I pulled down another inch, then another, exposing more of his hard, smooth shaft.

"Jesus, Amy," he growled.

"I know you like my perceived innocence."

He shook his head. "There's nothing perceived about it. It's a fact." He stroked the underside of my chin with his fingertips.

"But the fact is, I want *you*." I gave a final tug and his bottoms fell to the floor, leaving him gloriously naked. "And I want *you* to see all of *me*."

He stepped from his discarded clothes and I simply stared. With his jutting erection right in front of me, I realized I'd never seen a man this up close and personal before.

Every experience before Roman had been clinical, awkward, and honestly, I'd kept my eyes closed most of the time. Not now. Not with him. From day one, he'd brought passions out in me that I hadn't known I could feel. There was too much I wanted to experience. And I wanted him right there with me, learning from me as I did from him.

"Wow," I said again. Thick and long. Velvety, yet strong as steel. Keeping my gaze locked on him, I bit my lip and ran my palms up his thighs.

"You're torturing me," he whispered. "Staring at me like that, licking that sweet mouth." His cock twitched, pulsing even harder. I smiled up at him. "Just looking my fill."

Keeping my eyes on his, I leaned in and ran my tongue along the head. He hissed, and his fingers dove into my hair. Not pushing or pulling, just tangling. I licked the underside then sucked on the crown briefly, watching his reaction.

His chest tightened and his jaw clenched. He must've liked that. So I tried to go deeper.

"Fuck, Amy," he muttered, pushing his hips out to meet me, slowly burying himself in my mouth, inch by amazing inch. And I loved every taste, every sensation. I couldn't take him all the way, so I wrapped my fist around the base and pumped.

"That's so good, sweetheart." His fingers wove more tightly into my hair, and I loved the tremble in his strong hands, as if he was finally giving up some of that control. Even though I was the one on my knees, I felt powerful. I could give him this kind of pleasure. I could help him let go.

I moved my mouth up and down, sheathing him over and over between my lips. Sucking hard while flicking my tongue against the head. If possible, he grew even harder, so I did that again and again until he was rocking on his feet, meeting my mouth with gentle thrusts.

"Fuck, sweetheart, you're going to make me come."

I worked faster, wanting to take him all the way. Show him I could handle anything he could give me.

"Pull back," he grated. I didn't. Instead I bore down, taking him as deeply as I could. He didn't fight me, just kept his hold on my head as his release overtook him. "Ah, God!"

I took everything he gave. Drinking him down and feeling more alive, more needed, more desired, than I ever had in my life.

He was breathing hard when I drew away. Slowly unraveling my hair from his grip, he looked down at me. Cupping my shoulders, he sank to his knees.

"You can't ever just do what I think you will, can you?" he said, and kissed me hard.

"I like to keep you guessing," I said against his mouth.

In one quick move, he pushed me to my back, spread my knees with his hands, and drove his tongue into my core.

"Oh, God!" My hips flew up to meet him.

It all happened so fast I could barely keep up. He wrapped his arms around my thighs and pulled me closer, thrusting his tongue even deeper. I arched and moaned his name.

"You're wet, sweetheart," he said, then licked madly at my clit. "You like sucking me off?"

"Yes," I cried to the ceiling. "So much."

He growled in approval and continued to devour me. Yanking me so close that his whole face was buried between my legs, he ravaged my sensitive flesh. Eating at me like a wild man tasting sugar for the first time.

Tremors surged through my body, and I didn't even have time to prepare for the orgasm, it just hit me—hard and fast.

I clawed at his shoulders and sobbed his name as wave after wave of ecstasy overtook me. My whole body shuddered and convulsed against him as he didn't stop, just kept drawing it out.

"Roman . . ." I said on a strangled whisper.

He slowed his pace, allowing me to catch any breath I could and come down slowly. He kissed my inner thighs all the way to my knees.

I hadn't really registered that my eyes were squeezed shut and we were on the rug in front of the fire until Roman picked me up. Cradling me into his arms, he walked to the bed and laid me down.

"Look at me," he softly said, stroking my hair.

When I did, I saw nothing but intense, dark eyes staring back at me. He looked at my face for a long time, as if trying to decide how to say whatever was going through his mind.

Finally, he ran his thumb over my mouth and whispered, "You've changed everything, sweetheart."

Chapter Fifteen

·······

Y our approval rating is up five percent," I said, reading the front page of the paper as I puttered around the kitchen. "Seems a lot of people like you." I winked at him across the island.

"That's what I've been trying to tell you, Amy. I'm a likeable guy." He smiled, and I had to check the urge to sigh.

Seeing him standing there in his steel-gray three-piece suit and dark-blue tie was enough to make a girl want to play hooky. But after spending the whole weekend with him at his house, it was time to get back to the real world. Which I kind of wanted to whine about because damn it, the man had been more open and relaxed in the past forty-eight hours than at any other time since I'd met him. I didn't want it to end, mostly because I didn't want things to change.

I opened the fridge and took an apple out of the bottom drawer, along with some turkey and mayo, and set it all on the island.

"What are you doing?" he asked.

I grabbed a knife and bread. "Making you a sandwich for lunch today."

Leaning against the counter drinking his coffee, he looked so comfortable. Happy to take the morning slowly. The weekend had been beyond amazing. We'd slipped out of the campaign events the second Roman had shaken all the hands he'd needed to, and spent most of what little free time there was lounging around and cuddling. The Giants had played on Sunday, and during halftime we'd had our own little entertainment show.

At some point over the last few weeks, Roman had bought a few outfits and necessities for me to keep at his house, a pleasant surprise. However, I hadn't been home all weekend, and likely had two room-mates waiting to hear the details about that, and how serious my relation-ship with Roman was. Problem was . . . I didn't know what to tell them.

"You don't need to make me lunch, sweetheart."

"I like to." I glanced up at him. "Unless it bothers you?"

"Not at all."

"Packed lunches are just comforting sometimes. Lauren used to pack mine." The moment the words left my mouth, I couldn't believe I'd said them. I hadn't talked about her, other than to reference the night she'd died, in a long time. For a brief moment, it was nice to remember the good times. Think of her life instead of her death.

I continued to build the sandwich, and Roman set his cup down and came to stand behind me. Wrapping his arms around my waist, he peeked over my shoulder.

"She sounds like a wonderful sister," he whispered.

I nodded, and tried to fight the sudden sting behind my eyes. "She was. She took care of me when we were younger."

"I can tell." He brushed my hair to the side.

"How?"

"Because there is genuine love and kindness in you. I bet Lau-ren's influence helped build that. Just by knowing you, I get a glimpse of who she was."

I choked a little. It was the most incredible thing anyone had ever said to me. I'd only ever thought about how I'd tainted Lauren's memory. I'd never thought that carrying a piece of her inside me was a good thing. She was still a part of me. A good part.

"Thank you," I whispered. Looking over my shoulder, I kissed him. "I'm excited to meet your parents and see who influenced you."

Roman's smile faded. He released me, walked back around to the other side of the island, and resumed his coffee.

"We're not alike in the slightest," he said.

I frowned. "You're not like either of them? Isn't your dad a retired congressman?"

"Just because we're both in politics doesn't mean anything."

The tone of his voice conveyed far more than the words themselves. I tried a different approach while finishing the sandwich.

"What does your mother do?"

"A lot less than she used to," he said in that low voice he used when he was angry. I had no idea why, but apparently the mother route was worse than the father.

"Did she stay home with you growing up?"

He scoffed, although I didn't get the joke. "Sometimes she did."

Wrapping up the sandwich and apple, I put them in a paper bag and grabbed a cookie from the nearby jar.

"Well, hopefully my lunches can measure up to hers." I smiled, trying to lighten the mood. Roman just glared.

"There's nothing to measure up to, Amy." He grabbed his bag and quickly kissed me on the forehead. "Thank you for this." Then he walked from the kitchen.

If I had been nervous to meet his parents before, I was way beyond that now.

. . . • . . .

"Amy, this is my father, Michael Reese," Roman said, his voice echoing slightly in the massive foyer. I was at the Reese estate—Roman's childhood home—and he didn't look very happy about it.

"Pleasure to meet you, young lady," Michael said and shook my hand. He covered and patted it with the other, just like Roman did when he met people.

"The pleasure is mine, sir." I smiled.

"Getting started without me?" a woman said, her heels clicking and her arms spread as she approached us. I straightened my stance and tugged at the hem of my dress.

"Mother," Roman acknowledged. His tone was sharp, and his teeth didn't part around the word. "This is my girlfriend, Amy Underwood."

"Oh!" She didn't pause, just walked straight toward me and hugged me tightly.

A small "oomf" shot from my chest, because for a small woman, she had a viselike grip. I was taken a little off guard, but between the awesomeness of getting to meet Roman's parents and the magic of an anxiety pill, my nerves we manageable.

"I'm so happy to meet you, Amy," she said, pulling away but keeping her hands on my arms to examine me. Her smile reached her eyes in a true, genuine way that made me happy inside. She was so warm and motherly, I was instantly at ease.

"Amy, this is Regina, my mother."

"It's very nice to meet you too." I smiled.

She looked so polished. Her short, dark hair was simply and perfectly styled, and her expression was kind.

"Well, isn't this a treat?" she said and looked at her husband, gently smacking his shoulder. "Michael, Roman brought a girl home." She seemed really happy about that, and leaned in to whisper to me loud enough for everyone to hear, "Roman's never brought a girl home. You must be very special."

Her eyes were beaming with joy, and I felt like I was truly welcome.

Michael nodded and smiled. He seemed like a nice enough man. Not overly uptight or brooding, as I might have expected a congressman to be.

"Dinner will be in twenty. Why don't you show Amy around? Pick out a room to stay in," Regina suggested. There was something hopeful in her eyes, but it was quickly chased away by Roman's glare.

"We're not staying the night. Just dinner. My secretary arranged the details."

"Oh, hush." She waved her hand. "There's no reason to stay in a hotel when you can stay here."

"I don't mind if you want to—"

"No," Roman cut me off.

I looked from him to his mother, and whatever was between them was as thick as concrete. She shuddered a bit and took a step back, as if burned.

"May I help with dinner?" I offered, hoping to break the tension.

"That would be so nice!"

She acted like no one had said a kind word to her in ages, and I suddenly felt the need to hit Roman over the head. He had a mother who obviously loved him and wanted him around, a luxury of which I was envious. Why was he so rude to her?

"You hired caterers," Roman said in a bored tone.

Regina shot him a look.

"Yes, but I made the dessert," she said proudly. "You can help me frost the cake, dear." She smiled at me.

"I'd love to."

Wrapping her arm around my back, she led me toward the kitchen.

"I'll have her back soon so you can give her the tour, Ro," she called over her shoulder.

"That won't be necessary," Roman replied. "We're leaving right after dinner."

Regina sighed a little sadly and glanced at the ground. My God, what was going on with Roman? I'd never seen him so off-putting and outright cold.

"I'm sorry," I whispered, feeling the need to apologize for his rudeness. "I don't know what's gotten into him."

"It's okay," Regina said, walking into the kitchen. "This isn't new behavior."

I wanted to ask more, ask what the hell happened and why, but I felt out of place, and it technically wasn't my business.

"That looks wonderful," I said as we approached a double-layer chocolate cake.

"Thank you. It was my mother's recipe." She handed me a small tub of frosting and two pastry spreaders, and we both went to work.

"Is this homemade frosting too?"

"Of course." She smiled. "So tell me about yourself, Amy. I'm sure your life story has been in the papers by now, but I tend to stay away from that stuff."

My heart beat happily because actually, it was very nice that Regina had asked me about myself instead of scouring the press and following blogs. It made me feel like a real person who was dating her son.

"I want to hear how my son got lucky enough to have you on his arm." She winked at me and my chest instantly warmed. A mother's approval was an amazing thing, even though she wasn't mine. It was hard not to get caught up in it.

"I'm from Indiana. I met Roman at a gala and he literally swept me off my feet. Well, he took my shoes off, but there was definite sweeping." I grinned like a fool, happy to get to dish about the man I was seeing with a mother who seemed so happy for him.

"That's so wonderful. He is a charmer," she said. "Since he was young, that smile has gotten him almost anything he wanted."

Oh, I believed that. That thing was a lethal weapon.

"What do you do, dear?" she asked, continuing to frost.

"I work at New Beginnings."

Regina's eyes snapped to mine with a flash of horror. She recovered quickly, blinking fast and glancing away, then forcing a smile.

"That's a wonderful cause," she said.

I nodded, confused and hoping I hadn't somehow upset her. With her husband and son being in politics, the anti-drug issue couldn't be a secret. She was obviously aware, but something in her reaction was odd.

I tried to change the subject. "Roman told me you stayed home with him while he was growing up?"

"He said that?"

Well, sort of, but I nodded anyway.

"His father was in DC quite a bit when Roman was young. So it was just the two of us for the majority of the time. He was such a good boy."

She kept her concentration on the cake, but looked on the brink of tears. I felt like a horrible person. I couldn't seem to find a single thing to talk about that didn't upset Regina.

"Forgive me," she said, running a fingertip under her lower lashes. "I'm just being an emotional old woman."

I patted her shoulder. "I'm sorry if I upset you."

"Oh, no, dear, you didn't." Clearing her throat she smiled at me before returning to the cake. "Tell me more about you. You said you were from Indiana. Did you come to New York for your job?"

"Yes. It's technically an entry-level job right now, but I hope to make it more permanent. I'm trying to get a new center built in Arbor Hill."

"That's quite a goal." She sounded truly impressed. "I'm sure it will turn out wonderfully. We've been following Roman's campaign and he has the anti-drugs effort on the agenda. I assume you have something to do with that?" Her voice was soft and held such a sweet hope, it made my stomach twist.

"It's a team effort," I said. Of course, I couldn't tell her about the deal or how he'd gone to my boss and all that, but still, we were a team in this.

"He's never spoken for or publicly backed an anti-drug campaign. Especially New Beginnings."

"Really?" I frowned.

She nodded. "I don't want to intrude, but may I ask if there's a personal motivation for you in this?"

It was my turn to stare at the cake and hold back tears.

"My sister, Lauren," I started, glancing at Regina. She stopped what she was doing and gave me her full attention. "She died several years ago of an accidental overdose. She was eighteen."

"Oh, you poor thing." She pulled me into a hug, and now I really felt like crying.

Whenever I spoke of Lauren, guilt and horror flashed over me. Roman had just started to dispel the darkness and let in the light, enabling me to remember the good. Now with Regina hugging me, supportive and kind, I felt the weight of the guilt lessen a bit more.

"You are truly a sweet girl." She squeezed a little tighter.

"Ma'am," the caterer said, "dinner is ready to be served."

She released me and smiled.

"Thank you, Mrs. Reese," I said.

Holding my hands, she said, "We'd better get in there."

I nodded. As we walked into the dining room she whispered, "I'm so happy Roman has you."

. . . . . .

"Thank you for visiting, dear," Regina said, and pulled me into another one of her strong hugs. "I want us to meet again soon. Maybe I can come into the city and we can have lunch?"

Behind me, Roman clenched his teeth so hard I could hear it.

"I'd really like that." I hugged her back and was sadder to leave than I would have expected.

Regina opened her mouth, maybe to try once more to convince us to stay. But when she glanced at Roman, whatever she saw shut her down.

"Well, you two drive safely." She patted my cheek, and the small endearment made my whole chest feel a little less hollow. My own mother didn't even care to see me, while Roman's looked truly upset to watch us leave.

"Son," Michael said and shook Roman's hand.

"Thank you for dinner," Roman said to his parents. And that was it. A cool, short parting marked by cutting politeness and tense undertones.

Roman rubbed my back while escorting me out the front doors, but didn't say a word. Once we hit the fresh air, I went to take a deep breath, but Roman beat me to it. His chest struggled for a moment, then calmed. It was so quick, I wasn't sure if it had really happened.

"Are you okay?"

"Fine," he said and cleared his throat.

He led me to the garden around back. The estate was beautiful. An old, massive home on sprawling acres of land. The white wood and columns, complete with a wraparound porch, made me envision politicians gathering here to create laws. It looked so picturesque. Trees lined either side of the long driveway, and just past the manicured lawn was a dense forest.

"It's beautiful out here," I said.

He held my hand as we walked through the garden, making our way to the car that the driver already had running and ready. The smells of maple and grass danced in the fall air, and I wanted to curl up and take it all in. Yet while I felt free and peaceful out here, Roman looked more wired than I'd ever seen him. Tension and rage hummed from his body.

"What is going on?" I finally said, and stopped to face him.

"Nothing. Let's go."

"Wait," I said, literally digging my heels into the ground. "You haven't seemed yourself today. Did something happen between you and your mother? Because things are . . ."

"What?" he snapped.

"Weird. You're acting weird."

"You really want to talk about this?" Something in his expression changed. A darkness swept over him and devoured any sign of the sweet Roman I knew. A tremor raced up my spine, but I nodded.

"Yes. I want to know you. What is so bad about this place, about your mother, that you're acting the way you are?"

He closed the distance between us. His presence surrounding me, taking over the very air I breathed. He ran his hand from my neck down to my breasts, stopping between my legs to cup me roughly. The shock of his attentions didn't stifle the small moan that slipped out.

"You're going to need to be naked."

"What?"

"And in a place of my choosing." He pinched my nipple through my dress and I gasped. The sting of his touch lingered and spread shivers through my whole body.

"But that's for when we talk about . . ."

How to say that which cannot be said? It was like a riddle, and now my skin was burning so badly, crying out for Roman's attention, that it was hard to focus. But he knew what I meant.

"That deal was made for if and when I had questions about our relationship." I drowned the urge to air quote the last word. "Not to talk about your past."

"I'm changing the rules."

"You can't honestly think I'm wired," I said, challenging the ridiculous notion he'd used before to support his "naked talk time rule."

He simply shrugged.

I backed away from him, hating where this conversation was going. Even after the past several weeks together, it seemed I'd still made no progress in getting him to trust me.

"Maybe I just like talking to you when you're naked," he said, and walked past me toward the car.

Whatever was going on with him had some seriously dark roots, and I had a bad feeling those roots ran deeply.

All I could do was follow him and get in the car. He didn't say a word as the driver began the trek down the long driveway. As we wound between the trees on either side of the road, I watched the sun set over upstate New York.

"Roman?" He glanced at me, tension still radiating from him. "Will you talk to me?"

"About what?"

"About what happened back there."

"Nothing happened." He glared, warning me that he was serious about his threat earlier.

"I know what horror feels like. The moment we stepped into that house, you changed. And why on earth would you treat your mother that way? She's so nice and—"

"You don't know a goddamned thing about her!" He banged his fist against the privacy glass and the car came to a complete stop.

Throwing open his door, he grabbed my hand and exited the car, pulling me with him. Keeping a tight grip on me, he walked off the road and into the forest.

"What are you doing?" I asked, trying to keep up as he wound through the trees, taking us deeper into the dense woods.

"I made myself clear earlier, Amy. You want to talk?" He gently pushed me up against a big tree, and my back hit the smooth trunk. Standing in front of me, Roman began tugging at my dress.

"I don't like that house because I've spent plenty of time in it already, and as far as my mother goes, there isn't a responsible, trustworthy bone in her body."

Though my skin prickled with cold, my blood was hot, rushing through me quicker and quicker with every sweep of Roman's hands and yank on my clothes. Apparently unhappy with the sturdiness of my dress, he reached underneath it and ripped my panties away. My body responded to him in every way, just like it was trained to do. I cupped his face and tried to coax him to look at me.

"What happened?"

He paused for a moment and looked me in the eye. "Why is it so important for you to know?"

There was something so raw, so untrusting in his voice that it chipped another piece of my heart. I knew that he had trouble trusting people, that he didn't like talking about his personal life or past— that much we had in common. But this? This was something deep. Something that had shaped him.

"I just want to know you. To understand," I whispered.

He shook his head and went back to running his hands up my legs. Just the feel of him, all his strength and intensity, was enough to make my core throb and ache. There was the sound of a belt being unfastened, but I couldn't see. Between the dark gray evening sky and Roman pressed against me, all I could make out were his blazing eyes. His whole body was racked with tension.

"Why do you hate your home?" I tried again.

He scoffed. "That place has never felt like home. You know what does, though?"

He gripped my knee and brought it to his waist. There was no warning before he thrust his hard cock inside me. I gasped and gripped his shoulders.

"This . . ." He withdrew and surged back, filling me to the hilt once more. "This feels like home."

He kissed me hard. I was stunned. Dazed. Didn't know what to think, but didn't want him to stop. Yet he did. He pulled out completely, and I heard a rustling. When he returned, I felt him enter me once more, only this time, he was covered in latex.

For a brief moment, Roman and I had been connected with no barriers. And it had felt amazingly right.

Keeping a tight grip on my knee, he slowly thrust in and out. Coaxing my every breath to come quicker, leaving me panting for more.

"I was six when she started locking me in there," he breathed against my mouth. Darting his tongue inside, he took a deep taste, then buried his face in my neck. "For days at a time, she locked me in the closet."

I wove my fingers in his hair, his assault on my body making it difficult to process his words. But either because he felt vulnerable or strong enough to do so, he was finally opening up. I just wanted to be there, to catch him, help him, anything he'd let me do.

"Why?" I whispered.

His grip tightened, yanking my ass off the tree and holding me flush against him. He was so deep, so rigid, that my body smoldered around him.

"My father was in DC all the time," he rasped, and pounded even harder inside of me. "My mother would leave to see her dealer and end up being gone for days. Every time she left, she locked me in the hall closet with a loaf of bread and a carton of juice."

He pounded faster, harder. I held on to him, my heart breaking while my body burned. I thought of a six-year-old Roman. Terrified and locked away in a small space. In the dark, alone, not knowing what had happened to his mother or when he would get out.

Everything was coming together, but my brain was struggling. Distracted and consumed by Roman inside of me. Which was likely what he was going for. This way, I couldn't form questions. Couldn't think straight.

"I'm here," I whispered, the only thing that made sense to say. He held me closer.

Regina was paying for past sins that Roman might never forgive. For now, all I could do was wrap my arms around him, and hold on as hard as I could. Whatever he needed, I'd do.

"I'm here," I said again. "I won't leave."

My body was helpless against his, and a slow, intense release came over me, shuddering through my entire body. He was right behind me. I felt his strong muscles flex and harden and his breathing roughen.

"Amy," he said on his last thrust. Still inside of me, he leaned back enough to look at my face. Those blazing eyes were boiling black pits. "Don't bring this up again."

Chapter Sixteen

· · · • · ··

Here's your sweet and sour," Paige said, handing me a carton of takeout. "I've missed you around here."

Sitting on the couch, I forked my food and nodded. "I've missed you too. Have you been keeping crazy hours?"

Paige chomped on a dumpling and nodded. "I can't tell you how happy I am to be in sweatpants right now," she said around a mouthful.

Hazel had a late study group tonight, giving Paige and me a chance to catch up about the past week. Between traveling with Roman, playing house with him for a weekend, and the revelation in the woods, I didn't know where to start.

"Paige, you talked about how Roman's past gets dug into because he's running for reelection, right?"

She nodded. "It's usually worse the first time around. So far this campaign has been pretty smooth. No big skeletons."

How did I ask Paige about things and keep Roman's confidence? If Roman's mother had been an addict, wouldn't the press have found out? And what about all he had endured? I thought of the one question I'd asked Roman all those weeks ago when he'd proposed this arrangement:

Can something like this really be kept a secret?

I didn't how much Roman hid, but I did know he hid things well. If there was anything I could to help him, I'd like to know. A small flare of rage simmered low in my gut at the thought of what others might do with facts like those Roman had told me.

"Has there ever been an issue involving his mother?"

She stopped eating and looked at me. "Why do you ask?"

"Because I met her. She's really nice, but there's definitely some tension."

I was treading lightly because, again, I didn't know how much everyone else knew and how much was concealed. Judging by the look on Paige's face, she was privy to more than she had previously let on. I sighed and looked at my lap.

"I just don't want him to hurt. I don't know what's going on, don't know what to ask, and don't want to push too hard, but, Paige," I shook my head, "I saw something in his eyes. Something . . . broken."

There were so many things in life I wished I could fix. I wished I could have fixed Lauren, helped her before she'd ever had the opportunity to dive as deep as she did with drugs. I wished I could fix my relationship with my parents.

I wished I could fix myself.

But of all the things that were wrong in my little world, I wanted nothing so badly as to fix whatever was currently hurting Roman. There was pain, anger, and mistrust in him, and damn it, I wanted to take that away. I may have failed all the other times, but not this time. Not with him. There had to be something I could do.

"If I just understood . . ." I mumbled, more to myself than to my friend.

Paige stared at me for a long moment, then finally stuck her chopsticks in her carton and leaned in.

"There are sealed medical records and other files that have magically disappeared."

My brows shot up. "What files?"

"Records of rehab stays. Missing person's reports. Things like that."

My whole forehead crinkled, and I felt it go straight to my skull. Roman had said she'd gone to meet her dealer and stayed away for days. Losing track of time was not uncommon when an addict was high. But she had tried to go to rehab too? Something must have stuck eventually because she seemed sober now.

"And the medical records?"

"Rumors of stomach pumps, a laceration claim, and an overdose incident. There's nothing concrete, it's been covered up well," Paige offered and resumed eating. "We think the single actual sealed record is about Roman. He would have been about eight years old, I think, but we don't know what he was seen for or why. It's all just rumors at this point."

"Oh, my God. Why didn't you tell me sooner?"

Paige frowned. "Because this," she motioned her hand between the two of us, "is what's called speculation. If taken further, it could be considered slander. Not to mention, it's part of my job to keep shit like this under wraps."

"But you're telling me now," I said softly, so grateful Paige trusted me enough to speak about this.

She nodded. "Because things are different now, aren't they?"

She looked at me as though reading my thoughts, waiting for me to admit the truth. My chest tightened on every breath.

"I think I'm falling in love with him." I ran my fingers over my temple. "But every time I think we're moving forward, something stalls us. There are secrets, on both sides, and I feel the distance they bring. I hate it."

"It's hard to trust, Amy," Paige said like she knew firsthand. "People, for the most part, are assholes."

"I don't think so," I whispered.

Paige smiled. "And that's why you're different. After Warren, you have every reason not to trust men. You have no reason to trust your parents, because all they do is wrongfully blame you. It's easy to see why you'd have a hard time trusting. Yet you trust anyway."

I scoffed because holy crap, she was right. "I really am an idiot, aren't I?"

"No," Paige looked truly upset by my statement. "You have hope. The kind that is unwavering and that, honey, makes you strong. Not stupid."

"You're strong too," I said.

"I can't see people the way you do, Amy. I probably never will. And unfortunately, instead of rose-tinted glasses, Roman wears gray ones. Giving your trust to someone completely is a lot to ask."

"It's possible he may never give it, isn't it?"

She shrugged. "I don't know. But you have to decide how far you'll go for him. How much you can take before what he *does* give you is no longer enough."

"All I know is I can't hurt him. Can't not be around him. I just want him to be happy."

"Then he's lucky to have you."

I took a bite of my food, wondering if Roman would ever really open up to me. Ever start trusting. Because the problem was, I didn't know how much I could take. By the time I figured it out, it would be too late, of that I was certain. But walking away now wasn't an option. Now or maybe ever.

· · · • · ·

I clicked my fork against my plate and chewed quietly.

"You've been awfully quiet this week," Roman said from across the table. I kept my eyes on my food.

"So have you."

"I've had a lot of meetings."

"I know." Election Day was drawing closer. I pushed my plate to the side and folded my hands in my lap.

I could feel his stare on me. It was a small restaurant, echoing with the low hum of other couples, but all I could hear was the silence between us. Roman had made it very clear on more than one occasion that if he didn't want to talk about something, he wouldn't.

Since visiting his parents last week, he'd gone back to his method of minimal interaction, which was fine. I needed to put in a good week at work before I left for Indiana this weekend.

"I've missed you," he said. I glanced up at him.

"I've missed you too." He didn't move, not even his gaze from my face. "You realize this isn't normal, right?" I said.

"What isn't?"

"You and me. This." I motioned between us.

He crossed his arms over his chest and sat back in his chair. "Explain."

I wanted to laugh. One quick word, as though he were talking to one of his staff and expected this issue to be resolved as quickly as it had been brought to his attention. Too bad this wasn't a quick fix.

"We have these amazing moments together," I started.

"I agree," he said, those dark eyes running from my mouth to my breasts and back up. I stifled the rising tingles and forced myself to continue.

"Then something happens—like those amazing moments lead to a closeness, but that closeness ends up shutting us down. We don't see much of each other for a few days, and all the progress we've made gets wiped away. And we're back at square one."

And by that point, I was aching for Roman too badly to think straight. The rest of it, like trying to figure out the feelings between us, was pushed to the back of my mind, and all I wanted to do was show him how desperately I wanted him. Needed him.

"I don't know which square you are on"—he inflected his words so they stung straight to the center of me—"but I'm not on one."

I wanted to throw my hands up and beg him to give me something. Elaborate. Divulge details. I wanted to call his bullshit because he knew, just like I did, what I meant. You can't go from zero to sexy to uncertainty in less than sixty and not have whiplash. Taking a deep breath and a page from Roman's book, I remained still, calm, and said a single word.

"Explain," I said.

His mouth turned up at the edge in amusement. We both knew this was now a battle of wills. The reality of our situation was jumping back and forth between us, even without being acknowledged.

"I think of you all the time. Your smell, your smile, the way your lips tremble against mine right before I sink inside of you," he said.

My breath caught in my throat, but Roman didn't even blink. I'd wanted an explanation—apparently he'd raised that to full disclosure.

"I don't like you knowing certain things about me. I can see it on your face: always thinking, trying to figure things out, just like you are now. What's worse is, I'm giving you information I don't typically share."

"And you don't like that?" I asked, repeating his words, my stomach hurting from his admission.

"No. Yet, I still do it."

"You give me pieces," I agreed.

But those pieces left more questions. All I wanted was to feel normal, and to have him feel normal with me. As I knew and had pointed out, little was normal about the relationship between me and Roman. It would have me flying high with happiness, burning hot with desire and lust I hadn't known existed, then leave me confused. The high was amazing, but the crashes were becoming increasingly difficult to handle.

"Pieces are better than nothing," he stated, as if he'd just won the discussion and was ready to move on.

"The problem is, you're not happy. Don't you see how that is an issue?" I asked.

"I never said that. I said I didn't like sharing certain things with you."

Okay, that time I did throw my hands up. "Problem. That is a problem."

He leaned in and ensnared my attention with a look so deadly I shivered. "Yet, I still do it."

"Then you ignore me." I shook my head, which hurt all the way to the base of my neck.

There was no way to win. Roman was attempting to open up, yet he wasn't happy about it, and the few pieces of information he had shared had caused him to shut me out for the next several days. The cycle was exhausting and splitting me apart, because I didn't know what to fight for anymore. It was like I was going against him in order to save him.

"Don't do that," he said in a low voice. I looked up at him.

"Do what?"

"That." His gaze took in every angle of my face. "That look. Like you're hurting."

I was. But so was he. He just did a much better job of masking his emotions and burying the past than I did.

"God damn it," he mumbled, and his hands clenched on the table. "I don't know how to handle you, Amy. All I know is that you want something I don't want to give. And when I offer a middle ground, it still doesn't appear to be enough for you."

"I just . . ." I just what? Was falling in love with him and had no idea if he reciprocated any real feelings for me? Wanted to know him, be myself with him, and have him be able to relax and be himself with me?

"I don't want to be a complication. I don't want you to have to 'handle' me." The word tasted sour. "You obviously know what you don't want. So why are you still with me? Is it just because of our deal?"

Black fire blazed behind his eyes, but I didn't care. I had to know. Damn the rules.

"What I know is that I wake up in my bed and your scent is fading. You look at me like that"—he lifted his chin—"instead of with a smile. And I've been away from you more than inside of you." Keeping his stare steady on mine, he clenched his jaw. "And *that* is a real problem."

I folded my lips together and looked down because my entire body was stinging like it'd been freshly sunburned. Roman's words alone sent a spiral of hope through me, and I wanted to cling to him.

In his own way, he was trying.

"Will you come stay with me this weekend?" he asked, his tone much softer now.

I wanted to scream yes at the thought of another wonderful weekend when we could just be. Between his busy schedule and campaign events, I was dying for some alone time with Roman. But unfortunately, I was prepping for a few rather stressful days.

"I can't."

He frowned. "Why not?"

"Because I'm leaving tomorrow and going to Indiana for the weekend."

His eyes narrowed, and he was back to business Roman. "When were you planning on telling me?"

"I told Jean a week ago to make sure I wasn't needed for campaign work."

"But when were you going to tell *me*?" he said again.

"I guess I was going to tell you now."

A hardness cut through his features. Since he clearly didn't like my answer, I added, "I didn't think this was something you'd have an interest in discussing since it didn't affect you or your schedule. That's why I just cleared everything with your office."

"What you do and where you go is of great interest to me."

His statement and the ironic look that accompanied it made me realize something: I was just as bad as he was. I hadn't thought to include him or tell him the details of my life. The silence stretched on, making me colder. The realization of all the invisible lines between us that would never be crossed was suffocating.

. . . .

"I like the blue one," Roman said from behind me. I turned to face him, surprised that he was standing at my bedroom door. The man radiated so much power and presence, it took up all the space in my small room. "It matches your eyes."

I glanced at the sweater in my hand. After he'd dropped me off last night, I hadn't slept well. My flight left in a few hours and I was behind in packing.

"Hazel let me in. I hope you don't mind."

I shook my head. "Of course not."

I tossed the sweater into my open suitcase on the bed, then faced Roman. He took two massive strides, effectively wedging himself into my space, and the crisp, masculine smell of him made me want to moan.

"Thank you for coming to say goodbye," I said, my chest relaxing a little with the knowledge that he'd made an effort to see me off. With the way things ended last night—silence—I hadn't known what to expect today.

Running his fingertip along my jaw, he stared down at me.

"I'm not good at offering information or explaining things I'd rather not."

I laughed a little, because I was getting used to his blunt truth, though it still caught me off guard at times.

"Yeah, I know. We covered that." I sighed and looked up at the man who made me crazy. Made me happy. Made me feel not so . . . alone. "But I can't ask you for things that I'm not giving either."

He tilted his head slightly, his gaze doing that sweeping thing I loved so much that made me feel like he was really seeing me.

"So I'm going to do better." I placed my palm over his heart, needing to feel that steady beat to ground myself for what I was about to say. "I want you." I admitted, simply and honestly. "But I get lost in that sometimes. And when the fog clears, reality is difficult to return to. You're the only thing that grounds me. I want to be that for you."

"I can tell you honestly that you don't ground me, Amy."

My lungs shut off and small pricks stung my eyes like a swarm of bees. This was it. I'd asked him what this was for him, told him how I felt, and now he was ending it.

"You confuse the hell out of me," he said, gently brushing his mouth over mine. I stood in shock, prepping for the goodbye. Wondering if this was our last kiss. He gently shook his head, as if reading my mind and responding. "You break every tie that tethers me to my control." He nipped my bottom lip, "I don't want to be grounded, Amy. Because you take me someplace better."

I couldn't help it: A tear rolled down my cheek, and Roman followed it with his lips, gently kissing the wet trail it left.

"You . . . you aren't breaking up with me?"

I felt his smile against my skin. "Silly woman," he said. "I have so many intentions for you, none of which include distance."

"I want to know you," I whispered. "Share things with you. Be there for you."

"There are things I won't talk about, Amy."

I nodded. "I know."

"But I'm not alone in that." Hooking his finger under my chin, he raised my face to look at him. "You have innocent eyes, but they're also haunted. Are you ready to tell me everything, Amy?"

I swallowed hard. When it came to him and how I felt, I could put it out there. Just like he was now. But the rest? The sadness and shame of my past—of what Warren was trying to do—no, I wasn't ready to tell him. In fact, I was actively trying to find a way not to tell him. Because he was the only person who made me think of Lauren in a good way. Who didn't make me mentally berate myself every time her memory crossed my mind, tainting it with guilt and horror. And Warren's threats or not, I wasn't ready to let that go. But I was running out of time.

"Maybe you're right," I whispered. "Maybe the full truth is too much to ask for. At least right now. Maybe we're fighting a losing battle."

Or maybe I needed to finally wake up and stop clinging to an unobtainable man with an outrageous agenda and a life I'd never fully understand or fit into. But damn it, I wanted to fit, because it was with him that I felt the most at peace.

"How can you be upset when we agree?" he asked.

"Because I *would* let you in," I whispered. "Eventually. With everything. And I don't know if you'd ever do the same."

"You said you wanted me. Is it enough that I want you back?" he asked, and tucked a lock of hair behind my ear.

"Honestly? You've already caught me. I just feel like I'm still reaching for you."

Deep down I knew I'd give him anything. Including the truth that terrified me, if it came to that. But I didn't think Roman would ever fully let down his guard.

"Maybe my trip this weekend is good. Give us time to think," I said.

"What is it you want to think about?"

"I was talking about you having time to think."

"I'm not sure I appreciate your assumption that I don't think regularly." He grinned. I smiled and he pulled me closer.

"You know what I'm trying to say," I said.

He nodded. "You want me to evaluate my objectives for this relationship."

"Yes." Despite all the stipulations and how this whole relationship agreement had begun, that night—the first night we'd met—mattered. It was the reason I was standing here before him. There had been no agenda then. No expectations. Just two people with a fresh start.

Roman Reese was special, and made me feel special, like something more than a disaster outrunning darkness. And yet he was running from his own darkness.

"What if I want to think *with* you?" he asked.

"Well, that would kind of defeat the purpose."

"I disagree." He placed a soft kiss on my forehead and said, "I want to be with you, sweetheart. You want honesty?"

I nodded, barely brushing his nose with mine.

"The way you're talking right now has me nervous."

I cracked my eyes opened, not realizing I had closed them in a lost moment, and gave him a disbelieving look.

"Politicians never get nervous," I challenged.

He scoffed. "They do. The good ones just don't show it." I smiled and he kissed me again, then pulled away. "However, I did come here for a reason."

I groaned and spun from him, returning to my packing. "Of course you did."

He came up behind me, his big hands on my hips, his thumbs brushing just above my jeans and beneath my shirt. The small contact of his fingers on my skin sent shivers racing through my body.

"I came to ask if you'd like some company to Indiana?"

My blood pressure spiked so quickly, it ricocheted through my veins like a boomerang. I spun to face him, my eyes so wide they almost hurt.

"You want to come with me?"

"This is the anniversary of your sister's passing," he clarified, as if I didn't know. "That's important, and if you'll have me, I'd like to accompany you."

My whole body lit up like a cracked glow stick. I'd always gone alone. And even when I saw my parents, they had the uncanny ability to make me feel excluded in their presence. But to have support? To have Roman?

"You'd really do that?"

He looked at me like I was crazy. "Of course."

"But the election is right around the corner and you have meetings, don't you?"

"Nothing I can't reschedule."

Water lined my eyes and I launched myself into his arms. I hugged him tightly, and he wrapped those strong arms around me.

"So, is that a yes?"

"Yes," I smiled. "I'd love it if you came." This was a huge sacrifice for him, and I couldn't believe he'd actually take time from his overflowing schedule to come with me.

He kissed me. It was soft at first, then hot, needy.

"By the way," he said, his palms sliding down my back to grip my ass. "I really like you in jeans."

Chapter Seventeen

······

She's just so beautiful and kind. Really amazing and ambitious. She never failed at anything she set her mind to," my father said with pride in his eyes.

Roman nodded and smiled at me. My parents had been excited to meet the governor of New York when I'd called yesterday to tell them he was accompanying me, and had instantly invited us over for dinner. Now, as we all sat around the dinner table, my parents couldn't stop gushing.

"She's the best thing that ever happened to us," my mother said, reaching for my father's hand and squeezing. Staring right at me, she finished with, "And we miss her so much."

My chest constricted and I tried to keep breathing.

Roman just smiled at my parents. "Well, I'm so happy you have a chance to see her now. Amy's been working really hard, so I'm glad she can take a break to come visit you two."

He glanced at me, and both my parents' faces fell. I wanted to crawl under the table and die. Instead, I leaned in a bit and whispered to Roman, "They're talking about my sister."

His frown, which turned into a questioning glare, shot between me and them. It was sweet that Roman had assumed the kind words were meant for me, but no. I'd learned a long time ago not to expect such sentiments. Roman, however, looked kind of pissed.

"So tell me, Governor, how's your campaign going?" my father asked. "I hear you're the favorite in New York."

Roman cleared his throat. I stared at my plate.

"The campaign is going well. Thanks to Amy." He palmed my knee under the table.

The small squeeze of support was nice, but it couldn't combat the emptiness that was creeping in. It was the same feeling I got every time I came home. Hollow.

"She's working hard and helping to head up the anti-drug agenda we're launching."

"That's nice." My mother said, and took a bite of her food. "You two are leaving tomorrow evening?" she asked, even though she already knew the answer.

"Our flight is at six," I said.

She nodded. "So you'll be seeing Lauren in the morning?"

"Yes."

"Excuse me," Roman said. "I was under the impression that we were all going together?"

"No," my mother said quickly. "Shame, but Allen and I will be going in the evening, after your flight leaves." It was obvious that she wasn't upset by this at all.

"Why?" Roman asked, sharply enough to get both my parents' attention. A trickle of unease entered the room.

"Well, um, because we're busy all day tomorrow."

"Doing what?" he countered.

My heart rate sped up. I recognized this. The square shoulders and calm breathing, the short, terse words: He was in full-blown Roman Reese, "politician and everything alpha," mode. And he was calling my parents out from across the table.

"We have plans," my mother tried again, looking at my father, who wasn't offering any help.

Roman placed his hands on the table and kept his stare on my mother, challenging her to lie further. He was going to push her again. I saw it on his face, felt it hum from his body. He wanted her to admit the real reason she was being evasive.

I, however, didn't want to hear it. Because I already knew the reason, and I didn't want the one man who actually saw me as something special to hear it either. It was the dark truth I'd been running from. And my parents' obvious lack of interest in my life showed more than I had anticipated. My whole body churned as though on the brink of combustion.

"Please," I whispered and shook my head. "Don't."

His dark gaze snapped to my face. I had no idea what my expression was, but whatever Roman saw made him alter and soften his.

"It's getting late," he stated and turned his attention back to my parents. "Thank you for dinner, but we should be going. Amy?"

I nodded in agreement and we rose from the table. My father shook Roman's hand, but my mother didn't come near us. Instead, she backed away.

Walking through the front doorway I'd crossed so many times as a child, the same doorway I'd brought Lauren through that night, and through which I was now following the governor of New York, I felt a ping of ache and relief settle in my chest.

I had been trying for a long time to make things right, to make my parents care about me again, but I was out of ideas. So once again I reached for the truth, and vowed that I'd use it more often.

"Mom, Dad." Roman's hand clasped mine, and he stalled so I could turn to face my parents. "I love you."

There was more tension and silence between us than I had ever felt in my life. Turning back to Roman, I left, another piece of my soul shattering.

. . . .

"You want to tell me what the fuck that was about?" Roman said, shutting the hotel door harder than necessary.

"No, not really," I said and sat on the bed.

He slowly paced in front of me. "Really? Because I've never seen a display like that. How she treated you was unacceptable."

My gaze snapped up. "Are you serious right now?" He stopped right in front of me and crossed his arms. "You do the same thing to your mother!"

He just stood there, a perplexed look on his face. The fact that the similarities seemed to be lost on him was incredible.

"I do not, and that is an entirely different issue. There are reasons for the tension between my mother and I, but your parents? There is none."

"How do you know?"

"Because I know you," he defended. "You don't deserve that shit. I'm sorry they lost a child, but they have you. Why in the hell would they treat you like—"

"Because they blame me!" Tears gathered in my eyes, and Roman looked at me like I was the crazy one. "They blame me for what happened to Lauren, okay?"

"Why would they do that?" he said softly.

"Because I'm responsible."

The moment the words left my lips, a rush of terror surged and I clamped my hand over my mouth. No matter how hard I tried, I couldn't take back what had just slipped out.

The truth.

"Amy." He knelt before me, cupping my face and coaxing me to look at him. "Tell me what happened."

"It's my fault," I said.

The more I spoke, the lighter and more terrified I felt. But this was it. All of it. If Roman wanted to know, I'd tell him, because the alternative—keeping it hidden, pretending I wasn't to blame—was slowly killing me. I had to let him know. Then he could make of it—and me—what he would.

"I knew she had been using. I picked her up from a party and instead of taking her to the hospital, I took her home." More tears ran down my face and a lump stuck to my throat. "Sh-she had a delayed overdose . . . died in her sleep. If I h-had just . . . gotten her help—"

A strangled sob cut through my lips and gut-wrenching pain overtook me. Why had I done that? Why had I taken her home? If I had made a better choice, the right choice, she may still be alive.

I chanced a look at Roman. He was kneeling, looking up at with me with a mask of pure rage on his face.

"I-I'm sorry," I stuttered, terrified that I was on the brink of losing him too. "I never meant to—"

"Don't you dare apologize," he said and clasped my face in his hands. "You listen to me." He shook me gently, and I found myself locked in his intense gaze. "Amy, this isn't your fault. You hear me?" His face was so tight with raw anger, it burned all the way to his eyes. "I want to rip your parents apart for making you think this. You did nothing wrong."

"But I did," I breathed.

"No," he snapped. "Lauren took those drugs, not you. She made her choices. You loved her and tried to help her. This. Was. Not. Your. Fault."

I squeezed my eyes shut and more tears came, spilling to my cheeks, over my jaw, and down my neck. Everything began to blur together. I thought of how Lauren used to laugh. She'd been so like-able. So good.

"She's gone," I sobbed. "It doesn't get easier."

Roman pushed the hair off my brow and continued to hold my face between his hands.

"She's still a part of you. And living this way, with this kind of guilt, thinking only of her death instead of her life, is doing a disservice to her and her memory," he said softly. "You need to let go of the end, sweetheart, and hold on to how she lived."

My breaths were coming faster, the pain in my chest reaching an all-time high. No one had ever been so amazing. Paige knew and was supportive, but Roman made me believe that I just might be able to move on. Let go.

"I've been keeping this from you. The secret of my fault in it. I was ashamed. I don't want it to affect your campaign—"

"Shhh, sweetheart," he cut me off, not letting me finish my words, or the thoughts that had been plaguing me. He pulled me to his chest. I let myself get lost in the steady drum of his heartbeat. Finding a rhythm, a stillness.

It wasn't until I had met him that I'd started to realize I was losing Lauren all over again. Only this time, it was the memories. All the good memories. Roman was stopping that, bringing back the good and fighting off the bad.

I threw my arms around him and kissed him hard.

"I don't want to feel this way anymore," I admitted.

"I don't want you to either," he murmured against my mouth, and returned my kiss. He pushed to his feet, never taking his mouth from mine, and hovered over me. I kept my arms around him and lay back on the bed.

A spark of need rushed through me, so hot and heavy I couldn't stand it. And that need was for Roman. I needed him to be inside me, a part of me. Needed that connection. It was the only time I truly felt wanted. Felt whole and not alone in the world.

I tugged his shirt over his head and threw it to the floor. He must have sensed my urgency because he returned my attentions.

He made quick work of my clothes, and when the last pieces of fabric fell away, he placed himself between my thighs and hugged me tight. Skin against skin. Every part I could reach, I touched. His hardness was like a hot brand on my lower stomach, but he held himself still and just embraced me.

His strong arms wrapped around me, pulling me close. I wove my legs around his waist. Using every ounce of strength I had, I clung to him, tighter and tighter, while tears ran down my cheeks.

"More," I whispered. "Please, I need more of you."

Without taking himself too far from me, he reached for his discarded pants and pulled out a condom, quickly put it on, and settled back between my legs.

"Amy," he whispered, as he shifted his hips and positioned himself at my entrance. "You're beautiful." He pushed slightly, breaching me with only the crown. "You," he emphasized, "are kind." Another inch slid in. "You are ambitious." And another.

He kissed the tip of my nose, and more tears ran from my eyes down my temples and into my hair. All the things that were never said to me, about me, he was saying now.

He kept his eyes on mine. "You, Amy, are amazing."

With a final thrust, he surged home and I gasped, digging my nails into his back to keep him close. Praying he'd never move from that spot.

"I need you," I whispered against his ear, then bit the lobe. His body tensed and I arched my hips, taking him just a bit deeper. "So much."

He stirred himself in my depths, hitting every nerve and bringing out that amazing feeling of strength. Of trust. Of hope.

Right then, life didn't seem so bleak. The past didn't seem too daunting. Not with me wrapped around him and him within me. It was simple. Good. Just us. And I believed him. I'd known it the first night I'd met him, when he'd removed me from a place I didn't belong. I'd known he was different. Just like tonight, he'd saved me. Led me to something better. Led me to him.

"I need you too," he rasped and kissed me hard, devouring me. Consuming all I was, branding me with his kiss while he pushed and pulled at my body, demanding more. Taking me higher. Moving deeper. My body couldn't keep up, couldn't understand such intensity because it had never felt it before.

I splintered apart before I knew what was happening. Over and over I came, around him, with him. He clutched me tighter and I kissed him with everything I felt, everything I was sorry for, everything I was grateful for.

We shared one perfect moment of bliss when the world stopped spinning and the past and darkness fell away.

All that existed was us.

Chapter Eighteen

· · · · ·

The short grass crunched beneath my feet as I made my way toward the single slab of concrete that brought tears to my eyes: Lauren's headstone.

Roman's grip on my hand tightened, and the morning air brought scents of my childhood in its breeze. An Indiana sunrise was a beautiful thing.

"I'll give you some privacy," Roman said. With a final reassuring squeeze, he let me walk ahead to find Lauren.

"Hi, Sister," I whispered, and set down the flowers I'd gotten her.

Kneeling, I brushed the dew and scattered blades of grass and leaves off of her stone. The edges of her name, her birthday, and her death date scratched my palms as I smoothed them over the glossy rectangle.

"I miss you," I said. "It seems like time goes by so quickly, but then I come here, see you, and always remember how young we are."

Tears started to fill my eyes, but with a sniffle, I held them back.

"I want to start living, Lauren. Enough for both of us."

I ran my fingertip along the cursive letters just below her name. "Beloved," I read. And she was.

"I love you, and I wanted to tell you that I'm sorry. I know I say it every year, but this time, I'm saying it for a final time." I glanced to the sky, hoping somehow she could hear me. "Something that was said to me recently made me realize that grieving is okay, but thinking only of your death poisons your memory and takes away the goodness you left."

A single drop escaped my lower lashes and trailed down my face. "And you left so much goodness. I'll never let go of you, but I have to let go of the guilt . . . for both of us."

Hanging my head, I wiped my eyes and took a deep breath. A small laugh came forth. "Do you remember the time we stayed up all night watching *Pippy Longstocking*, and were convinced that our kitchen floor needed to be scrubbed just like they did it in the movie?"

Another burst of laughter came out as I held the memory.

"You convinced me that Mom and Dad wouldn't be mad, so we tied sponges to our feet and used an entire bottle of dish soap to skate across the kitchen floor."

I shook my head, giggling the same way I had that night.

"Mom was so pissed. But damn, that was fun. You always were fearless like that." I rested my hand against her name. "And I followed you anywhere."

Something warm and smooth filled my chest from the inside out. Deep down, I knew it was Lauren's presence.

I glanced over my shoulder and smiled at the man who stood several yards away.

"That's Roman," I said, looking down at Lauren again. "He's amazing. I wish so much that you'd known him, and that he'd gotten to meet you. He's made me realize things, and helped me move forward."

A breeze blew just then, kicking up the scent of the wildflowers, and I felt Lauren with me more than at any time in the past seven years. It was as if she'd actually spoken to me.

"I love you too," I whispered and rose to my feet.

Her spirit was too strong to be buried, and it was time I started listening to it.

. . . • . . .

"Thank you for coming with me," I said, as I fished my keys out of my purse and unlocked my front door.

"Thank you for having me."

I smiled and opened the door. Roman placed my suitcase right inside and stood to his full height. He stared down at me, his breath visible in the cold night air. I wanted to invite him in. Paige and Hazel were gone tonight. Judging by the text messages I'd gotten this afternoon, they wouldn't be home anytime soon. But after being shot down last time, I knew better than to ask.

Then, over Roman's shoulder, I watched his personal driver speed off in the town car.

"Um, I think you're being ditched," I said, but Roman didn't bother to look where I was pointing.

"I guess I'll have to call a cab." He shrugged. "Or perhaps I could stay with you."

My gaze shot to his. "Seriously?" I asked around a huge smile.

He stepped closer, all that yummy-smelling heat surrounding me. I was so excited and surprised, I couldn't help but mess with him a little.

Tapping my chin, I looked at the sky. "Hmm, you seem to be inviting yourself over an awful lot. Better be careful, or I may think you're getting clingy."

"Politicians don't get clingy."

"Well in that case, I'd love it if you stayed."

He followed me inside and hung our coats by the door. I'd missed my small apartment. It wasn't much, but it was cozy.

"Would you like some coffee or tea?" I asked over my shoulder, walking into the kitchen. Roman sat down on the couch and I rummaged through the cupboards. "Ooh, we have hot chocolate."

"Sounds great." He smiled.

I made the drinks quickly, brought them to the coffee table, and sat next to him. I wanted to snuggle into his amazing body and enjoy hot chocolate like there was nothing else going on in the world. However, a couple of lingering questions needed to be answered.

"Why did you change your mind?" I asked. "Last time I invited you in, you made it very clear that you weren't interested in spending the night."

Resting his arm over the back of the couch, he turned to face me. "I'm not ready to let you go yet." He chuckled and shook his head.

"What?"

"It's just surprising how easily the truth comes out when I'm with you. I'm not used to it."

"Is that a bad thing?"

"Could be," he said. "I always pick my words carefully, but somehow you have me blurting things out I'd typically keep to myself, or not bother to feel in the first place."

I scooted closer, hoping that Roman's open mood would continue. "What do you not usually feel?"

He looked hard at my face, like he couldn't decide if he was mad, confused, or happy.

"Trust."

It was everything I could do to keep from dancing with joy. He trusted me. Enough to admit it. Enough to stay the night when he wouldn't before. The idea filled me with so much hope. Maybe this whole thing could have some kind of happy ending.

"You trusted me with your sister and your past." He grinned a little, but his eyes remained serious. "Maybe you're a good influence on me."

Shock and happiness burst simultaneously in my body. The truth about Lauren, and how I had felt about it, was the hardest thing I'd ever admitted out loud. Especially in light of the way I felt about Roman, and how it could possibly affect his campaign. Yet he'd never once blamed me. He hadn't even brought up his campaign or the possible ramifications of my admission. He was simply there for me. No strings. No agenda. Just support. Honest support.

"I've done a lot of things I'm not proud of," he said. "I don't like being out of control or surprised in any situation. I learned quickly that if you can manipulate an event beforehand, the desired outcome is more likely. It's key, since I don't like others to have power over me."

I gave him a disbelieving smile. "I have a hard time believing that anyone could ever have power over you."

His eyes locked on me, and something very hot, very serious and heavy, surged through my veins, replacing my blood with thick anticipation.

"Not anyone," he said. "You."

I swallowed hard. And here I'd been thinking that Roman held all the power in this relationship. He thought I influenced him? Handing over control, giving someone else free rein with your emotions, was a big deal. I knew that, having had my own feelings stomped on before. I'd never do that to him. But now that I knew a little more about Roman Reese, his need for control and how it manifested made more and more sense. Because for so long, he'd been locked away, all of his choices taken from him.

"Is that why you have problems with your mother?" I asked carefully, hoping he would feel comfortable enough to continue talking.

His body tensed. He was on the brink of yelling, I could tell. Instead, his chest slowly drew in a breath, and he spoke in that low, gravelly tone.

"I have problems with her because she took my freedom and made fear a common, recurring emotion in my childhood. In that closet, I always felt like the walls were closing in. I didn't know where she was, or when she'd be back. I sat there, in the dark, my stomach aching from hunger and my skin dry from dehydration, and all I thought of was her. Whether *she* was okay." He snarled the last part. "And as it got worse, I watched her waste away. Watched her *choose* to do so instead of taking care of herself or her family. She disgusts me."

I folded my lips together. My heart ached for him. For his mother. For his broken past.

"She's clean now," I offered.

"Yes, she is." He nodded. "Fifteen years now she's been sober. Doesn't change what happened though, does it?"

"You didn't deserve that." I gripped his hand and kissed his palm. "Somewhere in her mind, even when she was crashing, I'm sure she thought she was protecting you. Locking you away from the world that was hurting her."

"I almost starved to death, Amy," he growled, and ripped his hand from mine. "The last time she left me, she was gone for two weeks! That final straw finally got my father's attention. And now you sit there and defend her?"

"No!" I moved to grab his hand again, but he went to stand. This was the moment I couldn't risk. He'd walk away, misunderstanding what I was trying to say, and all that we'd built would be ruined. He couldn't leave. Not this time.

I quickly launched myself at him, straddling his lap and cupping his face.

"Get off me, Amy."

"No," I said sternly. "You need to understand something, Roman. You won't let me hold on to the past anymore, and I won't let you either."

He gripped my wrists but didn't push me away.

"In my whole life, I have never wanted to take away something so much as I want to take away what happened to you. I wish I could take away the pain. But the only thing I can do is tell you that on some level, I understand. You have a mother who made terrible mistakes, but she loves you, and I will remind you of that regularly. But no matter what, I'm always on *your* side."

"And what if I hate her?"

"Holding on to hate will only drain all the light from your life."

"How would you know? I saw you with your parents, with Warren at the fundraiser. Despite all the shit, you still put on a brave face. You couldn't hate someone if you tried."

"I've hated myself," I whispered. "Every day since Lauren died." His eyes softened a little. "And it's been very dark . . . until I met you."

He searched my face for a long moment, as if trying to decide if I was telling the truth.

I leaned in and kissed him softly on the lips. When I went to pull back, he let go of my wrists and reached behind me, grabbing my ass and clutching me closer. Biting my bottom lip, he brought me back to his mouth and plunged his tongue inside. I moaned because with one kiss, the man had my head swimming.

"You're the one who pinned me here," he rasped. "You really expect me to let you back away now?"

He thrust his tongue back between my lips and dueled with mine. I rose to my knees enough to unfasten his pants. With some fancy moving and swaying, he worked my jeans off of me, then ripped my panties away.

By the time we'd clawed each other's shirts off, I was panting his name and desperate to have him. He yanked my bra off and instantly latched on to my swelling nipple.

"Oh, God," I groaned, dropping my head back and letting him suck and nibble. Diving my fingers into his hair, I pulled the silky strands.

A burst of hot, violent need shot through me. I wanted him. Hard. Rough. Until we couldn't breathe. When I pulled his hair harder, he bit down on my breast and I cried out his name.

"Fuck, you have me going crazy," he growled against my skin.

I rocked my hips against him. His hard cock slid along my folds, hitting my clit with every glide. I was already on the verge of coming and he wasn't even inside me.

He wrapped one arm around my back and used his free hand to cup my breast, bringing it closer to his mouth.

"You're getting me all wet, sweetheart," he said, thrusting his hips, grinding over my clit with more friction. With a firm hold on my breast, he sucked the entire peak into his mouth. I yanked again on his hair, which only made him suck harder.

"Condom," I whispered. "Now."

"I'm busy," he snarled against my breast. "You get it." He nodded at his pants next to us on the couch.

I didn't find anything other than his wallet, so I pulled it out and sure enough, there were two inside. I opened one quickly and, with him still nibbling on me, reached between us and slid it on him.

I positioned myself above him. He relinquished my breasts and gripped my neck in his hands. I wanted to forget all the darkness, the heavy past that we both carried. I wanted to unleash the aggression I had been carrying around for years. And I wanted to be Roman's catalyst for his release.

His hard stare told me everything I needed to know—he felt the same way.

I slammed down on him, his massive cock impaling me in one snug glide.

"Shit," he hissed. "So tight, every damn time." He leaned up and kissed me, though it was more of a bite than anything else.

Gripping my ass, he moved me up and down on him, faster and harder. My breasts bounced between us, my sensitive nipples raking along his hard chest. I pushed down, taking him all the way to the hilt, and stayed there, keeping him deep inside as I whipped my hips back and forth.

His fingers dug into my ass cheeks and his head fell back against the edge of the couch.

Thought was gone. The past was gone. All the pain—Roman's and mine—all the mistrust and hate. Gone. We gave everything we were to each other, slaking our mutual need for release. My body short-circuited like a scorched wire hitting wet concrete.

Sensations and emotions climbed with every move, every touch. He was right there with me, balancing on the brink. His tongue plunged between my lips, and I snagged a bite between my teeth.

We came together, Roman buried deep, filling me. His frame convulsed, and my whole body burst into flames of wildfire. Crackling and melting. Falling all around him. I let myself go. All of it. And I knew right then that this was different. The truth was between us. The trust established. The fresh start I'd been dying for since the night I'd met him awaited.

With my mouth hovering over his, I whispered the last piece of truth I needed to tell him.

"Roman . . . I love you."

Chapter Nineteen

The glow of the morning sun knocked on my eyelids like an annoying neighbor. I groaned and reached out beside me. The sheets were cold.

I opened my eyes to find Roman gone. But my cell phone lay on the pillow where he'd been. Sitting up, I opened it to find a new text message waiting.

I'm sorry I had to go. Early meeting. You're beautiful when you sleep ... and all the time. Last night was amazing.

I smiled at the screen and my stomach fluttered. Last night had been amazing. Roman had actually slept in my bed, and I had dozed off feeling taken care of and safe, wrapped in warm arms and strength. I tried—*tried* being the key word—to focus on all the good moments, and not to stress about the fact that I had admitted that I loved him, and he had said nothing back. He had just hugged me tighter, so I was hopeful that was a good sign.

I glanced at the clock. I still had an hour before I needed to head into work, but Paige and Hazel were probably already gone. The house was quiet, until a knock at the front door broke the silence.

Throwing my robe on, I rushed to the door. My first thought

was that Roman had come back. I ran to open it, nearly giggling like a moron, and—

All the blood left my face.

"Warren."

He looked livid, and his creepy glare made me tug my robe together at the collar.

"You got the governor to blow off a meeting with me for a piece of ass?" he sneered, and stepped inside.

I tried to shut the door, but he slammed it open. The doorknob punctured the drywall with a loud crack, making me jump.

"I don't remember you being that good of a lay."

The few times we had been together, no, it hadn't been good. But what I now realized was it had had nothing to do with me. It had been because Warren was an inconsiderate, horrible man.

"Get out of my house, Warren," I said firmly. "Now."

I couldn't afford to be scared. Wouldn't. I drew on everything I had to remain calm. I was done feeling weak.

"You are supposed to be convincing him to support me!" he yelled. "Not canceling meetings on me!"

"I'm not convincing the governor of anything."

He scoffed. "Fine. Then I'll tell him about Lauren."

"I already did."

His face fell, and that moment was priceless. Watching him sweat and realize he no longer had control over me, no longer had the upper hand, was worth a million bucks.

"He knows the truth. I told him what happened and you know what he did?" I stepped toward Warren and he moved back. "He supported me."

"You're bluffing."

"Why would I? Frankly, I don't care what you do with your life. But you're done trying to involve me in it."

"You whore," he growled. "You can't take this from me."

"I'm not taking anything, Warren. This is your doing. Man up and deal with it, because guess what? I don't have to tell anyone that you're an asshole. You let them know all on your own."

He stepped toward me, and I thought for sure he was going to slap me. My breath was shaky, but I raised my chin and faced him. He wanted me to cower, and I'd be damned if I'd ever give this man a single ounce of power over me again.

"Get. Out." I said.

He stared at me for a moment, and I knew he was debating how to end this. Whatever he was thinking, it involved bringing me pain, that much was painted clearly on his face. Never taking his eyes off me, he backed out the door.

"This isn't over," he grated.

"It is for me." I slammed the door in his face.

Chapter Twenty

· · · • · ··

It was four days until the election, and Roman was looking like the frontrunner. I also hadn't laid eyes on him since the night he'd stayed, but he'd made an effort to keep in touch with a few calls and texts. I knew he was bogged down with all kinds of things, so when he called me while I was on my way to work, I was happy to hear his voice.

"I'm sorry I've been so tied up, sweetheart."

"It's okay, I understand," I said, walking up the steps to my office.

I wanted to talk to him about that night. About what I had said. It wasn't lost on me that he hadn't said he loved me back, and I was focusing most of my mental energy on not letting that uncertainty mess with my newfound self-esteem. The self-esteem Roman had helped me find.

Soon, once we were under the same roof, the issue would be addressed. I hoped.

"I'm going to be in several meetings today, but can you come by tomorrow? We can go to lunch and celebrate."

"Celebrate?" I asked. "What is it we're celebrating?"

"Are you at work?" he asked.

"Yeah, just got here."

"Then I'll let you go. See you tomorrow." The line went dead before I had a chance to ask any more questions. I walked in, confused and wondering what he'd been talking about . . .

The entire office was buzzing. People were talking and laughing loudly and somewhere, I heard what sounded like a champagne bottle pop.

I wound through the crowd toward my cubicle.

"What's going on?" I asked Cindy, one of the interns, who sat two rows down.

"New Beginnings got the funding!" she said.

"What?" A huge smile broke over my face and I rushed to my desk, dropped my purse, and turned to find Marcy.

"Indiana!" Silas called. He was in the middle of a crowd of people in the meeting room, drinking from a Dixie cup. "Can you believe it? We got the money for the new center."

I smiled and nodded. "It's great."

"Yeah," he nodded and took a sip of his drink. "It is. I can't wait to get going on it."

I frowned. "You're helping with the new center?"

"I'm heading it up. Got the Level Two position!" His nice smile turned into a wicked grin. One that spewed victory and gloating.

Suddenly, the loud voices and chaos were overwhelming. I couldn't have heard him right. How had that kind of selection been made without an application process?

I couldn't think of what to say. Luckily, Marcy came up behind me.

"Can I talk to you for a moment, Amy?"

I nodded and followed her to her office. She shut the door, muffling the outside noise. She sat behind her desk and rubbed her forehead. "I'm so sorry, Amy."

"So it's true?" I asked. "Silas is heading up the new center?" My whole body felt chilled.

She nodded. "Not because I wanted to appoint him," she said quickly. "You are the best person for the job. You worked on this from the beginning, have the most experience, and would make this new center a success."

"Then why did you give it to Silas? I didn't get a chance to apply."

"There was no application process," Marcy said lowly. "I didn't have a choice. The governor's chief officer informed me of the funding approval and the specific stipulation that you could not be the one to head it up."

Chief officer? I swallowed hard. Bill. Something very cold and uneasy ran through my veins.

"I yelled at him for a good ten minutes," Marcy said. "I couldn't believe he'd just walk in here and do something like that."

"Wait, he was here?"

She nodded. "He just left."

My heart rate spiked. "I'll be right back," I said, and hurried from Marcy's office. Bolting for the front door, I was just in time to see Bill getting into his car.

"Bill!" I hollered.

He obviously saw me, but debated whether or not to acknowledge it. Taking his sweet-ass time, he finally got out of the car and stood on the sidewalk.

"Good morning, Miss Underwood."

"I know you don't like me, but why would you cheat me out of this job? I didn't even have a chance to apply."

He looked at me like he always did: Like I was lacking. "It is my job to think of the governor's interests and get him reelected."

"He's doing great. What does that have to do with this center?"

"How do you think it would look if the governor's girlfriend was miraculously chosen to head up a major project with state dollars behind it? Dollars the governor himself pushed for." Bill held up his hand as I opened my mouth, cutting me off. "I'll tell you: not good. It would look bad, actually, and I have enough on my plate to deal with."

"Does Roman know you did this?"

He ground his teeth for a moment, looking like he was on the brink of walking away and ignoring me.

"No, he doesn't. Look," he said, stepping closer. "If you care at all about him winning, about anything other than yourself and this stupid job, you'll keep your mouth shut. Because I guarantee you, Roman will take a hit in the polls if you head up this project. A bad hit."

He paused long enough for me to take in his angry expression.

"It wouldn't look good," he repeated. "Do you understand?"

I nodded, though I didn't understand.

"Good day, Miss Underwood." Bill said and got into his car.

Before he drove away, I saw his scowl deepen as he looked me over one last time. I reminded myself that reality sucked sometimes, but Roman mattered more. If losing this job and not being able to head up the new center would protect his image, that's what I'd do.

I'd consider his interests, just like I'd promised.

. . . .

"How was your day?" Paige asked as I walked into the living room. I hung up my coat and tried not to lose my cool.

"Fine. What are you doing home so early?"

Paige had her Blackberry in her hand and was looking between it and her laptop, which was sitting on the coffee table.

"The office has been crazy. Figured I could get some things done from here, where it's a bit quieter."

I nodded.

She glanced at me long enough to take in my crappy mood and ask, "You want to talk about it?"

Something like pity and guilt marred her pretty features.

"You know, don't you?" I asked.

She nodded. "I heard the funding came in and Silas got the job."

"I assume you heard that from Bill?" My tone was sharper than it should have been, but it was hard to let it go.

"He's right though, Amy," Paige said softly.

My gaze snapped to her, and my lungs imploded on themselves.

"He didn't even give me a chance to apply, Paige. I never assumed I'd be handed the job, but I thought I'd at least have a chance to prove myself."

"You threw that away when you started dating Roman."

My mouth dropped. "How can you say that?"

"I'm not saying it to be mean," she said. "It's just a fact. It wouldn't look good to have the governor's girlfriend head up a major project with state money behind it."

"You sound like Bill." Never before had I been so shocked or upset with Paige.

"Good! That means I'm doing my job," she snapped back. "Sometimes it's not about the best person for the job—it's about the lesser of two evils. A lot of people work hard to keep Roman in office. You know why? Because Roman is a good governor. But if he were to lose because it looked like he was doing special favors for his girlfriend, just handing her state money and a job—"

"That's not what he did. I work hard at New Beginnings. He put the funding on the bill, but the job itself is based on merit."

"But that's not how it would *look*," she said again. "This could really hurt him. The competition would spin it in a way that would drop his approval rating quickly. All the gains he's made in the polls over the past few weeks would be gone."

I let out a long breath. Hating this. Hating that I was fighting with my best friend. Hating that despite my best efforts, I'd still created a situation that had potential to affect Roman's job.

"I understand that," I said. There was only one thing I could do. "I'm letting it go. I don't want Roman to suffer because of me or how something may look. What's important is that the center is going to be built, and people will be helped."

Paige's eyes softened. "I know this is hard. I know you wanted it." I nodded. "It's just a job."

"What will you do?" Paige asked.

I shrugged. "I guess I'll need to find a new one."

"Just like that? Just walk away?"

My other option was what? Fight? Tell Roman? No. There was nothing to fight anymore. The center would be built, and people with addictions and their families would have a place to go. The name of the place didn't matter—the facility did. I had been letting go of many things lately and in the process, finding out what was really important.

It was time I let go of this too. Putting Lauren's name on the building wouldn't bring her back, and it wouldn't make my parents love me. The center would help others, and that was enough. The rest I could figure out. I would try to find a different job, one that would enable me to stay in New York, because Roman was my choice, and I'd bet on him every time. That truth, bright and blaring in my face, made everything else seem manageable.

"I love him, Paige," I said. "He's honest and strong, and New York is better with him. I'm better with him."

"Does he feel the same way about you?" she asked.

I shook my head. "I don't know. But I'll find out tomorrow."

I walked into my room and sat on my bed. I had lost the job and the chance to head up the project I'd been working on for more than a year, but somehow, it all seemed secondary.

I had Roman, at least for now, and that was enough. It would have to be.

. . . . . .

The moment I entered Roman's office, he walked right toward me, cupped my face, and kissed me so sweetly, so thoroughly, I couldn't breathe right.

I moaned against his mouth.

"Damn it, I've missed you," he said and kissed me again. Everything melted away. "You ready to go celebrate?"

After my talks with Bill and Paige yesterday, no, I wasn't really in the mood to celebrate.

"Thank you," I said. "I'm so happy the funding came in for the new center."

He stepped back and looked at me. "You're thanking me, but you look sad."

"No," I said quickly. "I'm not. I just . . . I didn't get the job."

He scowled. "What? That's impossible."

"No, it's okay."

"No, it's not," he barked. "I happen to know for a fact that you're the most qualified. You spearheaded the whole goddamned thing."

"And you pushed for the funding."

"Amy, I wrote it down and the house approved it, but you are the one who's been pushing."

"But your anti-drug stance over the past couple of months—"

"Has been largely due to you."

I took a deep breath. He was fighting for me. He was on my side, without question, and I loved him for it. Loved him more than I'd thought possible.

The doubt that had been circling my brain for the last twenty-four hours started to drift away, because I had Roman. There. Ready to defend me, even to myself.

But this wasn't about me. This was about him. I gave my best smile.

"I'm happy that the center is being built. That's what's important." He examined my face as if he didn't believe me, so I followed with, "Besides, it wouldn't look good if I headed up the project, being your girlfriend and all. So it's a good thing."

I truly believed that. Paige and Bill were right. Roman worked hard, and I wasn't going to be the cause of anything that could spur an assumption otherwise.

He crossed his arms. "What do you mean, 'it wouldn't look good'?" he said. Something in his voice was very, very scary. "Where did you hear that?"

"I . . . I just thought—"

Shit! I tried to backpedal. But when his eyes widened and his jaw clenched even harder, I knew he'd pieced it together.

"Fucking Bill!" he growled and yanked open his door. "Get Bill in here now," he barked at his secretary, then slammed his door shut again and stomped toward me.

"Roman, don't. It's not him."

"The hell it isn't. I specifically told him to stay out of this. Now he has you thinking the same shit he does. It's doesn't matter that you're my girlfriend, Amy. You are the right person for that job."

"I disagree," Bill said, entering the office. "Amy's involvement in any way with the state funding you initialized would reflect poorly on you and your campaign."

Roman opened his mouth, likely to yell at his chief officer, but I grabbed his hand.

"I agree with Bill, Roman," I said.

His gaze snapped to me. It hadn't been my intention to tell him about Bill's maneuver, but I obviously couldn't have lied to him and said I'd gotten the job. He'd have found out either way and if I'd lied, it would have jeopardized all that trust we'd built.

"I never meant for this to be an issue," I said, glancing at Bill. "I really am happy with how things turned out. I can find another job."

I hoped. Preferably before the last of my savings disappeared in a few weeks.

"No," Roman said and walked to Bill. "Creating a stipulation so that Amy specifically loses an opportunity is no better than giving her one based on the same pretense."

"It would look bad," Bill said, the same way he said it to me yesterday. Apparently this was the phrase of the week, but it was wearing thin. "We're hanging on to this campaign now, but one wrong move and we could lose it. Then what? It won't matter what the hell this woman does for a living, or how many times she's seen on your arm, because you won't be governor." Bill calmed his tone and cleared his throat. "We need to focus on what is important. The election is in three days. You need to announce your support for the house seat and—"

"I'm not supporting Warren Cunningham." Roman said. "I told you that before."

"Jesus Christ," Bill said, pinching the bridge of his nose. "A Cunningham vote on the house floor would give us the majority over the next four years. It's the smart move, and you're pissing it away because he dated your girlfriend!"

"I'm not supporting him because he's inexperienced, untrustworthy, and doesn't know a damn thing about the state budget. He wants the chair because he believes it's his right. He hasn't earned it."

Roman looked ready to massacre Bill, and I took a few steps toward the door. I didn't know what to say, if anything, but this seemed like a conversation to which I shouldn't be privy.

"If you don't give Cunningham your support, he'll go to the press about your girlfriend's . . . transgressions," Bill said, all his distaste for me obvious in his tone.

"What the fuck did you just say?" Roman was talking between clenched teeth, and the temperature of my skin skyrocketed to a thousand degrees. Whether it was from Bill's accusation or the venomous exchange between the two men, I didn't know. But my blood felt like it was turning into wet cement, and my stomach was getting queasier by the second.

"Cunningham came to me yesterday about her," Bill glanced at me. "Telling a story about her having a part in her sister's death."

Everything I'd been holding on to, the positive outlook and faith in something better, rushed from me. All I could do was glance frantically between Roman and Bill, shaking my head. I wanted to defend myself, but how? Why? I'd told Roman the truth, but I'd never actually thought this would happen—that Warren would take this kind of step.

"Accomplice to a teen death caused by drug overdose is not flattering," Bill said. He looked directly at me and I'd never felt so small—so dirty—in all my life. "You fucked this up from the beginning. How long has Cunningham known about this? How long have you been hiding it?"

"I . . . I didn't—" I started.

"That is total bullshit," Roman cut me off, putting himself physically between Bill and me. "That's not what happened, and it's disgusting that you or Cunningham would have the gall to spin such lies."

"Spinning is what I do!" Bill yelled. "It's also what your opponent's campaign does. You think the details matter? No. What matters is how it comes out, and trust me, it *will* come out."

My heart dropped into the bottom of my gut. Warren was a son of a bitch, but I hadn't known he was this low. Blackmailing me was one thing, but the governor and his staff?

Roman looked at me for a long moment.

"I'm so sorry," I whispered. My voice cracked. It hurt so terribly all the way down my chest.

Then, a kind of calm came over Roman, and he smiled at me before facing Bill again.

"He wants a story? Then I'll give him one. I'm supporting Mayor Stanton for the house seat. Cunningham can go to hell."

"God damn it!" Bill threw his hands over his head.

Tears came to my eyes. Roman stood, collected and not the least bit concerned, at my defense. Never had anyone done such a thing.

"I told you at the gala," Bill said, pointing at Roman, "that pursuing this woman was a bad idea. She has fucked with your mind!"

He then turned that angry finger on me, but it was the look on Roman's face that struck something deep in my soul.

The look of pure horror.

Bill's words sank in. Surely he had misspoken.

"The gala?" I asked. "The night we met? But you . . . you didn't know who I was until later."

Bill scoffed, and Roman instantly paled.

"Wake up, Amy," Bill said. "You really think he didn't know?"

"Shut the fuck up, Bill."

I didn't think my mind could get any more fogged. My knees suddenly felt weak, and my ankles were shaky. My heart refused to pump blood—my lungs couldn't take in air. This couldn't be correct.

"It was a setup . . . from the beginning?" I looked right at Roman. For the first time since I'd met him, the governor was speechless. "That can't be right. You said . . . at dinner, at Angelo's, that was when you . . . you were so mad at me for deceiving you."

"You honestly believe that the governor of New York didn't know every single person who stepped into that gala? That he didn't have a plan from the beginning? He wanted you for his image, that's it."

Bill's truth took the strength from every last bone in my body. Roman always had a plan. "And you played along?"

Bill nodded. "The morning I saw you standing in his office was a surprise. I didn't think he'd actually go through with it."

"That's enough," Roman said and turned his full attention to me. "Amy, all that was before I got to know you."

"Oh, but you did know me. Didn't you? And you manipulated me into thinking—"

My throat was closing, my body shutting down, unable to take the unbearable pain that was searing just beneath my skin. The one moment, the one night I'd clung to this whole time, had been a lie. He'd even gone extra lengths to make me believe I was the one responsible. Believe that . . .

"I was more," I whispered.

"You are," he said.

But I simply shook my head and willed my mind to hang in there just a little longer. To process this mess and not break down.

"The connection between us." I could barely get out the last word, because there was no "us." Not now, not from the beginning. "All of this was a setup. Lies."

These past few months, that night at the gala had been the one piece of truth I'd relied on. I'd actually thought I had glimpsed the real Roman that night.

But like everything else, I'd been wrong.

239

"Amy." He stepped toward me and I backed away, holding up my hand.

"Don't." Tears were in my eyes and I couldn't breathe. I couldn't hold on anymore. I needed to get out of his office. I couldn't cry, not there.

Everything about our relationship had been an even bigger sham than I'd known. And what was worse, everyone around me had known it.

What Roman had offered me, what we'd shared, had meant nothing to him. Bill, and God knew who else, had known the entire time.

Every moment Roman and I had spent together flashed through my mind. He had been adamant that to everyone else, we were real. But in reality, I had been the only one fooled.

The only one stupid enough to trust him.

My ribs were cracking and my body was folding in on itself. I was tired, tired with a kind of soul-deep exhaustion that inhabited every cell. Every ounce of sadness weighed heavily on me. I recognized this feeling: It was realization that life had just changed, drastically, and would never be the same.

Loss.

Total irrevocable loss.

But this time, agony in my chest packed an extra punch. Because for the first time, I was watching something die in me that I hadn't even known was possible.

Hope.

Whatever iota of that feeling I'd clung to over the past several years was gone. I looked at Roman. His body was tense as if ready to pounce, his dark eyes burning like freshly sparked flares.

"Amy," he rasped. "I love you."

I gripped my stomach, because his words shot a painful, invisible dagger right through my gut.

"I don't believe you," I whispered.

Turning from him, I took Bill's advice from yesterday and did the only thing I could. The only option I had left . . .

I walked away.

Chapter Twenty-One

· · • · ··

*B*ang. Bang. Bang.

The pounding wouldn't stop. After an hour, I wasn't sure if it was at my front door, or just inside my head.

Bang. Bang. Bang.

"Amy!" Roman yelled and pounded the door again.

I sank deeper beneath my blanket and tried to fade into the couch. Alone. Totally and completely alone, in an apartment that, come next week, I wouldn't be able to afford. And the man I'd risked everything for was on the other side of the deadbolt that I refused to open.

Clutching my cell phone, I stared at it. I knew what I was about to do was a terrible idea, but I couldn't help it. I dialed.

"Hello?"

"Mom?" I sniffed. "Mom, I know th-that things aren't perfect between u-us." I ran the back of my hand under my nose and tried to calm my sobbing. "But I really need you right now. I'm . . . I'm all alone. I've l-lost everything and I-I don't know what to do."

"Oh, Amy," she sighed. "I don't know what you want me to say. Whatever it is that you've gotten yourself into, I'm sure you'll deal with it."

Until then, I hadn't known a heart could break in more than one way.

"Mom," I begged, "Please."

Tears were running down my cheeks, and my head hurt so bad I was certain my brain was attacking itself.

"Just tell me," I whispered. "What will it take? What do I have to do for your forgiveness?"

"Amy, I don't think this is—"

"Tell me, Mom. For once, just say it. The truth. All of it."

"Nothing, Amy." Her words were sharp and steady. Like she'd known the answer to my question for a long time and had just chosen not to say it aloud.

"Nothing?" I repeated.

When she didn't respond, I knew that whatever fragile connection had existed between us had snapped. I couldn't say goodbye, mostly because my sobs had grown too violent.

So I hung up.

Because there was nothing left to say.

Nothing left to do.

Nothing.

I threw my face into the couch and screamed, as if my body were purging the last seven years. The cushion muffled all the shrieking pain that spewed forth.

"Amy?" Roman's voice rang out from behind the door. I hadn't noticed that the pounding had gotten softer. Had he heard my conversation? Did it matter?

No. Because it wouldn't change anything.

"Amy, I'm here," he said, repeating the words I'd said to him in the woods. But unlike then, I had nothing to hold on to. And I couldn't open the door, because if I did, I might sink to a deeper level of despair, and fall even further into the abyss.

"Amy . . ." his voice was softer, like he was right against the door frame. "I fucked up. But I'm here."

I squeezed my eyes shut, but the tears just continued to run. Silently. Never ending. This felt like a nightmare, one I had jumped into and was now stuck in. The more time passed, the more I replayed every moment I'd spent with Roman. And all of them had been lies. I'd been stupid, naïve, and used on a whole new level.

Nothing.

Whether spoken by my mother's voice, Roman's, or my own, the word skewered me just the same. Right through the very center of my being, leaving nothing but a gaping hole. The pain was so great, it made me numb.

I didn't know how long Roman stayed out there. His knocking became almost soothing, and my eyes were too swollen from crying to keep them open any longer. So I closed them. The last thing I dared to hope was that this was all a dream, and that when I woke, it would all fade away.

· · · • · ··

It wasn't light that woke me, it was darkness. I glanced at the clock. It was just past seven in the evening. I had slept through the day. Keeping the blanket wrapped around my shoulders, I did a quick check of the apartment.

Still alone.

With the election in less than forty-eight hours, I figured Paige would be basically MIA, and Hazel had finals coming up, so most of her time was spent at the library. I did not want to be in this apartment by myself right now, with only my thoughts for comfort. They were no comfort at all.

My bones creaked like an old house. My face was hot and tender, like I'd been slapped several times.

There was a light knock at the door. My heart stopped, thinking it was Roman, still outside. But a soft, sweet voice rang out instead.

"Amy?" *Knock, knock.* "Amy, it's Regina, dear."

Just the sound of her voice made the tears rise again. My own mother had disowned me, yet Regina was here.

I walked to the door and opened it slightly.

"He's not with me," she said softly as her gaze roamed over my face. "You poor thing. May I come in?"

I nodded and opened the door.

"C-can I get you something to drink?" I offered, feeling ridiculous but trying to hold it together and be somewhat hospitable.

Regina simply opened her arms and wrapped me in the biggest hug I'd ever experienced. It was so surprising and so welcoming that those stupid tears I'd been fighting came flooding out.

I hugged her back. She smelled like cinnamon cookies and kindness. Like a mother.

"Shh, it's alright, honey," she said. "Come sit down." We walked to the couch and she sat me down. "I'm going to make you some tea and toast."

Before I could argue with her, she walked into my kitchen and set straight to work, finding things and making me food while I attempted to pull myself together.

"There we are." She placed the tea and buttery toast on the coffee table.

"Thank you," I said and looked at her. "I assume you know?"

"Roman called me." She patted my hand. "But I'm not here to fight his battles."

I took a sip of my tea. "Thank you for coming anyway."

"Of course. Call it crazy, but the moment I met you, I knew you were a special girl. And whatever happens with you and Roman, it won't change the fact that I'm here for you."

"Why?" I asked. I wasn't trying to be rude, but today had made me gun-shy. It was hard to believe that everyone didn't have an agenda of their own.

"You're one of the strong ones." Regina rubbed my shoulder. "And a nurturer. I could instantly see an innocent ferocity in you. When you apply it to the people you love, it's a wonderful thing, but it can be hard on you."

I just shook my head. "I don't know who I am anymore."

"You're a fighter, Amy."

I looked at her questioningly because after only one brief previous encounter, there was no way Regina could know me.

As if reading my mind, she said, "Oh, I know all about you, dear. And I can tell you right now, only the tough ones survive the kind of loss you've had." She glanced at her hands and her lip trembled a bit. "It's hard to see the good when something so terrible happens. It's hard to let go of the anger, but you did. You strive to make others feel better, safer."

"I haven't done anything. I've failed."

"No, dear." She patted my face gently. "New Beginnings is growing because of you. People will get help. Like I did."

I frowned. "You were at New Beginnings?"

She nodded. "The world needs people like you, Amy." She let out a long breath and raised an eyebrow. "The world also needs people like my son."

"You mean the kind of people who take over your world," I muttered. It wasn't a question: I knew firsthand that Roman Reese was a force greater than gravity. And without it, the effects were brutal.

"Yes. You and my son have very similar qualities, he just acts on his differently. But he loves just as fiercely . . . and it breaks his heart. Which is why he hasn't, until now." She swallowed hard.

"Who broke his heart?" I asked.

Despite the current situation, the part of my brain I feared would never go away that was still wrapped up in Roman wanted to know who caused him pain.

"I did," Regina whispered. "Over and over, I broke his trust and his faith and replaced them with fear." A tear ran down her face, and her gold bracelet jingled as she wiped it away. "But you have brought out a softness in him. An ease. You are very important to him."

I shook my head. "No, I'm not."

I appreciated Regina's honesty, and I hurt to know what she and Roman had gone through. But I didn't know what step to take now. All I knew was that I had been a part of a scheme. A plan Roman had had in place the whole time. And that made everything we'd shared a part of that scheme.

Tears flooded my eyes again.

"Amy." She shifted to face me fully and clasped her hands together. "Roman hasn't asked me for anything in more than twenty years. I don't know exactly what happened between you two, but I can tell you that he cares more about you than anyone else."

"It was a setup," I whispered. I didn't want to go into the whole story, but the basics were simple. "It was never about love, it was all a plan. A means to a political end."

Regina took a deep breath. "That's my fault." I frowned and looked at her. "Up until you, dear, Roman hasn't trusted a soul on this earth. What I did to him—how I left him—" she shook her head, more tears in her eyes. "It's a defense mechanism. One I created in him. If you always have a plan, then you have control of everything and everyone in your life. You can't be hurt. Can't be blindsided. Can't be left."

"I'm sorry for what you both went through," I said. "I'm so proud of you that you got sober. It must have been so hard."

She looked at me and smiled. "Thank you, dear. But I've fought my battles and had my woes. And all that has led me here, to you. Maybe this time, I can take responsibility for my part in this and help my son. I don't want this to be the end of you two."

"He lied to me. From the beginning. You didn't make him do that," I said hoarsely.

"No, I didn't. But he trusts you."

"How can you know?"

"Because he called me. I am the last person he'd turn to for help. And on the phone, not once did he defend himself or explain his side."

"He didn't?"

She shook her head. "No. He didn't. He merely said, 'Mom, I messed up, and Amy's hurting and alone right now.' You were his first concern. He said he wanted you to know that you still had somebody. That you weren't alone. If you wouldn't see him, maybe you'd see me, and I could tell you that."

Fresh tears streamed down my face, and something very dangerous emerged in the shadows of my soul.

Hope.

"I know what withdrawal looks like, dear."

She brushed a lock of hair away from my brow, and the gesture made me think of Roman. He did that every time he was trying to be soothing, a trait he must have gotten from his mother. It made me sad for him, for her, for both of them. So much time lost, so many feelings hurt. So much grief.

"Both of you are struggling. The good things in life aren't always easy, but they're worth fighting for, if they're right."

"I love him," I admitted. Love had never been the issue for me, maybe from the beginning.

"I know you do."

"But how do I know what's real? It hurts so badly. I can't breathe, like my lungs are gone." I set my tea down and cradled my forehead in my hand.

She nodded and pulled me into another hug. "It's called addiction, honey." She hugged me tighter. "It makes you strong and weak."

More tears fell and I held on to Regina like a lifeline. There were two things I knew for sure:

I was at my best with Roman. Strong and happy. And without him, I'd never been so weak. So scared.

And whatever happened, I was certain I wouldn't survive another crash.

Chapter Twenty-Two

······

"Holy shit balls!" Paige said, pacing the living room, her thumbs flying over her Blackberry. I'd just stepped from the bathroom after a nice long shower. Yesterday, when Regina had been here, she'd given me a lot to think about.

I'd hoped that the hot water would somehow bring clarity and rational thought to my mind, but it hadn't. All I could do was feel the hollow ache in my chest that had been growing since I'd left Roman.

"What's going on?" I asked. Paige looked up at me and bit her lower lip, obviously debating whether she wanted to tell me.

"It's okay. I know it's about Roman. I can handle it," I said.

When Paige and Hazel had gotten home last night, I'd caught them up, minus the part about the "dating arrangement." He'd lied to me, broken my heart, end of story. Paige hadn't looked overly surprised but again, that's why she was good at her job.

"Roman just announced his support for the house chair. He gave it to Stanton."

My eyes shot wide and I gripped the towel around my chest. He'd threatened to back Stanton, but after the blowup in his office, I hadn't known what to expect. In Roman's position, it would have made more sense to go with Warren. Then he wouldn't have had to worry about my past and Warren's blackmail hurting his campaign.

"Warren will leak to the press now." I said. "The election is tomorrow. He'll ruin Roman's chances the day before the ballots get cast."

Paige shook her head. "Not if Roman leaked it first."

My brows came together so fast and hard, it hurt. Paige just started reading aloud from her handheld.

"'The opening of the New Beginnings drug counseling and rehabilitation center in Arbor Hill is due to the hard work and vision of Amy Underwood,'" Paige started. "'Amy lost her older sister to a drug overdose several years ago . . .'" Paige trailed off, her eyes darting across the screen.

"What?" I asked nervously.

She met my stare. "He relates what you went through. How you were scared, had nowhere to go." Her eyes went to the phone again. "'She did what any loving sister would do,'" Paige read verbatim, "'she took her home.'"

Just when I'd thought I had the crying under control, that damn sting popped up behind my eyes again.

Paige read on. "'This tragedy will not hurt another family in New York if we don't let it. Arbor Hill will be the place to go for all who need help.'" She looked up and, with her green eyes fastened on mine, said, "'No one will be left to fight this battle alone.'"

I put a hand over my mouth.

Paige flicked a few more buttons. "Amy, he follows it up with a whole press release about his mother's stay in rehab at New Beginnings."

"What?"

"It's all here." She scrolled some more. "The entire truth. There's even a picture." She held out her phone so I could see Roman, on the steps of the capitol in Albany, hugging his mother. The photo was dated this morning.

Paige looked back at me with a smile, then read, "'New York and all her citizens deserve a fresh start.'"

My heart sank and my stomach ached.

"Will this hurt him? His chances at governor?" I asked quietly.

"That's the question you ask? You're worried about him and his campaign?" Paige grabbed her purse.

"What else should I ask?"

She threw the strap over her shoulder. "I dunno, how about, does he love me?"

I looked at my feet because I didn't want to know the answer to that. Mostly because either way, I was certain I wouldn't handle it well.

"But," Paige sighed. "To answer your first question, I'm heading to the office now to check the damage report. But honestly," she said, glancing at her phone again, "if anything, I think this will help him. An honest admission of events that the average New Yorker can relate to? Roman just aired his dirty laundry, and I think it will end up securing the blue-collar vote."

I smiled sadly, but I was truly happy that this could be a good thing for him.

"Paige?"

With her hand on the doorknob, she turned to face me. "Yeah?"

"That second question, the one I should ask . . ."

She smiled. "Does he love you?"

I nodded, bracing myself for another dose of pain. Because if Paige told me this was likely another scam, a special spin they'd done to gain votes, I thought I just might melt into the floor.

"I *would* say yes," she said. "But that seems a little inaccurate." Pain bloomed in my chest, but she finished with, "I'd say hell yes, he loves you."

My entire chest relaxed as I released a breath I hadn't realized I was holding.

"I need to find him," I said.

"I'd suggest some clothes first, unless you really want to make an entrance." She winked. "He should be at home right now. If you hurry, you can catch him before he leaves to meet his campaign team."

I rushed to my room and quickly dressed.

I had a governor to go see.

Chapter Twenty-Three

The cab dropped me off in front of the governor's mansion. I was almost to the steps when Roman bolted through the front doors to meet me.

I stopped dead in my tracks.

He looked tired. He hadn't shaved in at least a day, and his dark eyes were red around the rims. His button-down was wrinkled, and there was no sign of his tie. Or, for that matter, the always crisp and composed Governor Reese.

It was just him. Roman. Exhausted and sad-looking.

"Amy," he said, and stepped toward me slowly, as if scared I'd dart away if he moved too quickly.

"I heard what you said," I started. Taking a deep breath, I tried to call on the last of my strength and say what I'd come here to say. "I never meant to put you in a position where you had to choose."

"You didn't. And the choice was easy." He stepped toward me. "Do you have any idea what you've done to me?"

My eyes shot wide with something like anger, shock, and just . . . what had he just said?! The man had the nerve to ask me that?

"What I've done to you?"

"Yes." He took another step. "I was fine before you. My world was controlled and predicable. Everything was my choice. My decision. I thought you'd be the same way. Just another pawn to serve my purpose."

Was he seriously saying this? After the story he'd launched about me and his mother, I'd thought things would be different. But the tug in my chest was informing me that my heart was threatening to break again. I was ready to scream, to throw something, to fall to my knees and beg God to make it stop.

Then he said, "But *you* are the one *I* serve, Amy."

And my whole body zinged with a flare of anticipation. His dark eyes bore down on me, fear and hope etched along their edges.

"I've never been more miserable than I have without you, sweetheart. You've changed everything. You have control over me. I hate it." He lowered his voice and kept that blazing stare on me until I felt it to the center of my body. "But I love you. So damn much. You can have it all. Everything I am. Just please don't walk away from me."

A sob broke low in my throat. "I want you to be happy." And it was the truth. Such an easy thing to admit when there was nothing left to hide. "I never played you. I would never want to."

"I know." He stepped closer, lifting his hands slightly as though cornering a frightened animal. "I'm the one who deceived you. There's no excuse. But I swear to you, I won't do it again. I'm so sorry, sweetheart."

"Politicians never admit defeat," I whispered.

He took the final step, so close I could feel the heat of his body.

"You defeated me that first night, and I'll concede happily if it means I get to keep you."

He gently cupped my face, and tears rolled down my cheeks and wet his fingers.

"I love you, Amy."

With a deep breath, I said what I'd come here to say. The truth.

"I love you, Roman."

He kissed me hard and I wrapped my arms around him.

Standing outdoors on a cold day in November, I felt warm and safe. Complete.

"It's crazy," he said against my lips. "How much I need you. It's like . . ."

"An addiction." I nipped his bottom lip and he smiled.

"Yes, an addiction."

Epilogue

.. . . ..

Living in sin with the governor isn't going to look bad?" Hazel asked with a wink as she unpacked a box in the middle of Roman's bedroom—now *our* bedroom.

"Technically we're not 'living together.' I'm just keeping some things here for an extended period," I said, reciting what Roman and I had discussed. Smiling, I hung up some clothes in the closet. For the first time in a long, long time, I felt at peace. Truly complete.

"I'm just glad the election is over. Roman won, and that douche Warren ran back home to his mommy with no chair to sit on." Hazel snickered, and I glanced at her from within the closet. "Get it, no chair, because he ran for house chair?"

"Oh, I get it." I smiled and joined Hazel where she was, unpacking in front of the fireplace. I was so happy for Roman. After we'd made up, he'd taken me with him to watch the results come in. When he was announced the winner, he'd given a speech and addressed all his supporters. It had been overwhelming how many people had turned out. So much of the last few months had been wonderful and crazy and in the end, Roman was the right man. For New York and for me.

This next step I was taking with the governor of New York was a permanent one. While my stomach fluttered with happiness, I looked at Hazel and said, "I'm going to miss you."

She looked up and patted my shoulder. "You're not going far, and we'll see each other all the time."

I nodded, then frowned as I saw what she was unwrapping. "What is that?"

She peeled back the newspaper to reveal—oh, God, no . . .

"It's the turkey collection! I saw you looking at them all the time. It's my housewarming present to you." She beamed, and went about setting up Stroky and his cohorts on the little table between the chairs.

"But, Hazel, you love those."

"Yes, but don't worry. Christmas is coming, and I have these great sparkly Santas made out of recycled milk cartons and baby food jars."

"Great." Hideous as those things were, I liked that a piece of my old home had followed me to Roman's.

"Have you heard from Paige?" I asked.

Hazel shook her head. "I don't know what's going on with Paige. She's been working late for the past week, and we haven't really had a chance to chat." She looked up at me. "You look happy, Amy."

"I am."

"It doesn't bother you that you have to keep pieces of your relationship secret? Say that you and Roman aren't living together when you are?"

I unrolled another turkey. "It's not secret. It's like our own language. We share the truth, just not all the details."

"That makes sense." She shrugged. "Your private life should be your own, but I can see how it could be difficult."

Yes, it could be. But he loved me. I had never been more certain of anything. And that made the adjustments easier, because we were doing it together.

"You excited for your new job tomorrow?" Hazel asked.

"I am. I'm looking forward to meeting everyone."

I was also nervous. The job was heading up the anti-drug campaign Roman had enacted. While New Beginnings was building the new facility, I was the consultant who worked with the state government and the non-profits it supported. I still got to help, make a difference, and be part of the process of cleaning up New York.

"I still can't believe you insisted on an application process," she said.

"It wouldn't have been fair otherwise."

"Good afternoon, ladies." Roman set down the large box by the doorway. Holy God, the man was hot. In his dark jeans, casual leather belt, and a white shirt that clung to his chest and abs so perfectly it made me want to swoon.

Though it was a chilly day, he had helped move my things, and I'd never seen a man look better while toting boxes.

"Getting all set up?" he asked, walking toward Hazel and me and examining the little table, which now had half of Stroky's flock on it. He looked like he'd just swallowed a spoonful of salt.

"It's Hazel's housewarming present," I said, hoping to wipe that look off his face before Hazel noticed. "Isn't that nice?"

He instantly plastered on a smile. "Very thoughtful. Thank you, Hazel."

Hazel stood and clapped a little. "I'm so glad you like them." She hugged Roman, and then turned to hug me. "I should be taking off, but let me know if there is anything else you need help with."

"Thank you so much." My eyes stung a little as I watched Hazel leave, shutting the door behind her.

Roman approached me and nudged my chin up with his finger. "I thought you were happy about moving in with me?"

I smiled and batted the water away from my eyes. "I am. So much."

"Then why do you look like you're about to cry?"

I played with the bottom hem of his shirt. "It's just, Hazel and Paige are kind of like my only family." After the call with my mother a couple of weeks ago, she'd never called back. Which was fine, because I had let her go, along with the guilt and the past. And it felt good. It also made me realize that the few precious people I had in my life, I wanted to keep around.

"I'm your family, Amy," Roman said. "No matter what, I'm not going anywhere."

Great, now the tears were back. But they were the happy, amazing kind that made the world slow for just a moment so that all I could hear, see, and feel was Roman Reese.

"I love you," I whispered, lifting to my tiptoes and kissing him softly.

He cupped my face and brushed his nose against mine. "I love you too, sweetheart." He chuckled a little. "Speaking of people who love you, my mother has called four times today asking about us visiting next weekend. If I don't give her an answer soon, I'm pretty sure she'll camp out on our front lawn."

I smiled. "I'd love to visit. If you'd like to?"

He nodded, and something very content glowed behind those dark eyes. "I would."

I gripped his shirt, so proud of him. So happy he'd found his own peace with his past. Over the past few weeks, he'd made a major effort to work things out with his mother. Now, he looked calmer than I'd ever seen him, and I was so happy that everything felt like it was falling into place. For both of us. Together.

He gently nipped at my bottom lip, and I drew away just enough to run my gaze down his entire body.

"Have I told you how sexy you look in jeans, Governor?"

He grinned and kissed me quickly. "I figured moving my girl-friend in with me is an appropriate time to wear them."

"I agree. However . . ." I ran my palms up his impressive chest. "You are a little sweaty. Maybe it's time for a shower."

"You don't like me sweaty?" He traced his tongue along the seam of my lips.

"I love you sweaty. I just want you naked and in the shower."

"Mmm, I like it when you're demanding, Miss Underwood."

"I thought politicians don't respond well to demands?" I ran my hands beneath his shirt, and his cut torso muscles jumped beneath my touch.

"I respond to you every time, sweetheart," he rasped against my mouth. "And I don't ever see that changing."

Without warning, he picked me up, and I laughed. Wrapping my arms around his neck, I let him carry me to the shower. Life was going to be good, from here on out, because I had found Roman and Roman had helped me find myself.

"I love you," I whispered against his neck.

He squeezed me a little tighter. "I love you too."

There, in Roman's strong arms, there was nothing I believed in more.

Acknowledgments

. . . .

Thank you, Maria, for being an amazing editor. Thank you to my awesome critique partner and BFF for all your love and brilliance. Thank you, Lindsay, for your rocking edits! Thank you to my family and friends for your support.

Read on for a sneak peek of the next
book in Joya Ryan's Sweet Torment series.

Only You

· · • · · ·

Thanks for manning the desk, Paige," Jean said, taking her glasses off and letting them hang from the chain around her neck. "Want me to bring you back anything?"

Jean was the personal assistant to the governor of New York and the closest thing I had to a mother figure.

"No thanks, I've got a protein shake." Plus, I had a lot of work to get done.

"Okay, then. I'll see you in a bit." Jean's gaze lingered a little, and I saw unease and pity in her eyes. Yeah. She knew. Everyone around here knew. And by tomorrow, the press would make sure the entire country knew.

My boss, Bill Vorse, chief communications officer to the governor, was involved in a sex scandal.

He was also kind of a douche. I had been on the receiving end of his unwanted advances a time or two in the year I'd been his assistant. But now it looked like he'd gone too far and, according to the rumor mill, with more than just one girl. And there were pictures. The story would break tomorrow.

And when it did, I would be out of a job.

I rubbed my temples, trying to ward off the oncoming migraine.

Letting out a long sigh, I looked at my protein shake sweating on Jean's desk, then at the bowl of candy.

Shake?

Candy?

Eff the protein.

I reached for a handful of Hershey's Kisses, but the bowl shocked my finger, making me jump and knock it onto the floor.

"Damn it."

Walking around to the front of the desk, I collected the chocolates and put them back in the bowl. On my hands and knees, ass in the air, I reached under the desk, trying to get the last chocolate wedged against the wall and making my skirt ride up my thighs.

"Is there a good place I can stick this?" A deep, husky voice came from behind me.

Directly *behind* me.

I shot up, barely missing cracking my head on the edge of the desk, and scrambled to my feet.

"Excuse me?" I said, shuffling a bit unsteadily on my heels.

I tugged the hem of my skirt down, tucked back the few strands of hair that had come loose from my bun, and prepared to address the man—

Only my words dried up, while the exact opposite happened to my mouth—and panties.

Tall, built, and one hundred percent bad boy. He sported a pair of worn jeans and a white T-shirt that hugged bulging biceps and obviously chiseled abs. The cotton looked just slightly sweaty, but he smelled like cologne and spice and man. He held a small brown box for delivery, and I had never been caught more off guard by a package in all my life.

A SAVAS SHIPPING ball cap was tugged low on his head, but thick, jet-black hair stuck out and curled around the back of the band. Some sort of tribal tattoo peeked out from under his left T-shirt sleeve, and when those intense blue eyes locked on my face, a flash of heat radiated through my whole body. As his gaze traveled lower and landed on my breasts, I completely melted. And forgot to exhale.

"You alright there, sweetheart?"

My eyes snapped to his, and I realized I had just been staring at *his* package. He grinned, and his expression was so confident it could have had its own personality.

"You're breathing a little hard there."

"I, ah . . ." I shook my head, trying to regain my composure. This man, with his sexy smile and even sexier tattoo, was making me feel something I hadn't felt in a long time. Lust. The kind that started a slow simmer in my blood. Then I shook my head slightly. *Nope. Not going to happen.* Time to pull the composed Paige back together.

"Is there something I can help you with?" I asked with all the professional polish I possessed.

Apparently unaffected by my "serious" voice, he openly scanned my entire body and licked his lower lip, giving me the sudden urge to do the same.

"Yeah."

He just stared, blue eyes blazing. Silently assessing. A small smile revealed a set of amazing dimples.

"Ah, okay." I tried again. "What is it?"

"This." He held up the small box. "It's for Roman Reese. I'll just drop it in his office."

"I don't think so," I said. "We don't let delivery boys actually drop items off to public officials. You can leave it with me."

He balanced the box between his hip and forearm, raised a single eyebrow, and unleashed the sexiest expression I'd ever seen. "Delivery boy, huh?"

I tried to size him up in return, show him that he didn't affect me and that I meant business, but that was a mistake. Mostly because it made me drool a little, a problem I had just gotten under control.

I knew his type. Man, did I know his type. Way too good looking for his own good—and he obviously knew it. He was cocky and tattooed, and I'd lay ten-to-one odds he owned a motorcycle. He was exactly the kind of guy I would never go for again. The kind of guy I'd been screwed over by before. The kind I'd left back in Indiana, right along with my past.

I'd figured out a long time ago that if I wanted to get off the trailer park I'd grown up in, I'd have to start dressing, acting, and living the life I wanted—not the life I had.

And that life entailed upstanding gentlemen who wore suits and had ambition.

"Well, angel, I don't think the governor would mind if I just popped in."

I stepped in front of him. "He's not in. And I mind."

"What's your name?" he asked with a little tilt of his chin that signified he thought my protest was cute, at best. If there was one thing I understood, it was silent mockery.

"You can call me Miss Levine."

"Oh, I can, huh?"

I lifted my chin and crossed my arms, which only seemed to amuse him more.

"I'm Leo," he offered in a sugary tone that I recognized. It was the voice a man used when he was preparing to butter up a woman. Too bad for him I had been on the losing end of men all my life, which was why I steered clear of them.

"That's nice," I said.

He took a step toward me and his gaze dropped to scan my body again, leaving tingles on my skin. "I think we got off on the wrong foot here, Miss Levine." Never taking his eyes from mine, he knelt down and picked up the candy dish. "Roman is expecting this," he indicated the box in his other hand, "and me."

"He's not in," I said again.

"I'm a bit early." He shrugged. "But I can wait. Maybe you'd be willing to entertain me?"

My jaw dropped and my forehead hurt from how hard I was scowling at him.

"I'm not here to entertain anyone. Especially—"

"A delivery boy?" he said.

I glanced at my feet. I knew how people judged you based on your station or job in life. Which was exactly what I was doing to him.

I just needed to get out of this conversation and away from this man. Everything about him was bad news, and I didn't have the patience to deal with it. Or the hot flush he sent rushing over my skin.

"Just leave it here, and I'll make sure the governor gets it."

"Alright, Miss Levine." Leo set the box on Jean's desk. "How about a kiss for all my trouble of coming in here only to have you send me away?"

My mouth dropped. This guy and his ego needed a big check. "You've got to be kidding me? I've heard better lines from a—"

He handed me the candy dish, effectively cutting me off, and took a Hershey's Kiss from the bowl.

"Oh . . ." My face flared hot, and I didn't need a mirror to know how mortified I looked.

I put the candy dish on the desk, walked around it, and sat down. Partly because my legs were a bit shaky, and partly because the closer this guy was to me, the more I could smell him. Hot and delicious. It made me realize just how long it had been since I'd had a man.

Stupid body.

Stupid day.

"You're kind of sexy when you're irritated, Red."

He winked, and I immediately went back to studying the computer. My defenses weren't top-notch against charm like his.

"Come on. You have to admit that line was better than the kiss one."

Who was this guy? Whoever he was, he had balls to hang around the governor's office like he owned the place. Or at least as though he belonged—something I'd been trying to accomplish for the past several years with no such luck. But this guy? Two minutes here and he was right at home: confident, charismatic as hell, and with an easy charm that I desperately wanted in my life right now.

No. Scratch that. I wanted the life I had built. The life I had worked hard for. The life that proved I was better than where I'd come from. The life that he was currently distracting me from.

"What are you doing tonight?" he asked.

Never taking my attention from the screen, I said, "Working."

He nodded. "Well, maybe when you're done, there's this great pub right down the street. Best hoagies in the city. They even have a sign that says so. I'd like to take you there."

"You want to buy me a sandwich?"

Great. Just great.

Last night I'd been stood up by an accountant I had gone out with a few times. He'd made it obvious that his upper-middle-class life was more glamorous than I was.

"Yeah. I want to buy you a sandwich," Leo said with a wide smile.

I wanted to scoff, but the way those dimples flashed and his hips shifted just enough to reveal a peek of his black leather belt made me think twice.

"No, thanks," I said quickly before I could change my mind. Because a sub and casual conversation with a hot guy sounded better than anything I had going on later.

He stood to his full height, which was a couple inches over six feet, and adjusted his ball cap.

"You just broke my heart, Red," he said, putting a palm over his chest. "But I'm not giving up on you."

I just gave him an exasperated look and waved him off. Problem was, the view of his ass as he left was amazing—and depressing to watch walk away.

About the Author

Joya Ryan is the author of the Shattered series, which includes bestseller *Break Me Slowly*. She loves to cook and is a terrible dancer, though that doesn't keep her off the dance floor. Currently, she lives in California with her husband and two young sons.

Made in United States
North Haven, CT
25 August 2024

56525466R00168